GALLOWGATE

GALLOWGATE

K. R. ALEXANDER

SCHOLASTIC PRESS / NEW YORK

All rights reserved. Published by Scholastic Press, an imprint of Scholastic Inc.,
Publishers since 1920. SCHOLASTIC, SCHOLASTIC PRESS, and associated logos are
trademarks and/or registered trademarks of Scholastic Inc.

Library of Congress Cataloging-in-Publication Data available

ISBN 978-1-338-80648-9

10 9 8 7 6 5 4 3 2 1   23 24 25 26 27

Printed in Italy   183

First edition, August 2023

Book design by Stephanie Yang

FOR THE KIDS WHO JUST
NEVER SEEM TO FIT IN.
YOU WILL. I PROMISE.

THE DESCENT BECKONS
—WILLIAM CARLOS WILLIAMS

O

Sebastian Wight was cursed.

Truly, legitimately cursed.

Not like he had bad luck. Even though he did.

Not like middle school was hard for him, though his curse definitely made it harder.

No. This was a major curse.

Like, sometimes he'd open his locker to find a floating head. Or he'd walk down the hall and the doors would start to bleed. Or he'd pass a playground and the only kids on it would be transparent.

That sort of curse.

He couldn't tell anyone. Not even his aunt. Even she would think he'd lost it.

He tried everything to keep it a secret from his classmates.

Which meant everyone in school knew, of course.

It was hard to keep something like that secret, when he'd cried out more than once at something no one else saw.

But it wasn't the curse that had him worried.

No, he'd seen the ghosts for as long as he could remember.

It was the fact that the ghosts no longer seemed content to just scare him.

It was like they'd finally realized he could see them. And they didn't like it.

The ghosts had begun getting more active. More violent.

It wasn't enough to haunt him.

Now they wanted him to join them.

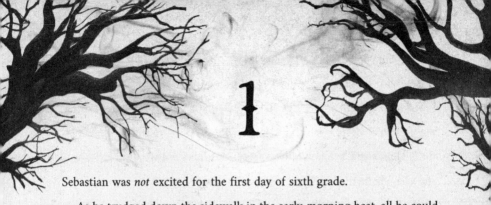

1

Sebastian was *not* excited for the first day of sixth grade.

As he trudged down the sidewalk in the early-morning heat, all he could think about was how he would much rather be indoors. In the AC. Ideally playing a video game or reading a graphic novel. Despite the warmth, he wore a knit cap over his choppy, bone-white hair, hoping it would help him blend in. He'd tried coloring his hair a normal shade more times than he could count, but the color never stuck. Ghosts weren't the only thing he'd been cursed with; after his parents died, his hair had gone white from shock. With his white hair and skin that never seemed to hold a tan, his aunt sometimes called him a little ghost in the winter months.

His classmates laughed and gossiped as they all walked toward the middle school. He overheard stories of campouts and sleepovers, vacations and summer drama.

None of them stopped to ask him if he'd done anything exciting or gone anywhere cool. No one asked how Aunt Dahlia was doing, or if he'd had—you know—any more *episodes*.

That was fine with him. It was better to be ignored.

He knew it was naive to hope that a new school would mean a new start, when he was with the same kids he'd known his entire life. But he still hoped it.

He needed this year to be different. This year, *he* needed to be different.

He was a few blocks from school when he saw it. *Her.*

A girl in a blue dress, about his age, facing away from him. She stood in the middle of the road, staring up at the clouds.

Sebastian stopped and looked up. But there wasn't anything interesting up there—no planes or UFOs or comets hurtling to the earth. Just big fluffy clouds and an open blue expanse. He wondered who the girl was, if she was new here.

He looked back down just in time to see the car squealing around the corner, half a block away from the girl.

The girl who was still looking up at the clouds.

"Look out!" Sebastian screamed. He took a step forward, toward the street, but it was too late.

Without even slowing, the car slammed right into the girl.

And continued driving.

Right through her.

It was then, and only then, when the car was past and she still stood in the exact same spot, that she turned around to face Sebastian.

His heart froze in his throat.

She didn't have any eyes, and her mouth was a jagged slash above her chin.

Sebastian yelped.

The girl stared at him sightlessly for a moment, that horrible mouth turning down into a crooked frown. As if considering him, and not at all liking what she saw.

"What you staring at, Freak Show?" someone jeered behind him.

Sebastian turned and realized everyone else on the street had stopped to stare at him.

The blood drained from his face as he realized what had happened.

He looked back to the street, but the girl was gone. Of course she was gone. She had never been there to begin with. Not really.

She was a ghost.

"I said," the same kid—an older boy named Billy Horwath—persisted, "what are you staring at, *freak?*"

Sebastian swallowed.

Took a hesitant step back . . .

And tripped off the curb, stumbling into the street.

Thankfully, there weren't any cars coming, but he still felt stupid as he fell back on his butt.

That broke the spell. Billy and the rest of Sebastian's classmates erupted into laughter, and Sebastian knew their excited chatter was no longer about summer break.

Billy looked down at him, something close to pity in his eyes. For a brief moment, Sebastian thought Billy would help him up. They'd been in Scouts together, years ago. Friends, almost. But Billy just turned and left, leaving Sebastian in the street.

Sebastian picked himself up and brushed himself off and pushed himself forward. He sensed someone watching him from across the street, but when he looked, there was no one there.

By the time he got to the front doors, all he knew for certain was that everyone in the middle school was going to hear what had happened. Everyone who knew him would be reminded why they avoided him, and anyone who didn't would quickly learn why they should.

Sebastian Wight thinks he sees ghosts.

Sebastian Wight is a freak.

So much for a new start.

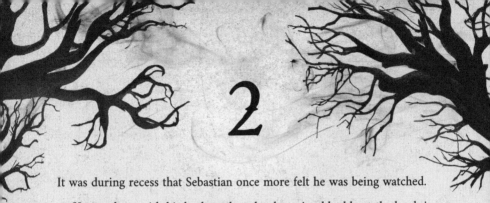

2

It was during recess that Sebastian once more felt he was being watched.

He sat alone with his back to the school, staring blankly at the book in his hands while everyone else played around him. He didn't look up. People had been staring at him and whispering behind his back all day. The best he could do was keep his head down and hope that some popular kid would start projectile vomiting and everyone would talk about that instead.

But after a few more minutes of trying to ignore it, the sensation still hadn't gone away. If anything, it felt stronger. The hairs on the back of his neck rose as he realized that whoever had been staring at him hadn't stopped, not since he had stepped outside.

He glanced around the playground. No one seemed to be paying him any attention. A pack of girls looked over at him and giggled. That was all.

He went back to trying to read.

A few pages later, a shadow fell across him. He looked up, expecting to see Billy cornering him for another round of taunting. Instead, the boy standing beside him wasn't anyone he'd seen before. What was more, the boy seemed entirely solid, and entirely alive.

"Hey," the boy said.

"Hey," Sebastian replied awkwardly.

"What are you reading?" the boy asked.

Sebastian had never seen the kid before, but maybe he was new? Maybe he hadn't heard the rumors about Sebastian's *episodes*, after all?

Sebastian held up the book to show the boy. It was part of a fantasy series he'd started over the summer, an epic tale of knights and magic and dragon riders, one of those thick paperbacks that looked like a brick.

"No way!" the boy said. He flopped down on the ground beside Sebastian. "I read that one last year. That whole series is so good. Have you read the spin-off stories about the were-tiger yet? Oh, I'm Aaron, by the way."

The boy spoke very fast, and Sebastian—who wasn't used to anyone but his aunt and a few teachers talking to him—took a moment to piece it all together.

"I haven't," Sebastian said, then introduced himself.

"You're the kid who sees ghosts, right?" Aaron asked.

Sebastian felt his smile slip, but tried to stop it from slipping too far. *So much for him not hearing about that.*

"Um . . ."

"That's so cool," Aaron continued. "My cousin says she saw a ghost in her basement once, but I think she was just trying to make me scared, because she also swore her dolls moved around on their own at night but I never saw it happen."

Despite himself, Sebastian started to grin.

"So you don't think I'm weird?"

"Oh no, you're like *totally* weird," Aaron said. "But who says that's a bad thing? I mean, you're reading *that.*" He nudged Sebastian's book, and Sebastian laughed.

Maybe this year wouldn't be so bad, after all.

"What's the scariest thing you've seen?" Aaron asked.

Sebastian tried to hold back a shudder. He knew Aaron wouldn't want the real answer. No one wanted to know that Sebastian had been there when his parents were shot. No one wanted to know of the grisly, terrifying things he'd seen during and after.

"Once I saw a skeleton," Sebastian said. "In the closet in my fourth-grade class. The teacher opened the door to get craft paper and this two-headed skeleton walked out. It still had bits of skin hanging off. She didn't see it. No one did. I nearly peed myself."

It was true. But it wasn't the scariest thing he'd seen. Not even close. He knew, though, that he didn't want to scare Aaron off with the truth. He also knew that making his curse a joke was the only hope he had of making friends.

He'd fantasized about a moment like this for years.

"Creepy," Aaron said with an elaborate shudder. "Have you seen anything recently? Like, are there a bunch of ghosts playing dodgeball on the playground right now?"

Sebastian looked around. Even though the uneasy sensation of being watched hadn't gone away, he said, "No . . . I don't think so."

"Dang," Aaron said.

Sebastian realized in that moment that although it was nice that Aaron didn't think he was making up stories, the boy didn't really understand.

Aaron *wanted* to see the dead.

Sebastian very much did not.

Thankfully, they shifted to talking about the books they were reading and the video games they were playing, and soon the bell rang and Sebastian and Aaron stood to go inside. It was the first time in Sebastian's life that recess hadn't seemed to drag on forever.

They started walking toward the doors when Sebastian felt it again, stronger than ever.

The eyes on the back of his neck.

And with them, a sensation, almost a smell—the tang of electricity, the crackle of static. Something sharp and dangerous.

He turned.

And this time, he saw it.

A shadow on the very edge of the school grounds. Standing beside a large oak.

Sebastian's blood went cold.

The shadow moved. Shifted. Drew closer.

One moment it looked like a man. The next, its shape blurred, twisted. Tendrils stretched out to become spider legs, then spread like bat wings as it moved nearer. With every inch, the terrible smell and the chilling cold intensified.

The shadow didn't have a face. Instead, it wore a porcelain mask in the shape of a doll's head. A mask with smooth white eyes and a terrible, painted smile.

Fear raced through Sebastian's veins, and he flinched back, knocking into Aaron. The boy steadied him for a moment.

"What is it?" Aaron asked, peering out toward the emptying playground, his eyes squinting. "What do you see?" He almost sounded excited.

When Sebastian looked again, the shadow was gone.

"Nothing," he lied. "Just . . . thought I saw something."

Two in one day . . .

He'd never seen two ghosts in one day. And he'd never seen anything quite like the figure he'd just seen. It hadn't just been coming toward him.

It had been coming *for* him.

That, too, was something new. Generally, the ghosts he saw didn't seem to care he existed. Like wild animals, they tended to vanish the moment

9

they realized he was watching. But this one . . . this one seemed to relish that Sebastian could see it.

It had seemed to take pleasure in his fear.

The bell rang again.

Sebastian hurried inside with Aaron.

Even within the school's walls, he didn't feel all that safe.

He never did.

3

Sebastian felt hunted—*haunted*—the rest of the day. But he didn't see the shadowy figure again, even though he felt its eyeless gaze on the back of his neck. When school was done, he hurried home, not even pausing to see if Aaron wanted to hang out. He didn't like being away from home any longer than he needed to be.

It was only when he walked past the front hedges of his aunt's house that he truly started to feel safe.

"Aunt Dahlia?" he called out as he took his shoes off in the entryway. That was one of her rules—no shoes in the house.

Aunt Dahlia had a ton of rules. None of them were super strict, but many were rather . . . strange. Then again, everything in her house would probably seem strange to an outsider.

Sebastian walked down the hall and to the kitchen, passing the dream catchers and crystals, the wooden masks and ancient stone carvings that were artfully arranged on every available surface. The walls were painted deep orange and royal blue, with small hand-painted embellishments along the ceiling and wooden floor. Late-afternoon light filtered through the windows, making the various herbs and flowering vines on their sills glow a rich green.

The kitchen, too, was a chaos of artifacts and instruments and contain-ers. An entire wall had been converted into wooden shelves for jars of herbs (Aunt Dahlia loved her teas), and decanters of various infusions lined the top of the fridge.

"Aunt Dahlia?" he called again, to no response. She worked as an archaeology professor at the local university, and it wasn't uncommon for her to be called in at any hour to help unpack a new shipment of artifacts and catalog them.

Sebastian grabbed an orange and sat at the large kitchen table to start his homework. But it was hard to focus. Every once in a while he would glance over his shoulder and look out the window, expecting to see the frightening shadowman lurking outside. He never saw it, but that didn't make the itch between his shoulders go away.

Hours passed, and it wasn't until nearly nine o'clock, when Sebastian was reading in the large wingback chair in the living room, that Aunt Dahlia came home.

If Aunt Dahlia's house was eclectic, she was even more so.

Tonight she wore a blue paisley blouse, a chunky necklace of red stones, a marigold skirt, brown boots, and a dozen bangles on her wrists. Her patchwork handbag was slung over her shoulder. She was like a ray of irrational sunshine in an otherwise boring world.

Sebastian noticed something was off, though. The brown eyes behind her turquoise cat-eye glasses, usually sparkling, were shadowed tonight, and her beehive of salt-and-pepper hair was frazzled.

Plus, unless he was very much mistaken, she smelled like woodsmoke . . . and it definitely looked like there was ash on her tan cheek.

"Are you okay?" he asked.

"What?" She blinked a few times, as if just now seeing him. "Oh yes, dear. Rough night in the office. Would you be a doll and brew me some tea while I change?"

She didn't even wait for his answer before hurrying upstairs.

Sebastian stood there, mildly stunned. It was rare for Aunt Dahlia to come home without giving him a hug.

And even stranger, she hadn't taken off her shoes . . .

Still, he went into the kitchen, boiled the kettle, and selected five herbs from her collection. Chamomile and valerian, hops and lavender, plus a bit of mint. Something to calm her nerves and wash away whatever had happened at work. Her fluster was almost enough to make him stop thinking about the strange ghost he'd seen at school. Almost.

Aunt Dahlia came down in a great floral velvet robe and striped pajamas, her hair undone and most of her jewelry taken off. The ash on her cheek was gone. She still looked distinctly frazzled, however.

Sebastian handed her the tea, and she settled onto one of the kitchen chairs with a sigh.

"I'm getting too old for these late nights," she said, flashing him her telltale mischievous grin. "Academia will be the death of me."

"What happened?" Sebastian asked.

She waved her hand. "Nothing of interest, little bird. Just a few PhD students causing trouble. How was your day?"

"I . . . I think I made a friend," Sebastian said.

Aunt Dahlia's eyes lit up. "Did you, now? Tell me all about them."

Sebastian told her a few things about Aaron. He also wanted to tell her about the haunting beings he'd seen. The shadowy figure. The ghost girl on the street. He wanted to tell her that things felt strange, that he felt like he was being watched.

But although Aunt Dahlia knew he didn't have any friends, she didn't know *why* that was the case. Or if she did, she never admitted it.

He'd never told her about the ghosts. He never would.

She was the only family he had left, and he didn't want to risk her looking at him the way everyone at school did.

After they talked some more about his classes, Aunt Dahlia gave him a funny look. Like she was appraising him.

"Your parents would be so proud of you, you know that?"

Sebastian's throat constricted.

He didn't say anything, and neither did she. But it was a comfortable sort of silence. They rarely spoke of his parents. After their murder seven years ago, when she'd taken him in as her own, she'd tried to keep them focused on the future. *We either move forward, or we fade away. There is no other option,* she'd said.

"Well, little bird, it's way past my bedtime," she said after a while. "And yours, too, I believe. Don't worry about the dishes. I'll tidy up in the morning."

He nodded, still feeling off—talk of his parents always made his heart tie up in knots. He couldn't remember *exactly* what happened, thankfully. His brain had blurred the shooting out. But even that fuzzy spot in his memory was enough to fill him with sadness.

Aunt Dahlia gave him a hug and went up to her room. Sebastian stayed behind, setting the mug on the sink and turning off the lights. Then he went upstairs to brush his teeth and go to bed.

His bedroom had once been her study, and he'd kept some of her artifacts on the walls when he moved in. But it had definitely become a boy's room in the years since: piles of clothes shoved into the corners, stacks of fantasy books on his desk. The only note of cleanliness was his made bed, and the neat array of crystals arranged on his windowsill. Two more of her rules: Never leave the house without making your bed, and keep your crystals tidy and rinse them in salt water every new moon.

Sometimes, even *he* thought Aunt Dahlia was a little . . . odd.

But he went over to the crystals, anyway, and shifted a large chunk of amethyst so it lined up with the smoky quartz, watching it glitter as it caught the light of the streetlamp outside.

Sebastian froze.

Something. Was moving. Outside.

At first, he thought it was a stray dog—maybe Mrs. Russell's greyhound had gotten loose again. It sniffed around the streetlamp, pausing just outside the entrance to their house, right between the hedges. But it didn't move like a dog.

As he watched, the shadow stood, slowly, unfolding itself like some cursed origami to reveal the ink-dark figure of a man.

A man with a porcelain doll mask for a face.

Sebastian was frozen to the spot. He couldn't back away for fear the beast would see his movement. Its head swung this way and that. As if trying to sense him. Trying to *smell* him.

In his shock, Sebastian's hand brushed against an agate on his window. The stone tumbled over with a muffled thud to the carpet, so soft even he could barely hear.

The shadowman's masked face snapped up.

Stared straight at him.

Without opening its porcelain mouth, it screamed.

The sound was terrible, like emergency sirens and screeching tires, piercing glass and howling dogs. Sebastian staggered back, his hands to his ears.

He fell back to his bed.

The scream seemed to go on forever.

Then, suddenly, it stopped, and all that was left was a terrible ringing in his ears.

Sebastian cowered there, barely daring to breathe. He waited for Aunt Dahlia to rush in. Surely she had heard that. Surely the whole *neighborhood* had heard that. He expected to hear emergency sirens and car alarms and slamming front doors as the nosy neighbors inspected the disturbance.

But the seconds ticked by, turning to grueling minutes. And finally, Sebastian slinked off his bed and made his way over to the window. He peered cautiously over the sill, staring between his crystals, and looked outside.

The shadowman was no more.

Sebastian heaved a sigh.

Then, before the figure could return, he replaced the agate and jumped into bed.

He didn't turn out the lights as he yanked the covers over his head. He lay there, terrified and shaking, unable to move or peer out from the sheets. As he waited for sleep to come or the shadowman to break in, Aunt Dahlia's words echoed through his head.

"Your parents would be so proud of you," she'd said.

He knew in his heart that it wasn't true. Who could be proud of a twelve-year-old coward like him?

4

Sebastian didn't sleep a wink that night. He stumbled through breakfast like a zombie, mildly grateful that Aunt Dahlia still seemed too distracted by whatever was going on at work to notice.

But as he was leaving, she stopped him just outside the front door.

She peered at him, and then beyond him to the street. Her nostrils wrinkled momentarily, as if she smelled something gross. But the look passed, and she smiled warmly at him.

"Give your aunt a hug before you go," she said. He nodded and trudged over to her, keenly aware of the other kids on the street, who were probably watching and snickering about this.

She wrapped him tight in her embrace.

"I'm proud of you as well, little bird," she whispered into his ear. "We don't always get to pick our family, but I would have chosen you over all the rest."

She tightened the hug.

"Be safe out there," she said.

"I will," he replied. He didn't know if the whole interaction seemed weird because he was so tired, or because it was, well, *weird*.

She let him go and smiled again, though this time she seemed sad.

"Safety is the one thing in this world we can't truly promise," she said as he turned to go. "And though we promise it, anyway, we always eventually break it."

Sebastian said nothing. Maybe she hadn't slept much, either.

It was only when he neared the hedges that he realized that she'd been staring at the very spot where the shadowman had been standing last night. His heart gave a little flip.

He looked back to her, thinking maybe he would ask her about what she'd seen.

But she was already back inside, and he was alone once more.

Aaron found him at lunch.

Sebastian was at his usual spot, alone at the end of a long table, a five-foot gap between him and anyone else.

"Hey," Aaron said as he sat down opposite Sebastian.

"Hey," Sebastian responded.

"Are you feeling okay?" Aaron asked.

Sebastian nodded. He felt like he'd been hit by a truck, but Aaron didn't need to know that, or why. He didn't want his only potential friend to learn what a scaredy-cat he was.

It didn't help that the feeling of being watched hadn't gone away. It had only gotten worse.

"Have you seen anything strange and unusual?" Aaron asked in a conspiratorial whisper.

It hit Sebastian, then, that maybe Aaron *did* think he was a freak . . . just not in a negative way.

"No," Sebastian lied. "I was just up late playing a video game."

"Oh cool," Aaron said. "Which one?"

Sebastian told him about the RPG he'd been working his way through over the summer, which got Aaron talking about what he'd been playing, and for a brief moment Sebastian was relieved to be having a conversation that didn't have to do with him seeing dead things.

But the dead things wouldn't leave him alone. The moment he started to be comfortable, that terrible, crackling smell from before filled his nostrils, and something in his pocket gave a sharp, cold sting.

He jolted and reached in, pulling out a small silvery-black stone, no bigger than his pinkie. The stone was ice-cold and seemed to buzz with static.

"What's that?" Aaron asked.

"Hematite," Sebastian said, looking at the stone in confusion. He hadn't put it in his pocket.

Then he remembered his aunt, requesting that long, somewhat awkward hug. Had she slipped it in without him noticing?

"Can I see?" Aaron asked.

Sebastian shrugged and handed it over.

The moment it left his hand and fell into Aaron's fingers, the room flooded with cold, an icy chill so powerful Sebastian felt his very limbs freeze. But more terrifying still was what happened to Aaron.

The boy shuddered, as if shaken by invisible hands. Shadows writhed around him, sank into him, and as they did so, his eyes frosted over, became a glowing moon-white.

Aaron's fists tightened around the stone, and his mouth cracked into a wide smile, too wide for his face, his teeth bared and gums pooling black blood.

No one else in the cafeteria noticed. They milled around and chatted while Aaron's smile widened, while the boy squeezed his fist and ground the hematite stone to dust. Sebastian knew, in some distant corner of his mind, that this was no longer his friend—Aaron had been possessed. And Sebastian couldn't do anything about it.

"*Her trinkets will not save you any longer, Sebastian,*" Aaron said. His voice was not his own. The words sounded hollow, like they were spoken down a long hall, spoken by a dozen different people all at once.

Aaron let the dust of the hematite fall to his tray. Leaned over, his mouth cracking wider. He crept up on to the table, knocking aside the trays, his movements jerky, spiderlike.

When he spoke again, his lips didn't move. But his breath was that horrible, electric tang, the scent of rotted meat and frayed electrical wires. Sebastian wanted to puke.

"*We have found you,*" Aaron said. "*We have* tasted *you. And now that we have marked you, you will never escape.*"

A great green-black tongue unfurled from his mouth and swept a slimy trail along Sebastian's cheek. Sebastian couldn't even flinch back. He was utterly paralyzed. His eyes darted around the room, hoping someone—even *Billy*—would see him, would help him, but they all ignored him, as if they couldn't see a thing.

"*Come,*" the spirits possessing Aaron cooed. Aaron reached over and grabbed Sebastian's throat. His grip was cold as ice and strong as stone. "*We shall bring you to him. Your death awaits.*"

Aaron's grip tightened, and Sebastian's vision exploded with stars as an even deeper, heavier cold filled his veins, seeping down his neck like oil, pouring through his heart and out to his fingertips.

The cafeteria around him began to fade. Colors leeched out, becoming a hazy grayscale. The beige walls and linoleum floor washed to near-white. The colorful posters became shades of black. The afternoon sunlight became a weak, sickly white. And his classmates . . . his classmates faded out of sight entirely, until all that was left was a series of blurred tables in a colorless room.

Colorless, save for the acid-green glowing monstrosity in front of him.

Sebastian didn't know what was happening—this had never happened before—but it was like he had fallen into a place outside of reality, a nightmare. And in this new terrible universe, the creature in front of him no longer looked anything like Aaron.

Instead, it was a beast made of a dozen bodies. Its transparent flesh writhed and twisted, never settling, so that one moment Sebastian could see a half-dozen faces leering out from its flesh, and then nothing but hands, or eyeballs, or fangs. Like multiple creatures all fighting for control over one form.

The only constant was the hand clenched around Sebastian's neck. And from the corner of his eye, Sebastian saw there were other limbs wrapped around him, tendrils or tongues or tentacles, binding him in place.

The monster's white eyes flared in victory.

"We shall call him," the monster crowed. "The master of death will reward us well!"

Sebastian tried to struggle, tried to break free, but the binds were tight. He didn't know who they meant by master of death, and he definitely didn't *want* to know.

The monster screamed, an unearthly wail.

Against the pallid wall, shadows began to ooze and form.

They congealed into the shape of a man.

A man with a porcelain mask.

The shadowman.

21

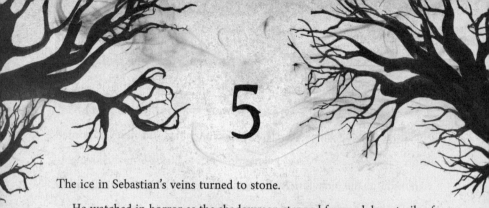

5

The ice in Sebastian's veins turned to stone.

He watched in horror as the shadowman stepped forward, long trails of black sweeping around him like wings, or a terrible cloak. His eyeless mask seemed to peer into Sebastian's soul, and his doll-like features smiled at the cowardice he saw within.

Sebastian knew, in that moment, that if the shadowman got to him, he would never be seen again.

As the thought hit him, and as the shadowman moved closer, another image filled his mind. His aunt, smiling at him. Wrapping him in a hug.

Your parents would be so proud of you.

No.

He wasn't going to die. Not here. Not like this.

He wasn't going to leave her alone.

He struggled harder. The memory of his aunt, her warmth, filled him, made the blood in his veins flow again.

"*You cannot run from this, Sebastian,*" the shadowman said. His voice was a terrible, rasping thing. "*You have been marked for death. You will not escape me again.*"

He stalked closer, enjoying Sebastian's struggle.

I'm not going to die. I'm not. I'm not!

A new sensation flooded Sebastian. A tingling warmth, a curious static.

The green monstrous ghost holding him screamed again. But this time, in pain.

Sebastian's eyes widened. Purple light was arcing around him, glowing through his limbs. And judging from the wails of the monster, it was burning his captor.

He didn't know how he did it, but he focused on the light. Focused on the electricity coursing through him. It built under his skin, buzzed between his fingertips. With a great yell, and a flash of power, more light burst from him.

Purple filled the gray void, and the monster clutching him screamed as it recoiled.

"*No!*" the shadowman yelled as its henchman was flung to the side in the burst.

The shadowman himself didn't seem nearly as affected. He lunged for Sebastian.

As the terrible porcelain mask loomed closer, Sebastian squeezed his eyes and thought only one thing: *I want to go home!*

"Hey," Aaron said. "Hey, are you okay?"

Sebastian's eyes snapped open.

Everyday sound and sensation flooded back.

He was in the cafeteria, the noisy, crowded, sweaty cafeteria. Kids were milling around him. And Aaron was sitting across from him, concern clear in his eyes.

"I—" Sebastian began. *What was that? Was I hallucinating?* Because no one else seemed to have noticed what had just happened.

Aaron's eyebrows furrowed.

"Maybe you should see the nurse," he said. "You look like you're getting sick."

Sebastian raised a hand to his forehead. His skin was cold and clammy, despite the heat of the cafeteria. Since when had it gotten so hot and claustrophobic in here? He felt like he couldn't breathe . . .

"And . . ." Aaron looked away. "I swear, for a moment, your eyes, like, turned purple."

Sebastian looked down at Aaron's tray. A fine pile of hematite dust spread over Aaron's lasagna.

Sebastian jerked backward, falling off the bench with a loud clatter.

It was real. It was real!

As he scrambled back up to standing, panting frantically, he realized that everyone in the cafeteria had finally taken notice.

Everyone. Was looking. At him.

"What—" Aaron began.

"Get away from me!" Sebastian yelled. "Just . . . just stay away!"

Aaron flinched back. Sebastian started walking backward, looking at everyone in the cafeteria like they might become possessed next.

It was real. The shadowman was here. The shadowman is close!

He knew he wasn't safe. Knew he couldn't stay here.

As he edged back, his fears were confirmed.

One by one, the kids around him shuddered.

Their eyes burned with white flame.

And, one by one, they lifted off the ground.

Sebastian hurried toward the door, dodging this way and that as his classmates hovered off the ground, their white eyes burning into him.

"*You cannot escape me!*" they howled in unison, the shadowman's voice sending fresh goose bumps over Sebastian's skin. *"You can run, but you will never escape!"*

His classmates began hovering toward him.

Sebastian hesitated only a moment. He caught sight of Aaron, who was still looking at him with pain and confusion. Then Aaron's eyes glazed over once more.

Sebastian reached the cafeteria door. And ran.

Sebastian ran all the way home. He didn't stop to look back when teachers called out to him, didn't pause at crosswalks. He nearly got hit by a car, but he ignored the angry honking and darted around it.

He didn't stop until he got home.

And even then, he didn't let himself breathe a sigh of relief until the door slammed shut behind him.

He stood there, leaning against the door, panting. Tears streamed down his cheeks. And finally, *finally*, the fear overtook him.

He collapsed down, curling his knees into his chest and rocking back and forth as wave after wave of fear and panic raced over him. His arms shook. His breath hurt.

He thought he was going to be sick.

He flinched when a hand rested on his shoulder.

"Sebastian?" his aunt asked.

He looked up to her, still crying. *Why are you home?* he wanted to ask, but knew if he opened his mouth he'd throw up all over her gold brocade house slippers. She dropped to her knees and pulled him into a hug.

He cried even harder.

"Shh," she cooed, holding him close and smoothing his hair. "Everything's okay. Everything's okay."

But it wasn't. It wasn't.

After far too long, he was finally able to calm his sobs. Though every time he blinked, he remembered the shadowman's smiling mask. The terrible burning possession of his classmates. The hurt in Aaron's eyes when Sebastian told him to get away.

"Tell me everything, little bird," Aunt Dahlia said. "Whatever it is, I can help."

Sebastian shook his head.

She'd never believe him. She'd think he was crazy.

"I . . . I saw . . ."

He swallowed and shuddered hard. He looked up into her caring eyes, then looked away, scared she would look at him the same way Aaron did.

"It's nothing," Sebastian lied. "Nothing at all."

6

Aunt Dahlia let him stay home from school.

She brought him tea and soup, and didn't question why he had come home crying. It was one of the things he liked best about their relationship—she didn't treat him like a little kid or question his every motive. He didn't think he could eat or drink anything ever again, as scared as he was, but he managed to get a few sips down.

After a while, exhaustion got the better of him. He fell into a restless sleep, jerking awake on occasion after dreams of his classmates' burning eyes, with the shadowman's promise that he could find Sebastian anywhere ringing in his ears.

At some point he awoke to find that the light outside had grown dim, and the house was silent.

His stomach rumbled, so he slipped out of bed and hurried downstairs to get a snack.

Aunt Dahlia wasn't home, and the clock said it was almost seven, so he made himself a PB&J sandwich and brought it back up to his room.

Aunt Dahlia never let him eat in his room, but she wasn't there, and besides—he deserved it after today.

He curled up in bed, but rather than pull out his phone or turn on the TV while he ate, he stared at a photograph on his nightstand. It was of him and his parents a few months before they were killed.

The three of them were in front of a water fountain, and his dad was pretending to throw Sebastian into the spray. His mom, holding the camera for the selfie, was laughing. He had her dimples, and had once had her auburn hair. His dad was howling with laughter, his black hair mussed and his glasses askew. Sebastian had inherited his dad's nose and pale skin; his mother's side was from Hawaii, not that you'd know that from Sebastian's propensity to crisp in the sun.

His dad had been full of tricks, always pulling pranks on Sebastian and his mom, but he was serious and caring when he needed to be. If Sebastian's parents were here, his mom would stroke his hair and listen to him intently. His dad would read a funny story or tell a joke to get Sebastian to laugh. But they were both gone. Gone like any chance of having a real friend. Gone like any chances of having a normal life in middle school.

He was alone, and that was never going to change. Not even Aunt Dahlia, no matter how hard she tried, could fill that void.

He was cursed.

He set aside his half-eaten sandwich and curled back up in bed, bringing the sheets over his head and obscuring the remaining light.

"I just want a friend," he whispered to the muffled darkness, tears filling his eyes. *I just want to be normal, to feel safe.* Then he closed his eyes and tried to fall back asleep.

In the dream, Sebastian stood in the graveyard at his aunt's side.

Rain poured down around them, drowning out the words of the pastor who spoke of unending life and other lies. If life never ended, why were his parents gone? If they were always with him, why did he feel so alone?

He stared down at the two graves. The smooth wooden coffins. The flowers he'd carefully picked out. No lilies for them. No. Sunflowers for his mother and snapdragons for his dad. Their favorites.

Not that they would ever see them. But he wanted to believe they could.

"I'll protect you, little bird," Aunt Dahlia said. "And you'll protect me. We're a team now."

He didn't say anything. He couldn't protect anyone. If he could, his parents would still be alive.

Something shifted just outside his vision, like clouds or mist swirling among the tombstones. A chill raced through him.

"It should have been you, little bird," Aunt Dahlia said. Her voice was strange. *"He should have taken you instead."*

Aunt Dahlia squeezed his hand. He looked up . . .

To see a porcelain mask looking back.

He yelped and staggered back.

When he looked around the gathered crowd, every one of them wore the mask of the shadowman.

"This is your fault, Sebastian," the masked congregation said in unison. They all watched him with their placid, eyeless stares. Their wicked painted smiles. *"All your fault."*

"No," Sebastian said. He took another step back and tripped over a toppled tombstone. Pain shot through his palms from where they'd landed in a thorny bush. Hastily, he hobbled back up to his feet and continued to back away. "No, this isn't real."

"If it isn't real," said one. The creature that had been Aunt Dahlia. It reached over and grabbed his hand. Revealed a scraped palm. *"Then why are you bleeding?"*

"No . . . No!"

He yanked his hand away and turned to run.

But the ground gave way beneath his feet, and he fell into a yawning pit of shadows and blackness, spiraling down, down, while the chorus of shadows laughed up above.

Sebastian jolted when he hit the bottom of the pit.

It took him a moment to realize it had been a dream.

"Just a dream." He sighed. He reached down to pull up the covers that had become tangled at his feet.

His hands.

They were covered in blood.

"No," he whispered. "This can't be real."

He pinched himself, hoping it was a dream within a dream. But he didn't wake up. He was still in his room, it was still dark outside, and his hands were still scraped by a thornbush that shouldn't have existed.

He got out of bed. He needed to clean the wounds. Needed to bandage them—

He froze.

Something was moving in his mirror.

He wasn't alone.

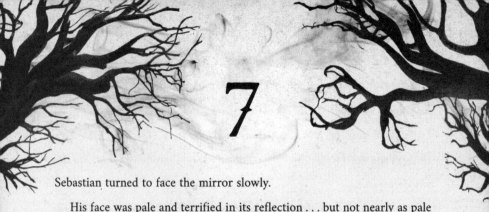

7

Sebastian turned to face the mirror slowly.

His face was pale and terrified in its reflection . . . but not nearly as pale as the mask that materialized in the shadows.

Sebastian took a stumbling step backward, knocking into his dresser. The mirror was between him and the door. He'd have to walk past it to get out. There was no way.

He couldn't even scream as the shadowman solidified in the mirror, as its blackened, skeletal fingers caressed the other side of the glass.

The mirror rippled, wobbled.

"*She can hide you no longer, Sebastian,*" the shadowman murmured. "*I can find you anywhere. Even here.*"

The shadowman pressed his hand forward.

The mirror bowed.

And the shadowman's hand pushed *through*.

The moment it did, the room was filled with the acrid stench of rotten meat and electric char. The curtains fluttered in an unfelt breeze. The bed rattled and rocked like a boat on the stormy seas. Every light in Sebastian's room flickered and flared and popped as his ceiling fan whirred and the figurines on his desk began a slow march. Even the books on his desk snapped like living creatures, and his clothes piles squirmed as if filled with rats.

"*You will be mine, Sebastian,*" the shadowman said. He reached his other arm through the mirror and gripped the frame. The wood charred where his fingers touched. "*As you should have been before.*"

Another pair of arms sprouted from his back, forcing themselves through the mirror glass and gripping the edges. Sharp talons dug into the wooden frame.

The shadowman lowered his head and pressed his forehead against the glass. The surface of the mirror wobbled as the monster's face broke through. Sebastian took a terrified step back, but he was stopped before he could get far—one of his shirts wrapped around his legs, binding him in place.

A seam appeared down the center of the shadowman's mask, splitting it neatly in two.

And as it widened, a long, black tongue rolled out.

Behind the mask was nothing but rotten black flesh and a tunnel of teeth, and the tongue that snaked its way toward Sebastian in a sinuous slither.

Sebastian finally found his voice and screamed.

The tongue raised itself to eye level and reared back, readying to strike, as the shadowman howled with victory.

The door flew open—

And into the room stormed Aunt Dahlia.

She didn't flinch when she saw the monstrous beast, didn't even startle when a book flew by her head. No, she stared at the monster with a quiet resolve, as if she had been waiting for—and dreading—this moment her entire life.

"You won't have him," she called out in a clear, strong voice.

She took a step forward and raised her hands in front of her, her fingers steepled in a strange gesture.

"You will leave this place. Now!"

As she yelled her final word, arcs of blue light sparked along her wrists and through her hands.

Sebastian's head spun as he watched lines of blue light trace themselves around the shadowman's wrists and neck, as a muzzle of blue wrapped around his split mask and slowly forced it shut. The tongue recoiled, snapped back into the shadowman's unending maw. But the creature didn't give up the fight.

Sebastian's room went wild. Bedsheets snapped from the bed and swirled around the room in an impossible windstorm, while books buffeted and toys went berserk. Even then, Aunt Dahlia didn't break, not as her hair billowed around her, not as books and toys tried to slam into her, rebounding off some invisible wall.

There was a shield around her . . . and around Sebastian as well. Even though he was still wrapped in clothes, none of the flying debris was hitting him.

"You cannot keep him safe any longer, Dahlia!" the shadowman roared. "I have seen him! I have tasted him! Your powers will never match mine, and you will never know peace again. I will have the boy!"

Aunt Dahlia didn't respond. She took another step forward. The lights around her fingers burned blindingly bright, as did the magical manacles wrapped around the shadowman. He struggled forward, tried to force himself the rest of the way through the mirror, his fingers scratching deep grooves in the wood.

Whatever Aunt Dahlia was doing was working. She took another step, and the shadowman was forced back. Farther into the mirror.

One of his hands slipped. Slurped back behind the glass. The clothes wrapped around Sebastian fell to the floor.

"He will never be yours," Aunt Dahlia said. Her teeth were gritted tight, her words sharp and biting. "Not so long as I live."

"*Your death,*" the shadowman said, "*can be arranged.*"

In one last effort, he lunged toward Aunt Dahlia, two of his four arms reaching out toward her. One taloned hand scratched her cheek.

"No!" Sebastian screamed, reaching for her.

Just like before, an unexpected power flooded him, a desperation made physical.

His hands tingled with cold as a billow of purple light burst from his palms.

The light connected, just as the creature slashed at Aunt Dahlia's face again.

The light pushed the monster back into the mirror. His hands slipped back through the glass.

The moment the shadowman had vanished beyond, the room went deathly still. The wind died, the books and sheets dropped from the air. Sebastian and his aunt stood there, panting, staring into the dark mirror.

Then Aunt Dahlia strode forward and raised her hand, drawing her fingers in an intricate pattern over the mirror's surface. A tail of blue light traced itself under her fingertips, creating a symbol that glowed an unearthly blue, a symbol that made Sebastian's mind spark with recognition, even though he was certain he'd never seen it before.

When she was done, she turned to face Sebastian, blood dripping down her cheek. The symbol faded into the glass. Now, the mirror showed only Sebastian's terrified expression.

"Well," Aunt Dahlia said after studying him for a long moment, "I think this calls for a pot of tea."

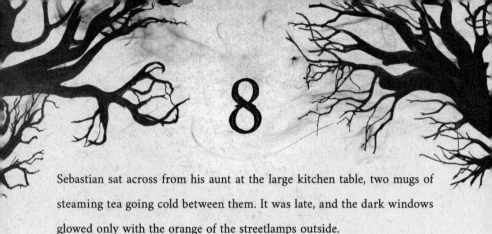

8

Sebastian sat across from his aunt at the large kitchen table, two mugs of steaming tea going cold between them. It was late, and the dark windows glowed only with the orange of the streetlamps outside.

Neither of them spoke. Aunt Dahlia watched him, a thousand thoughts clearly racing behind her eyes, while Sebastian stared numbly at the walls, wondering what was actually real. The only sound was the *tick tick tick* of a grandfather clock in the living room, and even that seemed to be working at an uneven pace.

"Can you tell me what is inside the tea?" Aunt Dahlia finally asked.

Sebastian's head jerked up.

"The . . . tea?"

"Yes," she replied. "What herbs do you smell?"

"I . . ."

He had just witnessed her confronting a terrifying spirit in his bedroom. A terrifying spirit that she had somehow not only known about, but had known how to fight off. With magic. He had seen his aunt doing magic. And somehow . . . somehow he had done magic, too.

This was no time for identifying the tea she had blended.

"There is chamomile, of course," she said, her voice light. She lifted her cup to her lips. "And lavender. Both good, calming herbs. But there is another note. Can you sense it?"

Now Sebastian worried it wasn't he who'd lost his mind, but his aunt.

He opened his mouth. He found he couldn't speak—the words just wouldn't come.

"Very well," she said. "I have also included a tincture of yarrow. Not the most delicious of herbs, but in an infusion it cleanses the soul of evil, and protects from dark spirits. I've admittedly been adding a few drops to your juice at breakfast for the last few weeks, just in case. I see my fear was merited."

She watched his eyes as she spoke.

She'd taught him the properties of dozens of herbs. But their medicinal properties. Nothing about evil, or ghosts. Sebastian's eyes widened. How much did she know? And how long had she known it?

Again, he tried to say something. And again, he couldn't even begin to find words for the countless questions he had.

"What happened in your room should not have been able to happen," Aunt Dahlia continued. She was normally warm, but her words now were emotionless. "I have warded this house against lesser and greater spirits, but apparently that is no longer enough to keep you safe."

Sebastian's tongue finally untwisted.

"But what *was* that?" he gasped.

"A spirit," Aunt Dahlia replied calmly. "And a particularly vile one at that."

"But it . . . it was after me. Why was it after me?"

Once more, she studied him with a cold, calculated detachment that was very much unlike her usual self.

"How long have you seen the dead, Sebastian?"

If he hadn't been sitting down, he would have dropped to his knees.

She knew.

"Forever," he whispered.

She swallowed, and the cold facade broke. She took a sip of tea, and when she spoke again, she looked not at him, but at the stained-glass window.

"I feared as much. Why didn't you ever tell me?"

Now it was his turn to look away.

"I didn't want you to think I was making it up."

Aunt Dahlia gave a short laugh that might have been a sob.

"Trust me, little bird," she said. "It would take much more than that."

She took another long drink, then looked to him and gestured to his cup. "Drink," she said. "Lavender has purificatory properties as well. You'll feel much better."

Sebastian did as he was told, and was mildly surprised at the warmth that seemed to flow out from his stomach when he took his first sip. He hadn't realized just how cold he was. Now that he had the mug in his hands, he couldn't stop shivering.

"There is so much I have to tell you," Aunt Dahlia said. "And so much I'd wished with all my heart I'd never *have* to tell you. But it appears I have no choice."

She set her mug down and looked at him.

"You can see the dead, Sebastian. As I can see them, and as your parents could see them. All children are born with the gift, though some are more open to it than others. Usually, though, the gift fades. By the time a child is thirteen, their connection to the world of the dead—what we call the *Æther*—is all but gone. But for some . . ." She took a deep, shuddering breath. "For those who have seen someone die firsthand, that connection is instead strengthened. Their tie to the Æther grows absolute. And with that tie comes a gift. A gift of magic. A gift that we use to keep balance between the world of the living and the world of the dead. A gift, my dear little bird, that your parents and I had hoped against hope you would not come to possess."

Sebastian's mouth had gone dry. He went to take another drink, but his mug was empty.

"Why . . . why didn't you ever tell me this?" he asked. All the pain and fear of the last few years . . . all of it could have been avoided if she'd said something.

Maybe she would have, if you hadn't been too scared to tell her what you saw, he thought.

"Because this gift is a curse," she replied. "To be an Æthercist—one dedicated to fighting back the spirits that wish to enter our world—is to not only live a life of constant danger, but to be an outcast, and to be burdened with knowledge that no mortal should have. Your mother hoped—as I had hoped—that you would be spared that fate. Clearly, no matter how hard we tried to prevent it from happening, we both failed."

"But . . . How . . . I felt . . ."

"Magic," she said. "What you did up there was an act of magic, an act of the Æther. And a clear sign that the path of gallows calls to you."

Sebastian's head spun. *I can work magic?*

"I have to be dreaming," he said. "This can't be real."

"It is," she said. "And the sooner you understand that, the better your chances of survival will be. Ardea was right all along . . ."

"Ardea?"

"*Madame* Ardea," Aunt Dahlia corrected. "She is the rectress of a school. A school where you can learn to fight the dead. Normally, students aren't admitted until they are thirteen. But it's clear we have no choice. I had hoped my powers could protect you, but it seems that I'm no longer enough to keep you safe."

Sebastian swallowed. None of this was connecting.

At least, that's what he told himself. But as she spoke, a part of him felt like everything made perfect sense. He just didn't want to admit it.

And then, out of nowhere, Aunt Dahlia began to cry.

Sebastian's heart broke. He got up and went over and wrapped her in a hug.

"It's okay," he said. "It's okay."

He knew, though, that it wasn't okay. Because this house had always been safe—he'd seen ghosts everywhere else, but never here. His aunt had protected him without his knowing. And now, the ghost that hunted him had promised to harm her if she got in his way.

It wasn't okay at all. Sebastian knew, deep down, that if he wanted to keep Aunt Dahlia safe, he would have to leave.

She patted his hand. She tried to smile up at him, but her lips quivered.

"Tomorrow," she said. "I'll reach out to her. I believe their term hasn't started yet. And there . . . there they can teach you everything. There, they can keep you safe." She burst into tears again. "I failed you," she said. "Just as I failed Danea. I promised your mother I'd keep you safe."

"You did, though," Sebastian said. He felt, with a horrible certainty, that a new and terrifying future was yawning open in front of him. "You tried. I . . . I want to go. I want to learn how to defend myself."

She squeezed his hand.

"Then we have one more night," she said. "And tomorrow you will fly away to Gallowgate."

9

Sebastian couldn't sleep. Not after that. Not after everything he'd witnessed, and everything his aunt had said.

She could see ghosts. She could *fight* ghosts. And she was sending him to a school with other kids just like him, kids who could see and fend off the dead.

He sat curled up on his bed, staring at the mirror, his thoughts racing.

He could just barely see the outline of the magical symbol his aunt had traced over the mirror, like the afterburn of staring at a bright light bulb, faint but there at the edge of his vision.

It was almost possible to believe it was a dream. All of it. The shadowman and his aunt's admission.

Except.

Except, whereas the symbol was faint, and the memory of their kitchen table conversation grew more and more surreal, there was one definitive truth he couldn't ignore: the burned grooves on his mirror frame, where the shadowman had tried to pull through. He stared at them with a heavy certainty, every splinter another jab in his fragile world. Every splinter a promise of future pain.

And he knew, then, that this wasn't a dream, and he wasn't waking up.

He could see ghosts.

There was a power inside of him that he could use to fight them.

And in the morning . . . in the morning he would leave here, leave everything and everyone he knew, and the one person he loved. The one person who had kept him safe. The one person *he* now had to keep safe. From himself.

Fear gripped his chest, made his guts churn.

The last thing he wanted was to leave. Aunt Dahlia's house had become his home. She was the only family he had left.

And why would he want to *fight* ghosts? He'd spent his entire life trying to hide from them. He never wanted this curse. He never wanted to be able to see the dead. And he most definitely didn't want to have to fight them for the rest of his life.

But then . . . then he thought of what would happen if he didn't go to Gallowgate. If he chose to stay.

He didn't think about the ghosts, or the shadowman, or what *might* happen.

He thought of what he knew *would* happen if he went to school in the morning, even if everything that had happened tonight had been a fever dream.

He knew everyone would make fun of him for what had happened in the cafeteria.

He knew Aaron—his only shot at friendship—would never speak to him again, and he'd spend the rest of middle school like he had elementary school: sad and alone.

And the more he thought about that, the more the sensations in his heart shifted.

He thought about what it might be like to go to a school where everyone was a weirdo like him. Where he wouldn't have to hide and pretend anymore.

Until, when light finally broke through the windows, Sebastian found that he wasn't all that scared, after all.

He was actually a little excited.

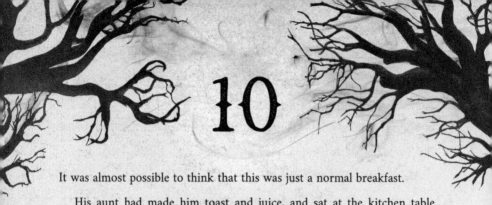

10

It was almost possible to think that this was just a normal breakfast.

His aunt had made him toast and juice, and sat at the kitchen table reading a book with a coffee in hand. It was almost possible, except for the fact that when Sebastian sat down to eat, his aunt waved her hand without looking up from her book, and the coffeepot hovered over from the kitchen and poured a fresh stream of coffee into her mug.

She grinned up at him when the pot finally resettled itself.

"I've missed being able to do that," she said.

Sebastian's jaw dropped.

"Will *I* be able to do that?" he asked.

"Not at first. Conjuring's a tricky field, and your first-year's studies will be devoted to, well, surviving the next few years of your education. But don't worry, you'll learn. It's in your blood."

She paused.

"Speaking of . . . Has anything strange ever happened to you?"

"You mean like seeing ghosts all the time?"

She bit her lip. "Not quite. Has anything else ever happened? Anything at all?"

He thought about what had happened in the cafeteria, about the world fading away to grayscale. But the way she was looking at him, that barely concealed concern, made him hold off. He didn't want to give her any more reason to worry.

"Nope," he said. "I think the ghost thing is weird enough."

She nodded, but he could tell she didn't quite believe him.

He had just taken a bite of his toast when a billow of smoke swirled out of thin air in the corner of the room. He nearly choked as it materialized into the form of a floating, translucent girl.

She hovered a foot off the ground, her hair and white dress billowing around her as if she were underwater. She looked like she was about his age, though from a long-gone era.

"Gh-ghost!" he managed. How had she gotten in here?

But Aunt Dahlia didn't seem the slightest bit concerned.

"Hello, Willow," his aunt said, nodding to the girl. "I take it Ardea got my message?"

"She did," the girl—Willow?—said. "And she questions whether or not it is safe for Sebastian to attend, given . . ." She trailed off and looked at Sebastian, but she didn't clarify.

"Pain me as it does to admit it," Aunt Dahlia said, "he is safer there than he is here. That . . . *thing* . . . should not have been able to get past my defenses. Gallowgate has stronger wards than I."

Willow just nodded.

"Besides," Aunt Dahlia continued, "although this wasn't the path any of us wanted him to take, it was the one we were presented. He has to take it. You know that better than most."

The ghost girl nodded again. "If that is your wish, then he is to come with me. The term begins this evening."

"At least one thing is working in our favor," Aunt Dahlia said. She looked to him, and although she smiled, he could tell it was strained. She may have been acting like this was all business as usual, but he could tell this was hard on her. "Go get dressed, Sebastian," she said gently. "I've never been good with long goodbyes."

"But I haven't started packing—"

"You will need only the clothes on your back," Willow interrupted. "We will see that the rest is taken care of."

Sebastian wanted to question, wanted to stall, but it was clear that Willow had no desire to answer any questions. Aunt Dahlia gestured for him to go. Her lip quivered slightly, and her hands shook.

He plodded up to his room to get dressed, his breakfast completely forgotten.

Now, truly, he felt like he was walking through a dream.

He changed into shorts and a T-shirt, and grabbed a hoodie just in case. He looked around his room, wondering when or if he'd see it again. He felt guilty about the unmade bed, the piles of clothes and stacks of books scattered on the floor. But Aunt Dahlia called out from downstairs. There wasn't time to linger and get all nostalgic. If he did, he'd never leave.

He looked to the mirror. The sight of the burnt claw marks emboldened him, just a little.

He didn't know what he was approaching, but he knew that he couldn't stay here. Not if he wanted to keep Aunt Dahlia—and himself—safe.

As he turned to go, however, the picture on his nightstand caught his eye. The one of him and his parents by the fountain.

Willow had said not to bring anything, but he wasn't going to leave this behind.

He ran over and grabbed it—as well as one of him and Aunt Dahlia on his last birthday—and wrapped them in his hoodie.

"Ready to fly, little bird?" Aunt Dahlia asked when he got downstairs.

She stood in the middle of the kitchen, Willow floating beside her, as if sharing space with a dead girl was the most normal thing in the world.

He nodded.

Aunt Dahlia smiled, and her composure cracked. She knelt in front of him and swept him up in a hug. Her shoulders didn't shake, but he felt a warm tear drop to his shoulder.

"Remember I love you," she said. "And that everything I've done, everything I've kept from you, was all born from that love. Now. Be brave. And do what Madame Ardea says. If you think *I* have a lot of rules . . ." She leaned back and forced herself to grin.

Sebastian sniffed back the wave of tears.

"Come," Willow said beside him. "It is time."

He nodded, and Aunt Dahlia stood.

His aunt looked to the kitchen door and raised her hands once more. Her fingers danced an intricate formation, and blue lights swirled around her fingertips. The space within the doorframe rippled like a stone thrown into a pond, and when it stilled, he could see nothing beyond it but blue mist and swirling shadow.

Willow gestured him forward.

Sebastian walked toward the door. Looked back over his shoulder once, to see his aunt crying silently behind him.

Then he stepped through, into the doorway, into the unknown, and his home vanished in a billow of blue smoke.

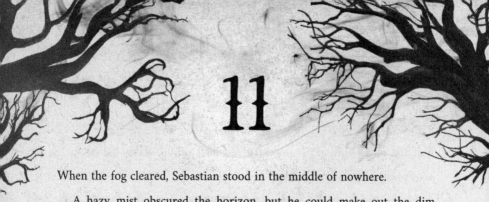

11

When the fog cleared, Sebastian stood in the middle of nowhere.

A hazy mist obscured the horizon, but he could make out the dim shapes of rolling hills in the distance. Somehow, even though it had been morning when he'd left home, it was twilight here: The haze was a steely blue, the hills purpled and bruised. Everything in between was marshland, low pools of water and small mounds of grass.

Willow was nowhere to be seen.

Had something gone wrong? Had his aunt sent him to the wrong place?

This definitely wasn't a school, and it didn't look like there was one anywhere in sight.

He stood on a wooden platform, the planks creaking loudly as he adjusted his feet to look around.

Behind him was a doorframe. Simple. Wooden. Though when he peered closer he saw that symbols had been engraved and gilded in it, shimmering a faint gold when they caught the dying light. The platform ended with the edge of the door. The only way forward was the narrow walkway that snaked through the marsh, though its destination was covered in heavy fog.

Sebastian stood there for a few moments. Didn't they always say that if you were lost, you should stay put? Let someone find you? Surely Willow would show up.

But as the seconds stretched by, another thought sent chills down his spine.

The shadowman had said he could find Sebastian anywhere.

Did that mean here, beyond the safety of his aunt's? If Willow could find him, he had to believe that the shadowman could, too.

He looked around one more time. Nothing stirred in the marshes. But he couldn't stay here. Just in case.

As quietly and carefully as he could, he made his way down the winding walkway.

Soon, the fog rolled in around him, and even the way back was obscured in mist.

Anything could be hiding in the gloom.

He walked faster and tried not to fall into the marsh.

As the fog shifted around him, he was able to make sense of small swathes of the landscape.

There were large stones on the hillocks surrounding him. No—not stones. Tombstones. Ancient and crumbling, some bigger than he was. They were strewn about the landscape. Was this whole sunken place a graveyard? Why had Aunt Dahlia sent him here?

He moved even faster.

The fog shifted yet again, and he was able to see where the path was heading.

A lake stretched out before him. A lake so large he couldn't see the other side. An enormous island, filled with dense trees and sloping hills, rose out from the center. Atop the tallest hill was a manor.

It looked like something out of a high fantasy, a sprawling beast of gray stone and steepled roofs and twisted towers. It had to be as big as a city block, if not bigger. Its windows were leaded and gray, the roof tiled with slate. But even from here, he could see the manor was in grave disrepair. Whole chunks had caved in, and more than one tower tilted precariously.

He felt his gut churn.

Was this Gallowgate?

For a split second he considered turning around. It didn't look like any-thing lived on that island. Even in the gathering darkness, he couldn't see a single light within the manor, or even a fire flicking in the forest.

Then the terrible scent of rotten meat and electric char filled his nos-trils, and he knew, before even turning around, that he had been found.

The shadowman stood on the walkway behind him.

"You think they will save you?" the shadowman asked. His four arms arced about him like spider legs, and his placid mask was a terrifying counter to the rage in his voice. *"You think you can learn to fight me? After what I've done? After the people I've killed?"*

Sebastian took a step backward and nearly fell into the water. In his stumble, the bundled hoodie he kept to his chest slipped.

The photograph of his parents slipped into the murk below.

The shadowman growled in amusement as it watched Sebastian's par-ents descend into the marsh.

"Such sentiment," he said. *"But fear not, Sebastian. You will join them soon!"*

The shadowman lunged.

Sebastian yelped and burst into a run, his footsteps thundering over the wooden planks.

Fog swirled thick around him, sometimes obscuring even his footsteps, and darkness descended like a cloak. He ran frantically forward.

Behind him, the shadowman's own footsteps were silent.

Sebastian didn't dare look over his shoulder to see how far away the monster was. It was too close. Way too close.

The shore loomed ahead.

Thirty feet.

Twenty.

A gateway arched up over the walkway's end, an imposing entrance of curling iron and heavy black spikes. There were words twined in the metal, but he couldn't make them out, and he didn't try.

He ran harder. Faster than he had in his entire life.

The archway neared.

Ten feet.

Five.

And he made the fatal mistake. He looked over his shoulder—to see the shadowman so close, his sharp fingers outstretched, that he could nearly reach him.

Sebastian stumbled and fell to his knees, but momentum kept him moving forward. He flipped over himself, curled tight into a ball, his eyes squeezed shut to block out the pain of the shadowman's sharp claws grabbing him, yanking him away.

But that pain never came.

After a terrified moment, he looked up and screamed.

The shadowman stood only a few feet from him. The monster stared down at him with that eyeless porcelain mask, but it didn't move, didn't lunge or try to rip him apart with those clawed hands. And it was only then that Sebastian realized—he had tumbled through the archway. He was crouched in the mud on the island, while the shadowman towered on the walkway.

The shadowman reached up one hand and stroked the space within the arch.

Blue light sparked at his fingertips. But he couldn't press his hand through.

Calmly, ever so calmly, the shadowman clasped his hands behind him.

"*It would have been better for you to die unknowing,*" he said. "*Now, you only delay the inevitable. And the longer you make me wait, the more I will make you suffer.*"

The shadowman dissolved in a curl of acrid black smoke.

Sebastian sighed in relief and flopped back in the mud, not caring that his only clothes were getting destroyed.

And as a light rain began to fall on him, he finally made out the words in the archway.

GALLOWGATE ACADEMY FOR ÆTHERIC ARTS

He'd made it.

Barely.

12

"What are you doing down there?" came a voice behind him.

Sebastian startled and looked over to see a boy standing by a tombstone a few feet away.

He was taller than Sebastian, though about his own age, with dark skin and short, curly black hair and a confused expression on his face. He also wore the strangest clothes Sebastian had ever seen.

A cloak with a cowl of raven feathers sat atop the boy's shoulders, and the clothes beneath were asymmetric jet black and covered in belts and buckles. He had a beaked plague doctor mask held loosely in one hand, its plate glass crimson eyes reflecting the light that came from a ball of white flame floating above his head.

Sebastian hurriedly stood, though any attempt at wiping the mud from his knees just made it worse.

"I—I—did you see that?"

"See what?" the boy asked. He took a few steps closer, his thick-soled boots squelching through the mud. He peered out to the walkway. Which was, of course, empty.

"There was a ghost . . ." Sebastian said.

The boy just chuckled. "Yeah. That's kind of why we're here." He grinned and held out his leather-gloved hand. "I'm Harold, by the way. Harold Watts. And you are?"

"Sebastian Wight." He once more tried to wipe his hands clean, but it didn't help. He shook Harold's hand, and Harold didn't seem to mind. In fact, Harold's gloves were also covered in dirt, and Sebastian realized there were plants drooping out of a satchel at his side.

"Welcome to Gallowgate, Bastian," Harold said. "Though you're a little late. Everyone's inside for the commencement dinner."

Dinner? Sebastian had barely had breakfast. Where *were* they? Also, no one had ever called him Bastian before. The name sent a small thrill through him.

"Come on—I'll take you there." Harold turned and began walking the dirt path that wound its way into the dark, mossy woods.

"But the . . . the ghost," Bastian said, hurrying to keep up. "It wants to kill me."

Harold looked over his shoulder. He didn't appear to be the slightest bit alarmed.

"Not unusual," he said. "But don't worry. Gallowgate has so many wards, no spirit can enter here unless they're summoned."

"Speaking of . . ." Bastian said. "There was another ghost that was supposed to be following me. Willow."

"I wouldn't worry about her. Chances are once you were sent to the Door, she wandered off. She's the liaison between Gallowgate and the rest of the world, so she's pretty busy."

They wandered up the hill, following the muddy trail. Bastian couldn't stop looking around. Part of him was terrified that the shadowman would come back. The rest was trying to come to terms with the fact that he was very much no longer in the Midwest.

The trees around them were old and gnarled, drooping with age, their branches glistening with rain in Harold's magical light. Large stones the size of Bastian were hiding in the ferns and brambles of the underbrush, and he noticed more than one tombstone peeking up through the misty gloom. He swore, too, he saw other shapes through the fog: shifting shadows, and flares of pale blue light that danced like fireflies. Harold brushed aside a long curtain of moss that hung over their path and kept it open for Bastian to hurry through.

"What were you doing out here, anyway?" Bastian asked. "I thought you said everyone was inside?"

"Hah, yeah. It's kind of a long story. I was out gathering some herbs. Belladonna. It loves the rain."

He patted the satchel of plants, but didn't elaborate on whatever the long story was.

"Where are we going?" Bastian asked. He wasn't normally this talkative around new kids, but the adrenaline coursing through him made it impossible to stay quiet. "I saw a manor before, but it looked pretty destroyed."

Harold just laughed.

"You'll see," he said.

A few minutes later, the forest thinned out, became a rolling lawn of green grass dotted with tombstones. The path changed from mud to cobblestone, and led straight up to the massive doors of the manor.

And it was *not* how it had appeared before.

Bastian stopped, his jaw dropping open in awe.

The manor was no longer a crumbling heap of abandoned gray stones. Instead, the series of interlocking buildings swept grandly over the top of the hill, their leaded windows glowing warmly with inner firelight. The derelict towers stood proudly, piercing the clouds that swirled around the highest turrets. The whole place was easily the size of two city blocks—Bastian couldn't even see the far sides, which dipped and disappeared into the trees. Iron lamps lined the cobbled walk, leading to a massive arched doorway that was easily three times Bastian's height and just as wide.

And as they walked nearer, Bastian realized the manor was even stranger up close.

The great lampposts they passed were topped not with lanterns, but with skulls whose eyes burned unearthly blue. At the base of each, twisted thornbushes grew, their purple flowers following the boys as they passed. Through some of the upper windows, Bastian could see staircases. Staircases that spiraled *sideways*. What he thought were normal formations on one of the towers turned out to be a row of tombstones lined up the side like a dragon's spine.

And he swore, when he wasn't looking, some of the towers moved.

They reached the great wooden doors. There, embellished in the wood, was a giant shield crest. Within it was a heron perched atop a human skull, a lantern in its beak and two fronds of plants curling up around it. Above the crest were three words:

MORS SOLUM LIMEN

"The school crest," Harold said. He flourished his hand, and as the light above him winked out, the doors opened of their own accord.

Warm air and firelight flickered out, and Harold led him into the hall. Bastian couldn't stop staring.

The space was enormous, easily half the size of a football field. Fireplaces as tall as Bastian lined both walls, their fires burning brightly. Leather chairs and sofas ringed the fires, along with small tables and patterned rugs in a myriad of colors. Stone pillars swept up to support the arched ceiling, and torches held in skeletal hands were embedded in the stone.

As they walked past, one of the hands actually waved.

Bastian nearly leaped out of his skin.

Harold led him onward, down the long crimson carpet that swept from the doorway to a grand double staircase at the far end. A fountain gurgled happily at the base of the stairs. It took Bastian a moment to realize that the statue with water flowing from its hands wasn't of just any girl. It was Willow.

"She was one of the founders of Gallowgate," Harold said, noticing Bastian's stare. "A couple hundred years ago. But don't ask her for a specific date. She gets touchy about her age."

"Noted," Bastian said. *Ghosts get touchy about their age?*

Harold led them upstairs.

"Normally I'd say you should change first," Harold said as he led them down a hall. He glanced at an enormous grandfather clock along the wall; it was made of black wood, and the pendulum rocking back and forth within was a bone studded with gold, while its face was an intricate clockwork of gears and crescent moons. "But there's no time. And I guess you don't have any other clothes with you . . . ?"

"Willow told me not to . . ." Bastian said weakly.

Harold grinned. "Don't worry about it. The manor provides."

Farther down the hall, Bastian heard the murmur of voices. His heart started to beat double time. He glanced down at his muddy and torn clothes, at his awkward bundle of muddy hoodie and carefully concealed photograph. Harold noticed the scared look.

"We'll sneak in the back," Harold assured him. "No one will notice."

Bastian nodded, the lump in his throat preventing him from speaking. It was one thing to imagine being surrounded by kids like him, kids who could see the dead. It was another thing entirely to be about to face them.

They reached their destination: another set of arched double doors, though much smaller than those outside. Bastian could barely hear the din inside over the pounding of his heart. How many kids were in there? Harold put a finger to his lips. Bastian nodded.

Harold leaned against the door and pushed it open slightly, just wide enough for Bastian to step inside.

The room was grand. More fireplaces blazed along the walls, their fires flickering between blue and purple, red and green, the light making the stained-glass windows above them dance. Or maybe the figures in the glass *were* dancing.

Bastian couldn't tell. His eyes were transfixed by the dozens of round tables scattered throughout the hall, each of them filled with kids of all ages laughing and joking. Save for the two tables nearest them, all the kids were wearing very strange uniforms. Above the tables, more skulls with glowing green eyes floated about, dancing and chattering to each other between flocks of fluttering bats.

Bastian's feet froze to the flagstones.

Harold nudged him, gesturing toward a table nearby, one with a bunch of kids about their age, all in normal clothes, who looked just as scared and excited as Bastian felt.

They were almost there. Then a Japanese woman wearing black robes embroidered in purple stood up from the high table. She had long curls of gray hair and sharp, piercing eyes.

"Sebastian Wight!" she called out, freezing him and Harold in place. Everyone cut off their chatter and turned around to face him. "You are late."

Bastian wanted to fall through the floor.

"So much for going unnoticed," Harold murmured.

13

The woman gestured for them to sit. Harold grabbed Bastian's arm and pulled him over to an empty spot at the nearest table, even though Bastian would have much rather turned tail and run out the door.

He sat, with Harold beside him, and the woman cleared her throat and began to speak. Slowly the curious glances of his new classmates shifted back to her.

"Welcome, students," she said. "Now that we are *all* here, we may begin."

Bastian glanced quickly around his table. The kids were definitely all new, like himself—they had the same nervous expressions, staring up at the woman with wide eyes. All except for a boy across from him, a boy with shaggy brown hair, thick black glasses, and dark olive skin, who was looking right at him. The moment their eyes met, Bastian felt his heart flip.

Both Bastian and the boy quickly looked away.

"Welcome to Gallowgate Academy for Ætheric Arts," the woman said grandly. "As many of you know, my name is Madame Ardea, and I am the rectress of this school. Over the course of the coming year, my fellow professors and I will train you in the skills necessary to fight and defeat the restless dead."

Bastian focused on the high table. The professors seated there were the strangest mix of adults he'd ever seen. There was a younger copper-skinned man in a leather biking jacket, with scars on his face and violent red highlights in his choppy black hair. The Black woman beside him was dressed like she was going to the Met Gala, in a luxurious red dress with a cowl that framed her smooth head. Beside her was an old sunburnt white man in grubby coveralls, who had a plague doctor mask similar to Harold's perched atop his curly gray hair.

Harold nudged him, and Bastian went back to focusing on Madame Ardea.

"Your studies will not be easy, but we expect you to take them seriously. The balance between life and death lies within your young hands. During your first year, you will be versed in the four pillars of the Ætheric Arts. And at the end of the year, you will undergo a series of exams to determine your focus for the rest of your education here. Those pillars are . . ."

She gestured to the wall, and a banner unrolled, revealing a blue tapestry of a spider in the center of its web. "Summoning."

Another flick of the wrist, and now a goldenrod tapestry of a scorpion unfurled. "Conjuring."

On the other wall, a green tapestry with a snake curled in a figure eight appeared. "Alchemy."

A final gesture, and a red tapestry of a moth with a skull pattern on its wings unrolled. "And Necromancy. At the end of the year, you will be sorted into your discipline during a ceremony called the Naming of the Guard. From there, your focus will become specialized as you train in your own unique skill. Each of the pillars is important; each will complement the others, which is why you will often work in teams when sent into the field to banish the dead. At Gallowgate, your education within these walls is only a fraction of your course load. The outside world is constantly under threat from wayward spirits, and you will be tasked with banishing them . . . soon."

She looked around the room, and Bastian followed her gaze.

He realized, then, that save for one other table of first-year students, everyone in the dining hall was grouped together based on their outfits. Under the scorpion banner, the kids wore leather jackets and ripped jeans, their hair funky colors, with chains and amulets draped around their necks. The groups under the spider wore black robes with intricate blue embroidery, much like Madame Ardea's, though they also had belts with charms and crystal daggers and bells at their waists. Those beneath the moth wore layers of gauzy purple and black, their necks and wrists laden with charms and bracelets and crystals. There was even a table of kids dressed similarly to Harold—the smeared coveralls, the bandolier of pouches slung across their chests, and plague doctor masks on the table before them. They sat beneath the twined serpent.

Maybe Harold wasn't a new student like Bastian. But Harold didn't look old enough . . .

"Remember, students," Madame Ardea said, and Bastian swore the lights in the room darkened when she spoke. "Ours is not an easy path. So many of you have faced terrible hardships to come here, and will face many more before your studies are through. The forces of darkness forever stir in the world beyond. But know this: Together, we will never be defeated. We are the guardians between the worlds. We walk where normal people fear to tread. We are Æthercists. Tomorrow, we submit to this ancient and arduous path. But tonight, we feast!"

She clapped her hands, and the doors behind her opened.

Trays floated out from the back rooms, laden with delicacies that made Bastian's mouth water: glittering silver dishes of roast chicken and beef, tureens of soup, platters of freshly baked bread, towering stands of pies and cookies and cakes. At first, he thought it was levitation magic, like his aunt had used only hours ago.

As one tray of roast chicken wafted over, however, Bastian realized it was being carried by a very faint ghost.

The ghost set its tray in the middle of the table, and others laid down their offerings until Bastian could barely see the boy across from him for all the morsels in between.

Apparently, that was the end of the opening ceremony, as around them, the older kids burst back into excited chatter.

Harold started grabbing food from the center, and the spell of silence broke.

"My name's Andromeda," said a white girl with purple streaks in her long black hair. "Andromeda Starr. Conjurer. At least, I better be."

Harold snorted at Bastian's side, but managed to hide it in a cough.

"Harold Watts," he said. "Future Alchemist." He nudged his mask with a fork—all of the cutlery was blackened silver, the handles shaped like bones. "Obviously."

"Can you choose?" Bastian asked after introducing himself.

"Not really," Harold said. "They select you based on your exams and the aptitude you show in classes. But alchemy's been my thing for, like, ever."

"How do you know all this?" asked a white boy with curly red hair named Roman. "I just found out I wasn't going crazy for seeing ghosts last week."

An Indian girl with her hair in a long ponytail laughed. "I nearly had a heart attack when a ghost showed up in my closet with the letter."

"I, um," Harold said, his dark cheeks flushing. "I've been here a while."

"A while?" Andromeda asked. She had a sharp, biting voice that cut through the din. She reminded Bastian of a female version of Billy. "What, are you, like, an orphan or something?"

Harold swallowed and didn't answer.

So many of you have faced terrible hardships to come here, Madame Ardea had said. If kids only saw ghosts after the age of thirteen because they'd seen someone die, did that mean everyone here was connected by that same terrible thread?

Thankfully, the other kids at the table picked up the conversation.

Bastian kept glancing over at the brown-haired boy across from him. *Finlay,* he overheard the boy say to the girl beside him. She had short blonde hair with pink streaks, and wore fingerless leather gloves—even while eating. Bastian never caught her name.

When they'd all eaten their fill, and Bastian couldn't have eaten another cookie if he'd been threatened, the ghosts came back and removed the trays. Madame Ardea stood up once more. The fires in the room dimmed to the faintest shade of blue. The crowd hushed immediately.

"The hour is late," she said. "And you must all be exhausted from your journeys. It's time for you to depart to your rooms. Everything you need for your time here will be supplied by the academy. Should you get lost, the halls are filled with spirits—like those you've met tonight. You need not fear them. Nothing within these walls will harm you. At least," she said with a wry smile, "nothing outside of your classrooms. Pleasant dreams."

With groans and sighs, the students rose from their seats and slowly made their way out the great doors.

Only Bastian hesitated. "Where do I go?" he whispered fiercely to Harold.

Andromeda was walking behind him—he didn't want to show her any sign of weakness.

Harold shrugged.

Just then, a hand clamped on his shoulder.

He looked up into the stern eyes of Madame Ardea.

"Sebastian, Harold," she said. "Come with me."

He'd been at Gallowgate for less than three hours, and already he felt like he was in trouble.

14

Madame Ardea led them away from the crowd and up a stone staircase to one of the highest towers. Bastian kept glancing out the windows as they walked—the forest far below was heavy with fog. Within it, strange lights floated and flickered.

Neither she nor Harold spoke, which didn't help his feeling of being in trouble. But he hadn't done anything wrong, had he? It wasn't like he'd been the only person getting mud everywhere.

At the top of the stairs was an office the size of his bedroom back home. The walls were floor-to-ceiling bookshelves covered in dusty leather-bound tomes, unusual artifacts, and large crystals. Candles dripped from every surface, and a large fireplace burned behind a great charred-black desk. Bastian did a double take. There were definitely skulls in the embers. And it looked like they were whispering to each other.

"Sit," she said, gesturing to two wingback chairs before her desk.

They did so, even though Bastian was keenly aware that he was still muddy.

"Well," the rectress said, looking between the two of them. "It seems we have another early arrival at our school."

Harold glanced over to Bastian, who just shrugged.

"Since you are not yet thirteen, Sebastian," Ardea said, "it seems we have two options. We can either keep you under Gallowgate's care until you are of age, though forbid you from taking classes, as we did with Harold.

66

Or . . . we let you study." She looked to Harold. "I thought it fair to ask your opinion, Harold. It wouldn't be right to offer Sebastian the chance to take classes when you yourself were forced to wait until you were thirteen."

"He said he was chased here," Harold said. He shrugged. "I don't see why he shouldn't be allowed to study. He seems ready."

That is so *not the case*, Bastian thought, though he was grateful to Harold for saying so.

"So be it," Madame Ardea said. "Sebastian, you will begin in the morning with the rest of the first-year students. And since you are at a slight disadvantage due to your age, I think it best if the two of you roomed together."

Harold grinned. But Bastian immediately felt bad—did that mean Harold was going to have a room to himself, before Bastian showed up? Just like he had when he first moved in with Aunt Dahlia, he felt like a burden.

Which reminded him . . .

"Is Aunt Dahlia okay?" he asked.

Ardea actually smiled.

"Dahlia? Oh, it would take more than an uninvited ghost to scare Dahlia Noble. She was one of the greatest Summoners this school has seen in a century. Though I can see why she sent you here; it is difficult to keep up wards at all times, especially when you're away from home. Yes, I know neither she nor your parents wanted to send you here, but this is for the best. Now that we know you can see the dead, and that the dead have noticed that awareness—well, you'd never rest easy again. As Harold knows all too well."

Harold nodded stoically.

"Right," she said. "I leave him in your care, Harold."

Bastian wanted to ask about the shadowman. But Harold had made it sound like being chased by ghosts was common, and even Aunt Dahlia had seemed relatively unconcerned by the ghost that had attacked him from his own mirror. Maybe the shadowman wasn't as scary as he'd thought.

They stood to go, obviously dismissed, when Ardea spoke again.

"And Sebastian? I do hope that you will seek me out if there are ever any . . . anomalies . . . in your training. Understood?"

He nodded, though he didn't have a clue at all. What would be considered abnormal when his new normal was magic and the undead?

Bastian tried to pay attention to the halls and courtyards Harold led him through. Most had flagstone floors and arched ceilings and windows overlooking the grounds. But at one point, Bastian glanced toward a side hall to see that it was twisted upon itself, so the kids chatting at the far end were upside down. And another stairwell was composed of floating tombstones that rocked slightly under his feet. Torches were held in skeletal hands, and more than one corridor was decorated with skeletons that waved hello, or golden sarcophagi that creaked open when they passed, revealing glowing green eyes within. Harold took it all in stride, even when a ghostly floating head burst from the wall beside them, quickly chased by a group of translucent children. Their giggles made Bastian's skin crawl.

"You need to watch out for that lot," Harold murmured when the ghosts disappeared. "They like playing tricks. Most spirits are banned from our dorms, but the kids don't really care about rules. And there's nothing worse than finding one of them hiding under your bed."

Bastian shuddered.

"We're at the very end," Harold said when they reach a corridor of plain wooden doors. "Last door on the left. Easy to remember."

Harold opened the door for him, and once more, Sebastian tried not to gasp in awe.

The bedroom. Was. Huge.

Like, easily the size of his aunt's ground floor. Two massive four-poster beds, complete with velvet curtains in an intricate skull-and-floral pattern, were set against opposite walls. Bookshelves reached high up to the ceiling, and a fireplace on the far wall burned brightly between two great windows overlooking the lake. There were more leather chairs, ornate rugs, and two grand desks laden with books and tools. Rather than a chandelier on the ceiling, a pale white tree grew upside down, its delicate branches holding hundreds of small candles.

While it was clear the room was more than enough for two people, it was obvious Harold had been using it as his own for a while. Clothes were thrown all over the floor. One of the beds, which Bastian assumed was his own, was tightly made but covered in books and parchment. Jars of dried herbs lined every available surface, and an intricate science kit of test tubes and beakers boiled away on both desks. More herbs hung drying from the beams of the beds, and the windowsills were crammed with herbs and plants Bastian had never seen before. The whole room had a pungent, medicinal odor that was oddly comforting. It reminded him of Aunt Dahlia's teas.

Harold grinned sheepishly.

"Sorry about the mess," he said. "I, um, wasn't expecting a roommate anytime soon."

Now it was Bastian's turn to say, "Sorry." He stood in the doorway awkwardly while Harold started running around, tossing clothes into a single pile and moving books off the empty bed.

"What? Don't be sorry! I've been so bored without a roommate. But Madame Ardea . . ." He shrugged. Then glanced around. "Well, I don't think she thought anyone could handle being my roommate."

Bastian walked over and looked at the plants on the windowsill. "Is this mugwort?" he asked, poking one of the leaves.

"Yup. Though that's nettle right next to it, so be careful."

Bastian pulled back his hand.

"You know your herbs?" Harold asked.

"Yeah, my aunt taught me. She said it was so I could make her teas, but maybe she was training me without my knowing."

"Makes sense. Alchemy's a huge part of being an Æthercist."

Bastian swallowed. Now that he was here, now that it was just him and Harold, the excitement was starting to ebb just a little. He'd never been so far from home before. He hadn't even had sleepovers to train him for being away.

Harold must have noticed his expression.

"It takes a while to get used to," Harold said. "But soon, this place will feel like home. Promise." He smiled, and Bastian attempted to smile back. *Home.*

"Look," Harold continued. "How about you take a shower? Your clothes should be in your wardrobe, and I can finish cleaning while you're washing up."

"Are you saying I stink?" Bastian asked.

"One hundred percent yes," Harold replied with a grin. "And that's saying something, coming from me. I've nearly lost my sense of smell a dozen times. That's why Professor Pliny gave me this, even though I'm not technically an Alchemist yet." He held up the beaked plague mask. "Bathroom's in there," he said, gesturing to a bookshelf on the wall. "Secret room. Just pull the book entitled *An Æthercist's Guide to Hygiene*."

Bastian raised an eyebrow, wondering if it was a joke. But sure enough, there was a blue book on the shelf with just that title, and when he pulled it, the bookshelf swung open to reveal a big bathroom.

"Remember to use soap!" Harold called out as Bastian pulled the door shut behind him.

Bastian laughed to himself, and the homesickness faded away.

He thought he might actually be making a friend.

And this one probably wouldn't get scared away by ghosts.

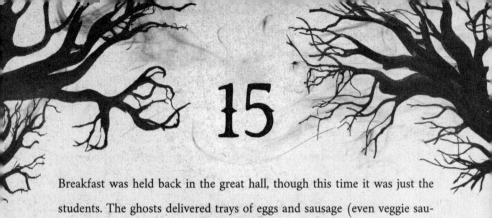

15

Breakfast was held back in the great hall, though this time it was just the students. The ghosts delivered trays of eggs and sausage (even veggie sausage!), biscuits and fresh fruit and donuts, carafes of coffee and tea and pitchers of juice. Sebastian helped himself to a little of everything.

They sat at the same table as last night; it was becoming pretty clear that the third- and fourth-years didn't have much to do with the first-years like himself. Today, at least, everyone *looked* like they went to the same school, even if Bastian and his classmates kept jumping at every ghost that appeared and every bat that swooped from the ceiling.

Much to Bastian's surprise, when he'd woken up this morning his wardrobe had been filled with clothes that all fit him perfectly. Everything was black, a post-apocalyptic chic, with ripped T-shirts and hooded sweaters that looked like cloaks and a myriad of belts and jewelry—silver amulets covered in runes, chunks of crystal that glowed with a pale inner light, bracelets of tiny brass skulls. Bastian, who'd spent the better part of his life trying to blend in (and failing because of his white hair), had been terrified to try anything on. He'd considered, briefly, going to breakfast and class in the pajamas that had been lying beside the bathtub last night—they, at least, were plain gray-and-black striped linen, with the school's crest on the pocket. If he'd worn anything at his old school like what he found in the wardrobe, he would have been beaten up.

But Harold had insisted pajamas weren't a great second impression, given he'd made his first impression late and covered in mud. So Bastian slipped on a few pieces that he hoped matched, put on a necklace of a silver raven skull with glowing purple eyes, and self-consciously made his way to the hall with Harold at his side. Bastian was glad he did, because all the first-years were in similar blacks. The pajamas would have been a strange choice.

His class schedule arrived shortly after the food. It was delivered by a large dog—or, rather, the skeleton of a large dog. It reared up on its hind legs in a perfect beg, the scroll in its mouth. When Bastian took the schedule, the dog thumped its tail a few times, until Bastian gave it a pet. The dog barked happily, then trotted off, chasing a ghost with a tray of bacon to the back room.

Bastian skimmed his schedule while everyone else chatted around him—they'd all gotten their schedules last night.

This was real. This was it.

He was here. And today, he was going to learn magic.

Instead of the normal, boring classes he'd endured before, like math and PE, this schedule made him grin with excitement.

BELL ONE: SUMMONING 1 : BONE CHAPEL, ARDEA
BELL TWO: CONJURING 1 : NORTH TOWER, FENNICK
BELL THREE: LUNCH
BELL FOUR: ALCHEMY 1 : LABORATORY 3, PLINY
BELL FIVE: THEORY 1 : LIBRARY, NICODEMUS
BELL SIX: NECROMANCY 1 : CRYPTS, LUSCINIA

"Crypts?" Bastian asked. "We have classes in crypts?" *And what exactly is a bone chapel?*

"Best place to contact the dead," Harold replied. "You'll get used to it. Pro tip, though: Wear layers. And, um, don't trust the mummies. They always try to prank first-years into letting them out of their sarcophagi—the old, *help, I'm trapped inside* bit—and trust me, you don't want to fall for it."

"Why not?" asked Roman, who'd been listening in. A few other kids were paying attention, clearly eager for any insight into their strange first full day. Even Finlay was watching from across the table.

Harold cleared his throat nervously; like Bastian, he was obviously not used to being the center of attention.

"Because they think it's super funny to jump out and trap the unlucky kid inside. Usually, when there are big spiders in there."

"I take it you know from experience?" Bastian asked with a grin.

Harold just focused on eating his donut, but Bastian was positive he heard him mutter, *Jerk*, before winking at him.

Harold may not have liked being the center of attention, but when it became known that he knew his way around the manor, he gained quite the following. He led Bastian and a gaggle of other first-years toward their first class, talking loudly as they walked and pointing out different parts of the manor.

"Down there," he said, gesturing toward a hallway that was completely flooded, and only crossable via stones that looked an awful lot like alligator skulls, "is the library. Just be sure to watch your step. The ouroboros gets . . . hungry." The murky black water rippled as he said it, as if something large and serpentine waited within. "And if you take the first corridor on your left up here, you'll make your way to the observatory. The tower only appears if there's a clear sky, however, so make sure you check your almanac beforehand. There was a group of Necromancers who got stuck up there a few years back during a long storm. Weren't able to return to the castle for a week and nearly missed midterms."

"Almanac?" asked the girl with purple streaks. Andromeda. "Why not just check a weather app or something? Does this place even *have* Wi-Fi?"

Harold paused and turned to look at her. "Why . . . Fie?" he asked, eyebrow raised in confusion.

Bastian felt himself flush with embarrassment for his friend. He knew Harold had been living here for a while—was possible he didn't know about the internet?

Then Harold grinned.

"There's no service here," he said. "Of any kind. All the Ætheric energy buzzing about interferes with the wavelengths or something. That's also why we don't have electricity. Rumor has it they tried installing it in the Alchemy labs once, but it ended up causing a huge electrical fire, so they reverted to candles and merelight."

"Merelight?" Finlay asked. He was only a few feet away from them. Bastian knew, because he was trying very hard not to look over too often.

Harold snapped his fingers, and a ball of white fire appeared above him.

"Also known as Saint Elmo's fire," Harold said. "Probably one of the first things you'll learn in Conjuring."

"So how did *you* learn?" Andromeda asked. "I heard you hadn't actually taken any classes here yet."

"Books," Harold replied evenly. "You know, the precursor to the internet. Doubt you've heard of them. But they're the only streaming service we have here, so I hope you're all caught up on your shows."

Andromeda glowered at him. Finlay chuckled.

"Oh," Harold said, pointing down another corridor. "Down there's the

Hall of the Fallen. Where all the Æthercists have been memorialized or buried. The ceiling collapsed a few years ago, so I'd avoid it."

Bastian glanced down that hall. He wondered if there would be any marker for his parents there.

They made their way outside, to the back garden. Or at least Bastian *thought* it was a garden. It might have been a cemetery, too, since the rows of flower beds were dotted with tombstones and statues. In front of them, rather than more forest, was a cliff.

Harold was leading them straight toward it.

"Are you as overwhelmed as I am?" Finlay asked in a quiet voice.

Bastian tried hard not to stammer his response. "Yeah," he said. "Just a bit."

"Yesterday I was in Arizona, sitting by the pool on my last day of summer break. And now . . ." Finlay gestured to the statue of a reaper beside them, with honeysuckle growing up its scythe.

"I know," Bastian said. "Have you . . . have you seen ghosts for long?"

Finlay bit his lip, and Bastian realized it might have been an impolite question.

"Ever since I was a little kid," Finlay said after a while. "You?"

"Same."

"It's funny. I spent all my life trying to hide from ghosts, and now I'm supposed to fight them."

Bastian wanted to say he felt the same strangeness, but they'd reached the cliff, and the gasps of his classmates cut him off.

Harold pointed to a lake below, then to a tiny building a few hundred feet from the shore, a steepled church of gray brick and bone.

"There," Harold said, "is the Bone Chapel."

16

"Welcome, class," Madame Ardea said. "I'm glad to see you all made it."

The church may have looked small from up on the cliff, but once they'd made their way down the precarious wooden walkway and across the narrow bridge, they'd found a building that was easily the size of a gymnasium.

It was obvious why it was called the Bone Chapel. Thousands of bones were pressed into every inch of the walls, packed so tight and artistically that Bastian couldn't see the stone behind them. Femurs in cosmic starbursts and swirls, finger bones spelling out phrases in Latin, rib cages forming crowns above dozens of skulls with candles glittering behind their open eyes. Pillars of stacked bones stretched up and arched high above to support the ceiling.

The ground, however, was concrete. Lines of clear blue stone crisscrossed it, forming a web. And in the center, inlaid in obsidian and more blue, was the spider that made up the Summoning sigil.

Madame Ardea swept forward, gesturing for the kids to gather around. Finlay nudged up beside Bastian. Bastian honestly thought his arm was going to burst into flames, in the best way possible.

"Now," Madame Ardea said, "there is much you will learn over the course of your studies here. But in all things, Summoning is the art that will prove most useful in your endeavors. It is the true backbone of any Æthercist's training. And that is why we start you here.

"Summoning is a threefold art. Here, I will teach you to summon, bind, and banish spirits, a trio of skills that are as indispensable as breath itself. Without these three skills, the other branches of magic are mere theatrics. Observe."

She waved her hand, and the lights in the room grew dim. Pale sunlight filtered through the stained-glass windows, but the majority of light came from the tiles in the floor, which had begun to glow bright blue.

"First," she said, "we summon."

Madame Ardea elegantly waved her hand upward, like she was conducting a symphony.

Pale green smoke curled from thin air before her hand. It twisted and billowed like a small tornado, becoming almost human in shape—Bastian could make out two skeletal arms and sharp fingers, a swirling torso, and a face of roiling smoke, its eyes black pits.

It turned on the spot, looking at the students. Then, with a horrible scream, it lunged straight toward Bastian.

He leaped back, knocking into someone else, but before the ghost got far, Madame Ardea calmly said, "Next, we bind."

She rotated her hand and clenched her fist, and two bright bands of blue light wrapped themselves around the ghost's arms—just like the lights Aunt Dahlia had summoned against the shadowman.

The spirit howled in rage, but it couldn't move. It floated only a foot away from Bastian. Finlay, who had also leaped back, laughed nervously.

"Finally, we banish," Madame Ardea said. She thrust her hand toward the floor, unclenching her fist and splaying her fingers wide.

With another angry scream, the spirit sank down into the floor where, with a ripple of blue light through the tiles, it disappeared in a wisp of smoke. The students immediately broke out into applause.

Madame Ardea bowed her head slightly.

"That was a simple spectre. A spectre, you will learn, returns from the dead only to haunt or frighten. They are somewhat malevolent, but mostly innocuous, and are banished quite easily. That said, there are as many types of spirits in the underworld as there are fish in the sea, and what is deadly to one would only empower the next. Not even I have encountered every type of spirit, and I shall die happy if that remains true."

She let her words sink in, casting a level eye on everyone in the room. Bastian was positive her gaze lingered on him longer than most.

"Today, we will begin by learning how to create a summoning circle. Within that space, a spirit may be safely summoned, bound, and banished. I will group you into threes. While one casts the circle, the others will watch. If any of you succeed, I shall teach you how to summon a shade—the cousin to the spectre, though one without a malicious bone in its body. Now, group up."

Harold immediately took Bastian by the arm. Bastian was about to open his mouth to ask Finlay if he'd like to join, when Robyn—the girl with pink streaks in her light blonde hair—stepped up and asked, "Mind if I join you two?"

Bastian looked over her shoulder to Finlay, who quickly grouped up with Andromeda and Roman instead.

"Sure," Harold said. "Want me to go first? I've had some practice, and I can maybe walk you through a few things."

Robyn snapped her fingers. Three tiny blue lights appeared above her palm, swirling lazily together.

"I think I'll be okay," she said. "My mom was an Æthercist and taught me a few things, before . . ." She hesitated, then quickly composed herself. "So, um, let's see what you two are made of."

If the rest of class was any indication, Bastian was made of Fail.

Robyn managed to create a full circle in mere moments.

She closed her eyes and took a deep breath and brought her hands to her chest. Blue light sparked across her palms, and when she opened her eyes—which Bastian swore glowed slightly blue—a line of searing blue light appeared on the floor, billowing like a heat wave.

Harold had gone next. It took him a few tries, and eventually—when his fifth attempt ended with only a few blue sparks dancing across the tiles—he pulled a vial from his satchel and said, conspiratorially, "Grave dust, sea salt, and ground myrrh. Don't tell Madame Ardea." He hastily poured it into a circle on the floor, and when he tried a sixth time, the salt flared blue and formed a wavering circle.

Then it was Bastian's turn.

He took a deep breath and tried to calm his fears so he could find the spark inside of him that Madame Ardea had droned on and on about. He closed his eyes—partly to concentrate, and partly to block out the sight of Finlay, who was on the other side of the room and trying his first circle.

Bastian visualized the blue circle burning to life on the floor, tried to will it into being.

Nothing happened.

He concentrated harder, squeezing his eyes shut.

"He's going to strain something if he keeps going like that," Robyn whispered. Harold hushed her.

Across the room, he heard a few classmates cheer, and knew that Finlay had succeeded in his circle.

C'mon, c'mon!

Bastian had always dreamed that magic was real, and that if it truly existed, he would excel at it. It helped him justify why he wasn't good at sports or art or anything normal, and why he'd always had his nose in a fantasy book.

The reality check was humbling.

"Come on," Harold said. "I know you can do it. You wouldn't have gotten here if you couldn't."

Suddenly, Bastian wasn't thinking about creating the circle. He was back in his bedroom, watching Aunt Dahlia as she faced off against the shadowman. His heart quickened, and his veins filled with terrified adrenaline.

Behind his eyes, he saw the shadowman pulling himself through the mirror, felt his fear turn into something tangible. A spark.

"That's it!" Harold whispered. "You're doing it!"

Bastian remembered that fear. Remembered how it had built inside of him, and how, when it released, it was a billow of purple.

"Wait . . ." Robyn whispered. She sounded so far away. They both did.

"What's he doing?" came someone else's voice.

He saw the shadowman coming closer, closer.

I have hunted for so long, the shadowman cooed. *And will hunt so long as you live.*

Terror filled Bastian's bones. Power flooded through him, but it no longer felt like it was under his control. He felt it spark and tingle against his skin. He felt it threaten to sweep him away.

"Bastian—" Harold said from a far-off hallway.

Then Bastian heard someone scream.

He opened his eyes and didn't know what he was seeing.

A half-formed circle glowed and sparked in front of him.

In its center was a writhing mass of purple-blue smoke.

From that smoke reached the dark, spindly hand of the shadowman.

Sebastian yelped and stumbled back, into Harold's arms. But even though the power within him cut off, the shadowman didn't disappear. The clawed hand snapped and snatched about like a writhing snake, and Bastian knew that it would break through if he didn't do something, fast.

"Now, now," came Ardea's calm voice. She swept over in a billow of black robes. "If you'll remember me saying, Sebastian—first we summon a circle. *Then*, we summon a shade."

She gestured toward the snapping arm. Blue lights laced across it, a mesh web that she forced down, down. Even though her voice was light, her brows were furrowed as she forced the shadowman back into the floor.

The arm disappeared into the cloud of blue smoke, and the remaining circle vanished in a flurry of hissing sparks.

"What—what was that?" asked Roman from across the room.

"Just a simple shade, dears. Nothing for you to worry about." The rectress smiled. "Though let that be a lesson on the importance of a strong summoning circle!"

Outside, a bell tolled, signaling the end of class. Everyone grabbed their things and began to filter out.

Madame Ardea didn't say anything to Bastian before the students walked out of the chapel and across the creaky walkway to the cliffs. It had begun to rain, and the waters of the lake rippled eerily.

"Nice one," Robyn said as she passed him. She grinned, but Bastian still felt ashamed.

He hadn't meant to summon the shadowman, and there was *no* way it was a shade. Had Madame Ardea mistaken it for a shade? Or did she know something she wasn't telling them? Maybe she just didn't want to worry him for nearly getting them all killed.

Maybe.

As he and Harold climbed the treacherous walkways back up the cliffs in stunned silence, Bastian looked over his shoulder to the Bone Chapel far below.

Madame Ardea stood outside the building, but she wasn't looking up at her students. She was facing the chapel. And as he watched, he saw her wave her hands in an intricate pattern. Blue lights spiraled from her fingertips, wrapping themselves around the building in webs and symbols. Symbols very similar to the ones Aunt Dahlia had cast over his mirror.

He knew, then, that he had his answer.

Madame Ardea knew the danger he'd nearly put them all in.

The question was . . . why hadn't she admitted it?

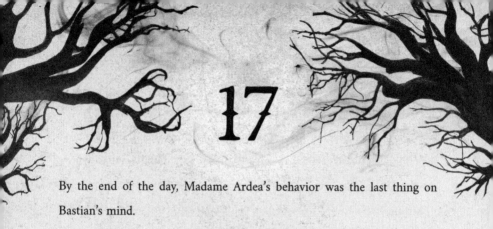

17

By the end of the day, Madame Ardea's behavior was the last thing on Bastian's mind.

He'd thought learning about ghosts and magic would be exciting—and it was—but he'd never considered just how exhausted he'd be after a single day of it.

He and Harold sat in the study hall—the huge room they'd tracked mud through last night, with all the fireplaces and the statue of Willow. A pile of books was stacked on the table in front of them, towering beside trays of tea and scones, beakers and vials of Harold's herbs and concoctions, and notebooks filled with furiously scribbled notes.

Bastian was trying to focus, but he kept glancing around at his classmates.

One table had a group of upperclassmen in shawls and charms seated around an oracle board. Necromancers. They spoke in whispers, for the most part—until one of them started to channel the voice of a spirit, and talked in a terrifyingly loud growl.

Another table had a group of Summoners—he could tell from the robes, but also from the fact that they kept summoning small spirits in the flames before them. Bastian shuddered and looked away. It reminded him far too much of what he'd done—or almost done—in class this morning.

Thankfully, after Summoning, there hadn't been any other close calls. Save for him almost setting Harold's head on fire during Conjuring, but that had *not* been his fault. They were supposed to be lighting candles, and Harold had dodged in front of him right when he was finalizing the spell.

Harold touched his hair at that moment, as if checking for any charred bits.

"It's all still there," Bastian said. "And for the millionth time, I'm so sorry."

Harold chuckled. "If I got upset over every time I lost some hair or an eyebrow, I'd be a mess. You should have seen what happened the last time I tried to transmute iron into gold. Nearly set the entire Alchemy lab on fire. I don't think I've ever seen Professor Pliny run so fast."

Bastian laughed. Pliny was so old he was practically a ghost himself, though his mind was sharper and held more knowledge about Alchemy than Bastian thought possible.

"Did it work, though?" Bastian asked.

"Nope," Harold said. "Just made a really charred lump of iron. The fire looked pretty cool, though. It was all green and sounded like wind chimes."

Across the room, one of the upperclassmen—a Conjurer, guessing from the clothes—cursed and stood.

"Already?" she proclaimed loudly, to no one in particular. Then she stormed off.

"What was that about?" Bastian asked.

"She was summoned to the field," Harold explained. "Remember what Madame Ardea said about studying being only part of our training? Well, upperclassmen, and underclassmen who have been through a fair bit of training, are often called out into the field to banish spirits. Usually nothing too dangerous, or else they'd let the adults do it. But it can get annoying. I've heard."

Andromeda and a few other classmates (including Finlay, whom Bastian was trying very hard not to stare at) were sitting at a table nearby. For the most part, they'd all been studying in silence. But when Harold finished, she leaned over in her chair and looked to them.

"Well, then," she said to Harold. "Better hope you aren't sent out with Bastian. He'd probably just end up summoning an even worse ghost than you were sent to fight."

"What's that supposed to mean?" Harold asked.

"You saw what happened in class," Andromeda said. "He nearly got us all killed."

"You heard Ardea," Harold said. "It was just a shade—"

"Shade, my butt," Andromeda interjected. "I know my ghosts. That was no shade. Ten to one Bastian gets himself killed or kicked out by All Hallows Eve."

Bastian sank back into his seat. He had never been good at confrontation, and Andromeda scared him more than most, which was saying something.

"It's happened, you know," she continued. "If an Æthercist is really inept or, like, a danger to others, they're either stripped of their powers and banished from the school or killed in the field." She looked at Harold. "You know I'm right. You've lived here. You've seen it. Heck, two kids died last year alone."

Harold swallowed.

"Is that . . . is that true?" Bastian asked. He'd known this place was dangerous, but he hadn't actually thought students would be killed here.

"How would you know?" Harold asked Andromeda instead. "You just got here."

Andromeda drew herself up proudly.

"I come from a long line of Æthercists," she said. "It runs in my blood. And I know enough about ghosts to know when I see a dead man walking. Or sitting, in this case."

Bastian noticed Finlay looking at him strangely. Like he was starting to see what Andromeda was saying.

"Well," Harold countered, "I've been here long enough to know a stuck-up jerk when I see one. Come on, Bastian. Let's go study somewhere else."

He gathered his things in his satchel and stood. Bastian awkwardly picked up his own supplies and, without saying a word in his own defense, followed Harold out the hall.

"It's your funeral!" Andromeda called out. She and some of the others burst into laughter.

Bastian glanced back only once, to see Finlay still watching him leave. He, at least, wasn't laughing.

Bastian stayed quiet until they were in the cold hallway leading to the Alchemy labs.

"Was what she said true?" he finally asked.

"What? No. Loads of kids have a rough start. Some of the best Conjurers I've seen here couldn't summon a flame for months, and—"

"That's not what I meant. Have kids been killed?"

The last word came out as a squeak.

Harold paused. They stood beside a shining set of armor. Three sets of glowing green eyes watched them from within the helm.

"Well . . . yeah," Harold admitted. "Like Madame Ardea said last night, this is dangerous stuff. But I wouldn't worry about it. Even if you *had* fully summoned that shade in class, it wouldn't have hurt us. The school is heavily warded. Nothing bad can happen here."

It reminded Bastian way too much about Aunt Dahlia's warning the other day, about safety being the one thing you couldn't promise.

"But it wasn't a shade—" Bastian began.

"What else could it have been?" Harold said. "Even if you had somehow managed to pull a *revenant* out from the depths of the underworld, and they're like the worst things out there, it wouldn't have been able to hurt you. Not with the wards and all the teachers around. Gallowgate is safe. Trust me."

Bastian swallowed and nodded.

"Andromeda's just trying to get under your skin," Harold continued. "I've seen plenty of kids like her come through here. Long line of Æthercists in their family, arrive knowing all the theory. But what she doesn't mention is that there's only one way to be an Æthercist—and it doesn't run in the blood. You have to see death firsthand. Which means her parents . . ." He trailed off and looked to his feet. His normally cheerful face fell dark.

Did her parents make her watch someone die? Bastian thought, his blood going cold. He couldn't imagine what sort of child that would create, how it would feel to grow up in that sort of family. It made him miss Aunt Dahlia even more.

"Some people will do anything for power," Harold finally said. "Even in our community. If anything, I'd be more worried about *her* summoning something she shouldn't. Now come on—I know a secret entrance to the pantry, and I want some cookies."

18

The next few days were a blur of classes.

Bastian was up every morning with the breakfast bells, and he and Harold would trudge groggily to the dining hall along with their classmates. From there it was nonstop learning and practice, before heading back to the dining hall for dinner with their new friends. Andromeda was never among them, and sadly, neither was Finlay. Ever since that first confrontation with Andromeda, she had avoided Harold and Bastian at all costs. And Finlay, well . . . he had taken to sitting apart from everyone at meals, his head stuck in a book and his glasses constantly slipping down his nose.

Bastian didn't have much time to wonder if he'd done something to upset Finlay, or if the boy was just a natural hermit. He had more than enough to distract him.

Like trying to remember the difference between a poltergeist and a ghast, or which herbs were best for protecting against banshees, or what phase of the moon was best for casting a summoning circle. Bastian thought there'd been a lot to learn at normal school. It was nothing, compared to this.

Every night, he and Harold would find a spot in the library or Alchemy labs or the study hall with a stack of books and instruments and a pot of tea, staying up way too late studying or practicing.

"I don't think I'm ever going to remember all this," Bastian said, dropping his theory book (*An Æthercist's Guide to the Underworld*) to the table and collapsing back in his chair. "Why is it all in Latin? No one even *speaks* Latin anymore."

Harold shrugged, but he wasn't really paying attention. He was too busy trying to figure out his carromancy homework.

"Do you think this looks like a heart or a ferret?" Harold asked, holding up the lump of cooled wax that dripped a grotesque red. Carromancy involved pouring wax into blood, and interpreting its shape. So far, it was *not* his favorite form of Necromancy.

"It looks like a piece of intestine to me," Bastian said, wrinkling his nose.

Harold grunted and scribbled that down in his notebook, then consulted the large tome beside him for the meaning.

"It's just . . ." Bastian continued, "there are dozens of types of ghosts, and four levels of the underworld. How are we supposed to remember it all when I can't remember the difference between the *Corpus* and *Velamentum Harmonium?*"

"*Corpus* is easy. 'Corpse,' like body. And *Harmonium* . . . think 'harmony,' like a choir singing harmony. Fa la laaaa."

"Please never sing again," Bastian said at Harold's intentionally (he hoped) off-pitch wail.

Harold stuck out his tongue. "You'll remember now, though. You can thank me later. And *Velamentum* . . . I dunno, you're just going to have to remember that it means 'Veil.'"

There were four Veils, separating the four levels of the underworld. Every level was host to its own unique set of spirits, and required a different sacrifice to reach it.

"You give up your body to pass through the First Veil, leaving a corpse," Harold said. "You give up your voice to pass through the second. Your memory starts to fade after the third, and then your soul vanishes after the fourth. Easy, right?"

Bastian grumbled and went back to his reading, sketching out notes in a blank sketchbook beside him.

He couldn't focus, and it wasn't just because the handwritten text was blurring on the page.

The more he learned about the underworld, the less appealing it all sounded. There was a river that pulled the dead through the various levels, until eventually they went past the Final Veil, from whence no soul had ever returned. None of the levels sounded particularly pleasant. Was that really all the afterlife was? What about the people who led good lives? What about . . .

"I was thinking," Bastian said.

"Don't hurt yourself," Harold replied.

Bastian stuck out his tongue, but he didn't smile. His thoughts were churning along with his stomach. He almost didn't want to ask this, but he wasn't going to stop now that he'd started.

"We've spent all this time learning about the ghosts that want to come back. And how the process twists them, makes them . . . well, makes them evil. We've learned that not all ghosts go past the Final Veil—some of them manage to escape the River of Death and just . . . linger. But what about the good spirits? What about . . ."

"What about your parents?" Harold asked.

Bastian nodded. He'd told Harold about his past a few nights ago, when they'd been reading in their room. Harold hadn't said anything about his own past, and Bastian hadn't pushed it.

"You want to know if you can bring your own parents back," Harold said.

Again, Bastian nodded, though he felt ashamed for some reason, now that Harold had voiced it.

Harold sighed and dropped his chunk of melted wax back in the dish of blood. (Bastian never asked what sort of blood it was. He didn't want to know.)

"Everyone wonders that at some point or other," Harold told him. "So it's best you get it out of your system now. The short answer is, yes, good spirits can come back. Like Willow, sometimes the 'unfinished business' a ghost has isn't all malevolent. But that's rare, because in order to go against the River, you have to go against the natural current of life. If you lost your parents a week ago, sure. They might still be lingering about and you could reach them, maybe even summon them. But it's been a few years now, and trust me when I say this: No spirit who has spent that long in the underworld is *good*. Even if your parents managed to escape the River, the levels themselves change people. And not for the better."

Bastian felt his chest constricting. Breathing was suddenly very, very hard, and he was all too aware that they were in the study hall, and there were other kids around, and the last thing he wanted to do was cry in front of everyone.

Harold put a hand on Bastian's shoulder.

"I'm sorry, man. Really. I know it's not the answer you want to hear. But your parents are gone, and that's for the best. You don't want them to linger."

"But it all . . ." Bastian's breath caught. He sniffed and pointed to the book, where the levels of the underworld had been drawn out in detail. Planes of twisted trees, or jagged glaciers or lurking shadows. "It all looks so grim. I can't believe that's all there is."

"It isn't, though!" Harold said. "Look." He pointed to the level beyond the Final Veil, labeled TERRA SINE ANIMA. Despite the label, nothing was drawn there. "No one knows what exists beyond the Final Veil, not really. No one has gone past and returned in . . . well, a very long time. But those who did said that the final realm is paradise. You have to have faith that your parents are there, and that's the best possible thing for them. For everyone."

Bastian sniffed again.

"Thanks," he said.

"Don't thank me," Harold said. "It's the truth. You'll quickly learn that just because you can't see something, it doesn't mean it isn't real. I mean, look around! Most people would never dream that a place like this existed."

As he spoke, a group of Conjurer kids a few tables over erupted into laughter when they made their classmate levitate in the air . . . and promptly turned him upside down and started tickling him.

Bastian felt himself grin. But the question still ate at him as he finished his homework, and when he went to bed.

Here he was, at the school where his parents trained. Their memories lingered in these ancient halls and dusty classrooms, had left impressions in the threadbare rugs and overstuffed chairs. Maybe one of them had slept in his very bed. He was walking in their footsteps.

It should have made him feel close to them, but in all truth, being here, realizing that everything he thought he knew about the world and his parents was wrong, made him feel further from them than ever before.

19

Despite being warded against evil spirits, it quickly became clear to Bastian that those wards did nothing to keep away bad dreams.

They weren't nightmares, not exactly. But ever since coming to Gallowgate, his dreams had become . . . different. Stronger. More vivid. Sometimes he'd dream of his aunt's house, and it would feel so real he would wake up smelling her baked brownies or brewing tea. Sometimes he'd dream about walking down the halls of Gallowgate, his feet taking him down dark, dusty passageways that clearly hadn't seen another soul in years. When he woke from *those* dreams, he was both shivering and covered with sweat.

But the dream that was the most vivid of all was the one he'd tried to block out ever since his parents' funeral. It used to only happen once or twice a month. But now, no matter what other dreams his mind concocted, he had this one nightly, without fail.

In the dream, he stood with his aunt in the sunshine, staring down at the two open graves. It shouldn't have been allowed to be sunny. Funerals shouldn't be allowed to happen in the sun. Didn't the world know that it had stopped?

He didn't cry. He couldn't let himself cry, not when he needed to be strong for his aunt. He stood there, holding her hand, while the two of them looked down in silence.

There were others around them—friends of his parents, older faces he knew but couldn't name.

The preacher was an older woman in long black-and-purple robes. Her voice was familiar, but her face was hidden behind a veil.

He didn't hear what she said.

Because in the dream, he heard something else.

He heard his father.

"Sebastian!" his father called out. *"Come to me, Sebastian!"*

One of the caskets slowly creaked open. Bastian tried to flinch away, but he couldn't move. He couldn't even close his eyes to hide from the horrors within.

Sometimes, when the casket opened, there would be nothing but shadows inside. Shadows that twisted and pooled to become the shadowman, rising from the grave and reaching out with clawed fingers until Bastian finally awoke.

Other times, he would look down and the casket would be without a bottom. Instead, a dark river of frothing black water raged far below. In those dreams, he'd lose his footing, and he'd tumble into the grave, careening toward the water. The lid would snap shut, and everything would fade to the deepest black as the water hissed and tore through him, and he would wake in the darkness of his room, frozen to the bone no matter how warmly the embers in the fireplace glowed.

Every night, he dreamed of his parents' graves.

Every morning, he couldn't decide which fate was worse: the raging river or the pale, patient smile of the shadowman.

20

Bastian was lost.

A few weeks had passed since he'd first arrived at Gallowgate, and although he knew his way to most of his classes thanks to Harold, he had gotten completely turned around. He blamed it on losing track of time while practicing Conjuring in the courtyard between classes. And the not-so-small fact that apparently the manor decided that the new moon meant a few new corridors he was certain he'd never seen before.

He trudged down one, a small ball of merelight hovering above his head. It was more a tunnel than a hall, but the other option was a hall filled with clown dolls, and there was no way in the world he was walking down that one alone. Especially since he saw more than one of them turn their head and smile while he debated.

There were no torches here, just small clumps of crystals in the ceiling and floors, and the steady, dank *drip drip drip* of water that made him feel like he was a million miles underground. His feet sloshed through a thin layer of water, making ripples dance in the wavering light. The crystals looked like twinkling stars in reflection, and his orb of light a moon.

It was then he realized that although the light showed up in the water's reflection, he did not. He forced himself not to look down again.

A full minute passed, and the hall didn't change. This had to be the right direction.

Right?

He turned around—maybe he could find a ghost to guide him, or a stray upperclassman who could point the way. He'd even take the clown hallway, if it actually *led* somewhere.

Except there was no exit. The hall had sealed itself. All that faced him was a rock wall.

Bastian cursed and kept going. It wasn't the first time something like this had happened, but it was definitely the least convenient.

Professor Fennick didn't seem to like him (or anyone, really) under the best of circumstances—being this late wasn't going to help.

The hallway tilted down, and he followed it until he was positive he was deeper underground than even the crypts where he took Necromancy. He could practically feel the weight of the school pressing down on him, and as the hall got narrower and his breath got shorter, he started to worry less that Professor Fennick would be angry and more that he might never get to class ever again. He started to jog.

Then he rounded a corner, and nearly had a heart attack.

The ground dropped off, and he stood on the very edge of a cliff.

Only it wasn't a cliff.

It was the side of the school.

He was on one of the upper floors, standing in a doorframe that led to nowhere. The lake yawned far below him, and the trees looked like stalks of broccoli. A gust of wind knocked past him and he took a hasty step back. When he looked over his shoulder, he faced a normal hall.

"Very funny," he muttered to the school. He held a hand to his beating heart. Seriously. That was nearly the end of him.

Maybe it was his imagination, or a passing ghost, but he swore he heard someone laugh.

His breath still pounding from his fear and the unexpected jog, he turned around and tried to regain his bearings. Fennick was going to *kill* him.

It grew colder with every step, and when he reached the next intersection he realized why. The hallway to his right had caved in after twenty feet. A large pile of stones filled the hall, and the fading afternoon sky was visible above.

Bastian paused. This was where the fallen Æthercists were honored. And despite his assurance to Harold that he wasn't going to go poking around in the underworld for his parents, he couldn't give up the chance to learn more about them in the mortal world.

The walls were covered in aged silver plaques, the edges blackened and the engraved words a heavy Gothic script. Although the plaques were crowded together, there were plenty of gaps. As if those spots were awaiting a plaque . . . or had been ripped out.

Despite the rubble in front of him, the floor was freshly polished and finely decorated. Inlaid shards of black stone formed four interlinking circles, with a curving, silver-gray river running through them. He knew before even reading the Latin inlays that they were the levels of the underworld.

On each of the plaques was the name of the Æthercist and a brief bio. Even though it was clear they were memorials, there weren't any dates.

As he searched for his parents, two nameplates caught his eye.

ADELAIDE WATTS

FABLED NECROMANCER AND SUMMONER

KNOWN FOR THE BANISHING OF REVENANTS

TYRONE WATTS

AWARD-WINNING ALCHEMIST

NOTED FOR HIS WORK WITH HOMUNCULI

Harold's parents. They had to be. So why had Harold never admitted that his parents were Æthercists?

Bastian kept looking, Fennick all but forgotten.

And there, near the very edge of the collapsed wall, he spotted it. His mother.

DANEA WIGHT

FIERCE SUMMONER

AND BELOVED GALLOWGATE PROFESSOR

"What?" Bastian gasped. "She taught here?"

"For many years," came a voice behind him.

Bastian turned to find Professor Luscinia standing at the hall's entrance.

As per usual, she wasn't dressed like she should be roaming the halls of a drafty old manor—she looked like she was just about to attend a very expensive party. Today, she wore a glimmering gold dress that fanned out behind her, with a simple gold tiara around her forehead. She looked every inch a queen, but the smile on her face was more mischievous than regal.

"Shouldn't you be in class?" she continued, gliding in.

"I, um . . . I got lost."

"And managed to find yourself in the Hall of the Fallen," she mused. "How convenient."

"Really! I got turned around and there was this hallway that turned out to be a tunnel that nearly dropped me off the side of the building."

Professor Luscinia chuckled and caressed the marble wall with a gold-manicured finger.

"Yes, the manor does get a little moody during the dark of the moon. As do we all. Full moons may be best for Summoning, as the Ætheric energies run wild. But on moon dark, the spirits wail ever louder." She stepped closer, her voice lowered. "So tell me, Sebastian. What have the spirits been saying to you?"

"I . . ." His dreams floated to mind. The graveyard. His aunt. The shadow-man . . . and his father's voice, calling him into the grave.

She peered into his eyes knowingly, and he wondered, for a brief, worried second, if she could hear his thoughts just as easily as she could hear the words of the dead. Her smile turned slightly sad.

"Your mother was an amazing Æthercist," she said, drawing herself up and looking to the plaque. "She was the Conjuring professor my first year, though she took some time off in my second when she had you." A twinkle came to her eyes. "I'll never forget that woman. She was the tiniest little thing, barely taller than you are now. But she sure could throw a fireball. And a punch, or so I've heard. She even brought you into class a few times. Set you in the corner in your crib, safe behind a protection circle. You'd just sit there and watch her work her magic, all your toys forgotten . . ."

She trailed off, staring at the plaques in silence, and all Bastian could think was that he had been here before. His mother had *taught* here. And then . . . then his parents had just hid Gallowgate and everything it stood for from him. Why?

Before he could ask, Professor Luscinia gathered herself and looked to him.

"Sorry, Sebastian," she said. "A sad trait of Necromancers, I'm afraid. Constant communing with the dead means it's easy for us to get stuck in the past."

Bastian's throat had constricted, his mouth dry.

"Did you . . . did you ever hear from her?" he asked. "After . . ."

Professor Luscinia placed a hand lightly on his cheek. The gentleness made him want to cry.

"No, dear, I'm afraid I did not. I was far too young, and she was gone far too quickly." She sighed and dropped her hand. "But enough of this sad talk. I believe I saw a few of your classmates hurrying that way a little while ago. If you run, you may be able to slip in before Fennick even notices you're gone."

"Yeah, because that's worked for me before," Bastian mumbled, thinking of his failure on his first night.

Professor Luscinia laughed. "Come. I'll take you there. Gallowgate knows better than to mess with me." She patted the hall's entry arch as they passed through. This time, he knew it wasn't his imagination: The manor purred in response.

It wasn't until she was leaving him at the Conjuring tower's door that he realized he hadn't seen a plaque for his father.

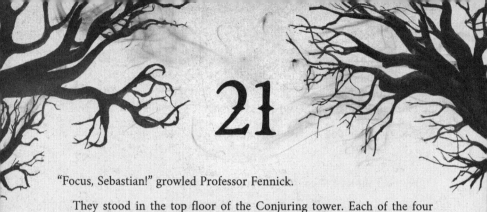

21

"Focus, Sebastian!" growled Professor Fennick.

They stood in the top floor of the Conjuring tower. Each of the four floors of the tower was dedicated to a single element, and today—as they had been for the last few weeks—they were trying to work with air. Which, according to Fennick, was "a lot less likely to get a pathetic group of idiot children killed."

Bastian gritted his teeth and focused on the candle burning in front of him.

But it was hard to *reach within* and *channel the element without* when Professor Fennick was growling and pacing right behind him. Professor Fennick couldn't have been older than thirty, his jagged hair streaked with red and his face covered in fresh scars. As per usual, he wore a leather biker jacket with studs on the shoulders and a chipped painted scorpion on the back, his jeans ripped and worn. He looked more like a lead guitarist for some punk band than a professor. He acted like it, too.

Bastian tried to block him out. Tried to focus on the candle flame. He willed it to flicker, to gutter out. Willed the air around it to move.

The flame flickered slightly. But that might have just been from Fennick's pacing.

"Come on," the professor said. He smacked the back of Bastian's head. "You call that focused? I've had farts more powerful than that."

Harold chuckled a few feet away.

"Think that's funny, do you?" Fennick asked. "I don't see you doing much better. And given how long you've been here . . ."

He trailed off as Harold blushed and stared even more intently at his candle.

Fennick stormed away from the two of them, muttering under his breath as he walked across the room.

Bastian glanced up to see Finlay on the other side of the round room. Finlay's candle flame flickered and, after a moment, went out. Robyn managed to douse her candle with a snap of her fingers. And Andromeda was extinguishing and reigniting her candle like she was flipping on and off a light switch. Frustration built inside Bastian. Even though he wasn't failing, he wasn't exactly *good* at anything, either.

Fennick clapped his hands.

"Alright, I can't take this anymore," he said. "Y'all are pathetic. So it's time for a little trial by fire. The real test of an Æthercist is in battle. Maybe making you fight for your lives will get your heads in the game."

Harold glanced to Bastian nervously.

"So," Fennick continued, "it's time to change tactics."

He clapped his hands, and a display case along the wall opened. Various oddities floated out and hovered in front of the students. Broken dolls. Bird skulls. Even an old bear trap.

Bastian was facing a stuffed bear that was missing an eye and half its fur.

Another gesture from Fennick, and the perimeter of the room glowed faint blue. He'd cast them all inside a summoning circle!

"You have two options," Fennick said. "You either finally get it through your sorry heads that we aren't just playing games, or you get hurt. Got it?"

Bastian swallowed and took a step back from the bear.

"Professor," Harold began. "You can't—"

"Don't tell me what I can and can't do in my own class, Watts!" Fennick roared. "I make the rules in here. And if I say you're all failing because you don't seem to grasp the importance of your education, then it's up to me to make sure you do. And after this, you will. It's time for you to face your first poltergeists."

"But—"

"Save your strength, Watts," Fennick said with a wicked smile, the scar on his mouth curling his lip. "You'll need it."

He gestured, and small curls of green fog appeared beneath each of the floating objects. The fog grew and coiled and flickered with sparks, and from the orbs Bastian heard the most horrible, high-pitched laughter. He watched in horror as two glowing green arms snapped out of the fog and latched on to the teddy bear, then yanked itself into the stuffed beast.

The bear's remaining eye burned virulent green. Its paws grew tiny crystalline claws, and it struggled toward Bastian. With Fennick's magic holding it up, it couldn't go anywhere. Yet.

"Remember," Professor Fennick called out as the other oddities became animated with evil, "poltergeists can only be banished when you destroy their physical form. And that's where your Conjuring comes in."

He took a step backward. Toward the door.

"I'll let you out at the end of class," he said. "At least, those of you who survive." He looked pointedly at Bastian and Harold. "Good luck."

Bastian watched as the professor passed through the glowing protective barrier and out the door, locking it shut behind him.

Harold muttered something about Madame Ardea having a thing or two to say about this, but there wasn't time to pound on the door or yell out for Fennick to release them.

The moment Fennick was out the door, the possessed objects dropped to the ground and began to attack. The class erupted into chaos.

Bastian yelped and ran as the grotesque teddy bear chased after him, and he wasn't the only one. Roman was backing away from the headless doll that stalked toward him, batting it away with a candlestick. Even Harold was having a hard time. He tried casting fireballs at the broken marionette that dragged itself toward him, but they just came out as small sparks.

"Forget it!" Harold growled. He started rummaging around in his satchel as he backed away from the marionette.

Bastian turned his attention back to the bear that raced after him. All around him, the room was a chaotic roar of students trying to run from their attackers. Only a handful were trying to fight back. Even fewer were succeeding, though it looked like Robyn and Andromeda were holding their own. Bastian tripped over a runaway doll and fell to his knees. Right beside Finlay, who'd just made the toy horse chasing him collapse into sawdust.

"Need a hand?" Finlay asked. Bastian's mouth lodged itself shut, but he managed to nod.

Finlay gestured to the bear, and a moment later it burst into flame. As the poltergeist tried to escape, Finlay gestured again, and blue bands formed around its body, whisking it down into the floor where it disappeared.

"Thanks," Bastian said.

Finlay grinned. "Don't mention it."

He held out his hand and helped Bastian stand up.

"How are you so good at that?" Bastian asked before he could stop himself.

Finlay blushed.

"One of the perks of not having friends," he said. "I get a lot more studying in."

Bastian swallowed. "I—"

But he was interrupted by the possessed bear trap, which leaped and snapped toward them. Finlay pushed Bastian back just in time. They staggered apart, while a girl named Tianna ran after the chomping trap, yelling out, "Get back here and let me banish you!"

Finlay grinned, and despite the nightmare around them, Bastian felt his chest go hot.

Andromeda whooped in victory on the other side of the room when the pile of bones chasing her burned to a crisp. Bastian looked over to see Robyn squaring off with her own nightmare—a bird skull with green spikes growing out of its head—before she, too, managed to destroy it in a blaze of fire. Even Harold managed to destroy his poltergeist—albeit with some strange substance he'd yanked from his satchel—which was now melting in a pile of bubbling green goo.

Finally, it was just Roman running away from his doll.

Andromeda stepped up beside him and snapped her fingers. The doll—and the spirit inside it—burst into flame and vanished in a high-pitched scream.

She looked straight at Bastian.

"This was your fault, loser," she said.

Bastian shrank back. He looked around the room. No one seemed seriously injured, but a few kids had slashes on their faces or arms, and even Harold was bleeding from a cut on his eyebrow.

"I'm sorry," Bastian managed. He didn't know if he was apologizing to her or the class.

"He doesn't need to apologize," Finlay said. "He's trying. Just like the rest of us."

Andromeda scoffed. "Tell that to whoever gets sent into the field with him. Trying doesn't cut it in this school. You either learn or you die, and you better hope you don't take down anyone else with you."

Despite his backup moments earlier, Finlay didn't defend Bastian. In fact, when he looked at Bastian again, he actually bit his lip, as if seeing Bastian in a new light.

Bastian knew that look well. He'd seen it on his other classmates, on Aaron.

Finlay was a little afraid of him.

The bells rang, signaling the end of class. Fennick didn't even bother coming in; the door opened on its own accord, and the class started filtering out. Finlay hurried off, and Bastian's heart sank as he watched him go.

"I'd rather be bad at Conjuring than be like her," Harold muttered as he came over to stand beside Bastian.

"She has a point, though," Bastian said. "If I don't improve . . ."

"You will," Harold said. He put a hand on Bastian's shoulder. "Some of us are just slower learners, that's all."

Bastian could only hope his friend was right. It felt like his life—and everyone else's—depended on it.

22

In his dream, Bastian wandered down the long stone hallway, tugged forward by a voice he could barely hear.

The flagstones were cold under his bare feet, and the skeletal hands along the wall held torches that burned purple, their flames impossibly billowing down, their smoke curling into a fog that obscured the ground. Forward, he walked. Down the Hall of the Fallen, the plaques glimmering and whispering in the torchlight.

Except . . .

In his dream, the hall didn't end in rubble. It ended in a door.

He moved closer. The door was emblazoned with twin herons, each holding an old lantern in its beak.

"Sebastian . . ."

He reached out. Touched the knob. The knob in the shape of a skull.

The door opened, and fog billowed out.

"I'll protect you, little bird," his aunt said. She squeezed his hand as they stared down at the caskets. She smelled of incense and drying herbs. "No matter what happens, I will protect you."

He wiped back his tears as he stared at the graves. He wouldn't cry. He wouldn't . . .

"See how far her protection got you," came a horrible voice.

Bastian looked up. In the ring of family friends stood a man. A man who wasn't a man at all. His painted porcelain mask stared at Bastian with a wicked smile.

"You will stumble into my arms, Sebastian. Sooner or later, you will join them."

He gestured to the caskets.

Bastian looked down.

The caskets were opening slowly, creaking, and black water rushed out, filling the pits, surging up toward his feet. In the distance, the church bells rang, louder and louder, until all he could hear was their terrible clanging and the roar of water at his heels.

Bastian bolted upright. His heart was racing as he took stock of his room. Embers burned in the fireplace. It still smelled like drying herbs. The moon was setting beyond the hills outside, pulling the night to deeper darkness. He was here, and he was awake.

So why were the bells clanging in his head? It wasn't breakfast.

Something shuffled, and on impulse he jerked his hand out. A tiny ball of merelight appeared above his palm. Its harsh white light filled the room and fell on Harold, who was rummaging through his desk.

"Watch it!" Harold hissed, shielding his eyes with an arm.

"Sorry," Bastian replied. He let the merelight dim, and a moment later the embers in the fireplace burned brighter and the candles in the tree growing above them flickered to light. "What are you doing?"

"Don't worry about it," Harold said. "Go back to sleep."

"How can I sleep through those bells?"

Harold stopped stuffing whatever he'd grabbed into his satchel and looked at Bastian.

"You can hear them?" he asked.

"Of course!" Bastian said. They were growing louder. "How is the whole school not waking up?"

"Because the bells only toll for those being summoned to the field. Only . . ."

"Only what?"

"No offence, but there's no way you're ready."

Bastian flopped back in bed and crammed his pillow to his ears. If anything, it only made the sound worse. He groaned. "How do I make them stop?"

"By heeding them," Harold said. He cursed under his breath and walked over, yanking the pillow away. "Come on. Get dressed. It'll help, trust me."

Bastian did so. He pulled on his school clothes, and as he did, the bells lessened. They were still there, but they didn't hurt so much that he thought his head was splitting in half.

Harold muttered to himself as he went around the room, grabbing jars of herbs, vials of potions, and various charms from their pegs on the walls. Bastian heard some of the words, like *liability* and *death wish*.

"I should have made you some protection amulets," Harold grumbled. "Stupid. *Stupid.* I should have known this would happen. But it shouldn't be happening. There's no way . . ."

He yanked something from his drawer and handed it to Bastian. "Take this. It's a smudge bomb—palo santo and bog myrtle and grave dust. It should repel . . . Well, hopefully you won't need it."

Bastian shoved the parcel into his pocket. He knew what this meant. He remembered seeing the upperclassmen—and even Andromeda and Finlay— jerking up in the middle of meals or in the study hall and storming out. Going into the field. To hunt ghosts.

But Harold was right: He wasn't ready. That merelight was about all he could manage, and he hadn't mastered even a basic summoning circle, and—

"Come on," Harold said. "We better hurry. We've already taken long enough, and if the bells think you're ignoring them, they get . . . nasty. And I do not want to get to the part with the vomiting."

He went to the door and held it open for Bastian, who'd just finished lacing up his boots.

Bastian hurried out and took one more look into the room, wondering if there was anything else he could take that would help, a book or an amulet or . . .

The bells gave a deafening clang, as if angry at his hesitation.

Harold grabbed his arm and led him down the corridor.

Bastian wondered if this was the last time he'd ever see his room again.

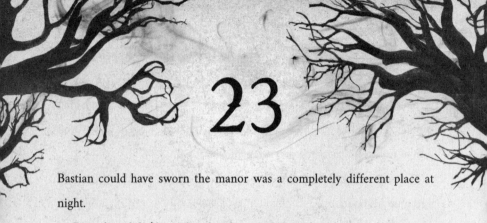

23

Bastian could have sworn the manor was a completely different place at night.

Even though he'd wandered and gotten lost in these halls multiple times, Harold managed to lead him to a corridor he'd never seen before—a hall that seemed to be built not with bricks, but tombstones, their weathered faces all but unreadable in the dim glow of Harold's merelight. Iron-barred windows looked out into a darkened courtyard, though it was impossible to see what lay beyond through the warped leaded glass.

Harold opened a door along the wall and stepped out into the frigid night.

It was the strangest courtyard Bastian had ever seen.

A large willow tree grew in the center, its bare, silvery branches glowing in the dying moonlight. It arched high overhead, the tips trailing down to a series of doors that were circled around it, like spokes on a wheel.

They were just doors. A dozen, maybe, each standing closed in its frame and facing the next like dominoes. Each was slightly different—plain wood or stained glass or rusted metal. And although they didn't move or creak or glow, something about them had a presence. A weight. As if they were alive.

"These are the Doors to Everywhere," Harold said, his voice tinged with awe. "They open to wherever is in need of our skills, anywhere in the world."

Now that they were here, Bastian realized that the bells had quietened. He could still hear them, but only faintly. He slowly walked around the doors. None of them opened. And none of them had any knobs.

"If they open anywhere in the world," Bastian asked, "why didn't my aunt send me through one of these when she portaled me here?"

"They don't work like that. Gallowgate has too many wards. The only way to come back through one of these doors is to leave through them. That keeps out evil spirits. Or mortals we don't want coming in." He paused and looked around. "I wonder if we're the only ones?"

"The only ones?"

In answer, the door leading to the courtyard opened, and out stepped Robyn.

They'd barely interacted since their first Summoning class. When she saw Bastian, it was clear she remembered that dismal failure. And all his failures since. Her expression fell.

"Hey," Harold said.

"Hey back," she replied, walking over to them. She paused and looked at Bastian. "What's he doing here?"

"He was summoned," Harold replied.

She laughed. "No way."

"He hears the bells."

"Well, send him back inside! You and I can handle this on our own. Or we can get someone else. He's not ready for the field. The last time I was out there I had to fight a banshee. A *banshee*! I couldn't hear for twenty-four hours after, and that was with two upperclassmen as backup."

The moment she said it—the moment Bastian *considered* leaving—the bells clanged in his head, louder than ever.

Clearly, Harold and Robyn heard them, too. They both clapped their hands to their ears and winced.

"Hear that?" Harold yelled. "He can't go back. When you're summoned, you're summoned. He has to come with us."

"Um, hello," Bastian said. "Still here. Stop talking about me like I'm not around."

"Sorry," Harold said. He winced. "I just . . ."

"Shut up!" Robyn hissed.

The bells had ceased.

The door in front of them began to open. It was a flat, gray door of rusted metal. And rather than the courtyard, a wall of darkness faced them through the opening. Bastian couldn't see an inch beyond the frame.

"Looks like it's just the three of us," Robyn said, casting one last look back to the courtyard entrance. Then she stepped over to Bastian. "Look. What's in there is going to be worse than anything we've covered in class, okay? So just stay in the circle and try not to get killed. We'll take care of whatever it is. Got it?"

Bastian nodded. A small part of him wanted to stand up for himself, to say that he had every right to go in there. But the rest of him remembered that he was a year younger and his training hadn't gone nearly as well as theirs. *That* part of him was terrified and didn't want to step a foot through that door.

Robyn glanced to Harold, then walked through the door. Once she passed the threshold, she disappeared entirely.

Harold hesitated. "I don't want to admit that she's right, but—"

"She's right," Bastian finished. He remembered Fennick's warning, about him being a liability. If the best way to keep his friend alive was to stay put . . . he'd stay put. "It's okay. Really."

Harold sighed. But he didn't say anything or try to refute him. Instead, he slid on his plague doctor mask and gestured Bastian into the doorway.

The moment they stepped through, the door shut, casting them in complete darkness.

Their way back to safety was gone.

24

"Where are we?" Bastian asked. His voice echoed in the pitch-black space.

Robyn punched him in the shoulder. "Shh!"

Silence descended. All Bastian could hear was his own frantic breathing. The bells were gone. The courtyard was gone.

All the wards and protections of Gallowgate were gone.

Robyn snapped her fingers and three balls of merelight appeared above her head, circling slowly.

Bastian wished they could just go back to darkness.

The lights illuminated endless rows of shelves, each stacked high with boxes. They were in a warehouse, possibly in a basement, with no windows and no doors and no way out. For a moment, the only movement came from the flickering shadows cast by Robyn's dancing lights.

Then, a few yards away, a box fell from one of the shelves, spilling its contents all over the floor. Robyn cast an orb of light out.

Doll heads.

Great, Bastian thought. *More dolls.*

"Well," Robyn mused, "it's clearly at least semi-corporeal." Semi-corporeal meant that even though it didn't have a physical form, it could influence objects.

She actually seemed a little excited.

"Poltergeist?" Harold asked.

"Probably. Not enough screaming for a banshee . . ."

Harold lifted his mask and sniffed. "The effluvium is pretty faint. But it's a big space. Maybe it's toying with us."

"Effluvium?" Bastian asked.

"Oh yeah. Haven't covered that in Alchemy yet. It's the scent of ghosts."

"And this isn't the time for a lesson," Robyn said. She looked to Bastian, who had begun sniffing the air as well. He *could* sense a faint tang in the air, an electric char similar to the shadowman's scent, but not nearly as bad. "Remember what I said. Don't. Leave. The. Circle."

"I know, I know," Bastian said.

Robyn closed her eyes in concentration and raised her hands to her chest, pressing her palms together. Then she took a deep breath.

One of the merelights floated down in front of her hands and turned a bright, crackling blue. A moment later, she flung her hands out to her sides. The light split into a fiery line that encircled the three of them, forming a giant, floating sky-blue ring. Heat waves wavered above and below the circle, obscuring everything beyond, and sparks danced to the floor.

Robyn opened her eyes. They glowed with a faint electric blue. Or maybe it was just a reflection from the circle.

"Right," she said, looking to Harold and winking. "Let's go hunt a ghost, shall we?"

Without waiting for an answer, she practically frolicked out of the circle.

Harold turned to Bastian and lowered his voice. "Look, I wish you could help, but I don't want you getting hurt. So just stay in here, okay? If worse comes to worst, use the smudge bomb. Toss it on the ground and it'll explode. That'll drive pretty much anything away, and also get our attention to come help."

He quickly rummaged around in his satchel, muttering the names of plants and potions under his breath. He grabbed a few vials.

"Back in a bit," he said. Then he slipped his mask over his face and disappeared through the circle.

Bastian stood there, blood pounding in his ears and the smudge bomb clutched to his chest. Now that Harold and Robyn were gone, he realized that—through the magic of the circle—he couldn't hear anything happening in the warehouse beyond. He could barely even see the shadowy figures of his companions as they wended their way down the aisles.

All he could do was wait. And hope. And think that standing in the center of a very bright circle in the middle of a very dark warehouse was like putting a target on his back.

The shadowman said he could find me anywhere.

If Aunt Dahlia's wards hadn't been enough to keep the monster out, he very much doubted that a first-year student's efforts would do much better.

He turned on the spot, trying to peer into the shadows, trying to summon his own merelight or fireball, but the fear coursing through his veins made it impossible. He couldn't even keep his knees from shaking.

All he wanted to do was run back to his room and hide under the covers.

Maybe he didn't have what it took to be an Æthercist, after all.

Light flashed to his right. He jerked and yelped as, beyond the circle, flashes and flames rose up between the shelves. It was eerie, like watching a silent movie—he knew there should be rumbling explosions, but it was entirely silent.

But that wasn't the only movement.

At first he thought it was a trick of the light. But then the *something* got nearer, and he realized that there were balls rolling toward him. Dozens of white and brown rocks, tumbling along the floor, swarming around him.

It was only when they neared the circle, not daring or not able to roll past its circumference, that he realized they weren't rocks at all.

They were the toppled doll heads.

He nearly tossed the smudge bomb then and there.

Because although they weren't moving past the perimeter of the bubble, they had him surrounded. And they were shaking.

Even without hearing it, Bastian knew they were laughing. He stared into their glassy eyes and felt his blood run cold. He was trapped. Their painted smiles reminded him far too much of the shadowman.

Light flashed in front of him, between the aisles, a bolt of acid green.

A second later, one of the great shelves near him began to topple.

It pitched to the side and slammed into the next shelf, which toppled into the next, which toppled into the next, and so on, like giant dominoes.

They were falling toward him.

The last one was going to crush him.

He didn't have time to think.

He leaped backward, right as the shelf crashed to the floor, demolishing the spot where he'd just been standing.

He tripped through the protection circle. Stumbled over the possessed doll heads.

The moment he did, sound and sensation came back—the electric char of effluvium, the distant roars of explosions, the terrible screech of metal as another shelf fell onto the circle.

The blue light winked out.

The vengeful cackle of the dolls' heads filled his ears.

25

Bastian ran.

He didn't know where he was going, but the shelves continued to collapse around him as the shadows seethed. All he knew was that he had to get away.

The trouble was, the only way out was the opposite direction from his friends.

The doll heads rolled and cackled behind him, leaping up and pelting him in the back. They acquired other body parts as they chased, pulling in legs and arms and torsos, until Bastian looked behind him to see hundreds of deformed dolls, their eyes glowing green.

He ran harder. Rounded a corner—

And hit a dead end.

He ran up to the concrete wall and smacked it with his palm, then turned and faced the dolls.

As he watched, their tangled bodies merged together into a larger construct. A horrible, monstrous figure rose above Bastian with hundreds of wiggling arms and legs, like a millipede made of doll parts. It scuttled toward him, trapping him completely.

"*He will be pleased!*" howled the legion of doll bits, mandibles quivering in excitement and dripping green goo. "*So pleased we have found you. So pleased we have brought you to him. Come, Sebastian. Your master awaits.*"

The dollipede lashed forward, wrapping its body around him. Bastian only had just enough time to throw the smudge bomb.

Smoke exploded amid a burst of fiery herbs that filled the aisle with thick, woody incense.

The dollipede screamed in frustration, chunks of it flying apart. For a brief moment Bastian thought he'd done it—he'd banished the poltergeist! But the pressure around his chest didn't lessen.

It intensified.

He felt a terrible lurching sensation, as if the poltergeist was yanking *through* his flesh.

A moment later, the world changed.

Color faded. Time slowed.

The world around him washed to grayscale, everything blurred and on the edge of fading, like a watercolor painting left out in the rain. Everything was murky, save for the monstrous poltergeist wrapped around him.

Only now, Bastian couldn't see the doll parts—he could only see the spirit within. It was vicious green and serpentine, a monstrous creature with five snapping heads and blinding white eyes. Its sinuous body wrapped around Bastian's chest. And as he struggled, as he looked down, he realized he was transparent as well.

It was like what had happened in the cafeteria. But he hadn't heard of anything like this in his classes.

"*You cannot fight this, Sebastian!*" roared the poltergeist. "*This is your destiny.*"

Bastian struggled. The poltergeist tightened its grip. And what Bastian thought was the rush of blood through his ears grew louder.

It sounded like water.

Like a river.

Like the churning, black river from his dreams.

From between the milky aisles he saw it: a surge of blackness, a rush of shadow.

The river of the dead.

He knew, then, where he was—he was in the first layer of the underworld, the world without form.

Which meant he was dead.

Panic raced through him as the river surged forward. He fought against the poltergeist, tried to struggle free, but none of his training seemed to work. He couldn't find the Æther to conjure or bind. He was cut off.

Shadowy water spilled across his feet, hissing and roiling, tugging his toes downstream, toward the next Veil, toward the next level of the dead. As the river rose, the poltergeist pulled Bastian farther downstream.

He looked to where the water was flowing.

In the stream, he saw a darker blot moving toward him, pushing upstream.

The shadowman.

Bastian yelped in surprise, and in the shock of seeing his nightmare manifest, he tripped.

Fell into the river.

Water surged up around him, frothing against his skin and blocking out the eerie half-light. It was cold and electric, heavy but also formless, washing around him and through him in a foaming hiss. All he could see was darkness and the acidic green coil of the poltergeist wrapped around his chest. The river carried them on, toward the shadowman, and Bastian knew . . .

He knew this was the end.

He could feel the river pulling away at him, dissolving the very parts that made him *him*. It fizzed and crackled through his body, humming deep within his senses: *Give in, let go, surrender.*

When his head bobbed out of the water, the poltergeist's green tails crushing his lungs, he saw the shadowman reaching for him, only a few feet away.

"It was all in vain," the shadowman cooed. *"Cease your fighting, and join me. I may even spare your friends . . ."*

Bastian knew that it was a lie. Knew that if he failed here, the shadowman wouldn't just stop with him—it would go after Robyn and Harold next. And since they had no clue what they were up against, the shadowman would tear them apart.

Bastian wasn't going to let that happen.

He reached again for the Æther, but this time, he felt something *else* at the edge of his awareness. A different sort of power. A cold electricity.

It reminded him of how he'd felt in his bedroom, trying to save Aunt Dahlia from the shadowman's grip.

He reached toward the power, and the moment it connected, energy flooded through him. A wild, frozen current that instantly made his skin spark with purple.

Distantly, he heard the poltergeist scream in shock or frustration.

The light pulsed through him, violent and violet, and when it reached a fever pitch he thrust it out, into the underworld.

Purple light rippled through the river, burned away the poltergeist and the shadowed current.

The poltergeist wailed. Now, *it* was trying to escape *him*.

The light consumed everything. Consumed him.

And between one furious heartbeat and the next, he was back in the world of the living.

Doll parts clattered to the ground around him. The air was filled with the pungent smoke of his smudge bomb. It was as if no time had passed at all.

As if he hadn't just died . . . and somehow come back.

"What . . . ?" came a voice from the shadows.

Light flared above him, and Robyn and Harold stepped out.

"What did you just do?" Robyn asked, her voice tinged with awe.

Behind him, he heard a creak. He looked over his shoulder to see a door in the wall. A rusted-metal door that definitely hadn't been there before.

Bastian didn't answer Robyn. He looked to her, and the shadows behind her started to move. To congeal. A dozen feet away, he saw the pale moon of the shadowman's mask.

"Run!" he yelled.

He lunged forward and grabbed Robyn's and Harold's arms, then turned course and yanked them through the door.

They stumbled in at his side.

Into the courtyard.

Into the frigid, silent night air.

They fell to the grass, panting.

"What—?" Robyn began, looking at Bastian.

"What is *that*?" Harold yelped. He scrambled back, away from the door, pointing.

The shadowman stood in the darkness of the doorway, its smiling mask pressed right to the invisible barrier separating them. Blue light rippled from the wards.

The monster stood there, examining them like a predatory animal.

Like he had all the time in the world.

Like he knew, eventually, they would all fall into his hands.

Robyn slammed the door closed, blocking out the shadowman's sneer. But Bastian still heard the monster laugh.

"Soon."

26

"We all just saw that, right?" Robyn asked.

For the first time since Bastian had met her, she actually looked unnerved. She paced back and forth in the back corner of the library—the only spot in the manor that seemed private, even at this time of night. It had been nearly impossible dragging her here; she had wanted to turn back and fight the shadowman. Bastian would have been perfectly fine running back to his room and hiding under the covers. Tea in the library seemed like an okay compromise.

Harold poured them each another mug. Valerian and chamomile—not the best tasting, but good for nerves. Bastian's hands shook when he took the earthenware mug. Clearly, he needed his nerves calmed. Either that, or it was from the ice that seemed to sludge through his veins. Even though he sat by the roaring fireplace, he had never felt so *cold*.

"We saw it," Harold said. He glanced to Bastian. "Though I'm still not entirely certain *what* we saw."

"That's what was chasing me here," Bastian said. "It broke through my aunt's wards. And I swear that's what appeared our first day in Summoning."

"Madame Ardea said it was just a shade . . ." Robyn began.

"That was no shade," Harold replied. "It also shouldn't have been able to find you again. Gallowgate's wards remove any sort of ghostly trace. Once you pass through them, any Ætheric ties between you and the spirit should have been severed."

"And yet . . ." Bastian said.

"And yet," Harold replied.

They sat in silence for a moment, Robyn still pacing, her tea untouched.

"So what *is* it?" Robyn asked. "I grew up reading stories about the ghosts of the underworld—" She made a face at Bastian's expression. "What? I was a weird kid, okay? I liked ghost stories. Especially the ones that were true. But I've never seen any ghost like that before."

"I've been calling it a shadowman," Bastian said. For a brief moment, he wondered what it would have been like to grow up knowing about all this. Maybe, if his parents hadn't died, he would have been as confident as she was.

"The shadowman," Robyn said. "Right. Well . . . it doesn't exist, according to every book I've read. It wasn't in *Denizens of Death* or *Grim Graves, a Guide to Ghosts and Ghouls*. I've read them front to back a million times."

"You're weird," Harold said. He grinned.

"Says the boy who collects poisonous plants," Robyn replied with a smirk. Then the smirk faded. "Does Madame Ardea know about this? I mean, I know it appeared in Summoning, but maybe she didn't connect the dots. Maybe she didn't know what it was?"

"She knew," Bastian admitted. "When we were leaving the Chapel, I saw her covering it in the same wards my aunt used to protect us."

"Why would she hide something like that?" Robyn asked.

Harold shrugged. "Who knows? I've lived here for most of my life. She's like a mom to me. But she isn't the most, um, expressive at times. Maybe she has a reason?"

"That reason nearly got us all killed," Bastian said. *If I knew what I was up against, I'd know how to fight it. Or at least how to avoid it.*

127

"Speaking of nearly being killed . . ." Robyn said slowly. She looked to Bastian, then glanced away. "That brings us to the giant undead elephant in the room. How *did* you defeat that poltergeist? You started floating, Bastian. And your eyes . . . your eyes turned purple, like you were possessed."

Bastian's heart sank.

"What do you mean?" he asked. "Isn't that normal?" His voice was a squeak.

"It's no magic I've ever seen," Harold said. "I swear the air dropped, like, fifty degrees around you."

"That would explain why I can't get warm," Bastian muttered. A shiver wracked through him, and Harold poured more warm tea into the mug.

"What actually happened, though? All we saw was you floating and glowing purple and then the poltergeist just vanished. No binding spells, no banishing. Just—" Robyn made a poof gesture with her hands.

Bastian didn't want to think about it. The moment he did, cold poured through him again. He could still feel the tug of the river. He still remembered how easy it would have been to just let go. How much a part of him had *wanted* to let go.

"I think I went into the underworld," he confessed.

Robyn snorted. When Bastian glanced at her, her humor melted.

"Oh. You weren't joking."

Bastian shook his head.

"Okay," Robyn continued, "well, that's impossible. I mean, that's the whole point of the First Veil—you have to renounce your body to pass through. There's no coming back from that."

"But I did," Bastian said. "I mean. I'm here."

"Maybe you were just imagining it. Shock or something?" Robyn asked.

"No, I saw it. I felt the river. It's happened before. I thought it was normal." He shuddered again.

"Maybe we should ask Madame Ardea," Harold offered.

"Maybe," Bastian said.

"If she wouldn't tell him about the shadowman, do you really think she'd explain this?" Robyn asked.

"It's worth a shot," Harold said.

"We can do it tomorrow," Bastian said. He wanted to stop talking about it now. He didn't want to think about slipping into the underworld. He didn't want to think about how close he'd gotten to the shadowman.

He didn't want to think about how close he'd come to joining his parents . . . and how close he'd been to letting it happen.

27

Bastian slept horribly.

Every time he closed his eyes, he was back in the underworld, back fighting off the shadowy river that ate away at his soul. He woke up coated in cold sweat and wondering if it had been a dream, or if he truly had been slipping away.

By the time he made it to Alchemy, he felt like he was sleepwalking. He hadn't had the courage to talk to Madame Ardea after Summoning. He told himself he would do it soon. When he was more awake.

Class was held in the greenhouses outside the laboratories. These weren't like the well-manicured greenhouses he'd seen back home; these were ancient plate-glass-and-ironwork constructions, with glass orbs of Ætheric merelight hanging from the ceilings and plants from every continent twining up the filigree, blocking out the clouded sky beyond.

Bastian knelt before a patch of earth at the very back of the greenhouse; he didn't want to try to make small talk, not today. The plant bed looked like a freshly churned grave, and a tombstone declaring the bed's contents (stinging nettle) rose at one end. The whole greenhouse was filled with similar "graves," though most, thankfully, were only filled with plants, not bodies.

A skeleton *had* reached out from the rosemary and grabbed Roman's wrist the first day of class, but that was just a practical joke.

"You know," came Robyn's voice, "you can get longer gloves."

He glanced over to see her standing beside him, a pair of extra-long work gloves in her hands and a freshly picked bundle of mugwort poking out of the satchel at her side. She knelt down and handed him the gloves.

"Thanks," Bastian said awkwardly. He peeled off his own gloves, which only went to his wrists. Red pinpricks from the nettle wrapped around his forearms. He'd tried being careful, but clearly he'd failed.

"You're going to want a salve for those," Robyn said, nodding to the rashes.

Bastian raised an eyebrow at her. Up until last night, she'd pretty much done everything she could to avoid or ignore him. Why was she seeking him out now?

"I'll have Harold make me one when I get back," Bastian said. Harold was in one of the advanced Alchemy classes, the only class they didn't have together. He wished Harold was here now; the moment he pulled the new gloves up to his elbows, the rashes started to itch and burn horribly. Not as bad as when he'd accidentally grabbed a bundle of poison oak in his bare hands, but close. And that hadn't been his fault—the tombstone declaring that bed's contents had been written in runes.

"Harold's really good at Alchemy," Robyn said.

"Okay, you can stop now," Bastian said. He wasn't usually one for confrontation, but he was too tired to care.

"What?"

"Being nice to me," Bastian said. "I mean, it's great and all, but . . ."

She dropped her gaze. "Look, I'm sorry I've been a jerk. Especially last night. It wasn't right. But . . . I don't know. I've been thinking about what you said, about what you *did*, and the more I think about it, the more impossible it sounds. Once your soul leaves your body, you're dead. There's no coming back from that."

"Are you calling me a zombie?" Bastian asked.

She snorted. "You kinda look like one right now. But I'm serious. What happened to you last night shouldn't have happened. And the ghost—the shadowman—shouldn't exist. You were out in the field one time, and two impossible things happened. Plus, Madame Ardea knew all of that when you came here, and she did nothing. Right?"

Bastian nodded. He'd never mentioned to Ardea that he'd slipped into the underworld. But maybe she'd known—hadn't she told him to tell her if anything abnormal happened during his studies? It was almost like she *knew* something about him was strange, but didn't want to say it. She'd wanted him to come to her.

"Which means we're being lied to," Robyn finished. "There's something strange about you."

"Thanks?"

She laughed. "My first pet was the shade of a cat we called Mr. Muffins. Strange is good. But it can also be dangerous. And like it or not, I'm a part of this now, and I refuse to be caught unawares again. So we're going to get to the bottom of this. Together."

"Are you saying you want to be my friend?"

"You just had to make it awkward," she replied.

Bastian grinned. "It's the one thing I'm good at."

She glanced at the welts on his arms.

"That," she said, "is obvious."

28

Even though Bastian could have happily avoided confronting Madame Ardea for at least another week, Harold wouldn't allow it.

"We're talking to her," he said, marching Bastian down the hall at the end of the day. He glanced to Robyn, who hadn't left Bastian's side since Alchemy. He didn't mention anything about their sudden friendship. Bastian figured that—like him—Harold was just grateful to have another companion.

"Can't we just not, though?" Bastian asked. "We're going to miss dinner." He hated how much that last bit sounded like a whine.

Harold glared at him, which wasn't exactly intimidating since it looked like a unicorn had farted on him. He was covered in a pink, glittery soot from some failed Alchemy experiment.

"I'm just saying," Bastian continued, "she didn't tell me anything before. What makes you think she will now?"

"Because now you have two other people corroborating what you say."

"Big word," Robyn commented with a grin.

Harold stuck out his tongue.

Together, they made their way out into the cold, rainy back lawn and down the cliffside walkways, out across the churning lake to the Bone Chapel. The door was shut, and heavy incense poured out when Harold stuck his head inside. There was still a class going on, but Harold gestured Robyn and Bastian in, anyway.

The upperclassmen were all clearly Summoners—they each wore the long, flowing black robes embroidered in blue and the dozens of chains and amulets and bells of their field—and they were all transfixed on the glimmering blue summoning circle burning in the middle of the room. The spiderweb inlay in the floor burned an electric blue as well, making everyone a ghastly shade of pale.

Especially Madame Ardea. When Bastian looked at her, confrontation was the last thing he wanted.

She stood at the far end of the chapel, her hands raised and blue light flaring around her palms. Her lips moved in a silent incantation. Her glowing blue eyes were fixed on the circle.

As he watched, the light within the circle bled out and became a thick shadow of the deepest black. A blue fog fell into the resulting void like it was a black hole, a hungry, terrifying emptiness.

From that all-consuming nothing came a horrifying roar that made the bone sconces rattle and dust puff down from the rib chandeliers. Bastian flinched against the wall, nudging against a skull that mumbled at being jostled. Robyn and Harold jolted, but they managed to remain composed. Even a few of the older Summoner kids took a step backward.

"I summon thee, wraith!" Madame Ardea called, loud and clear. "I call you forth from beyond the Third Veil. Arise!"

The mist swirling into the pit began to twist up, like a whirling tornado.

Then, with a crackle of light and a waft of effluvium so thick that Bastian choked, the mist became a humanoid ghost that floated and writhed within the circle. Humanoid, except its body looked like it had been rotting at the bottom of the sea. Its ghastly face was hollowed, its eyes pale glowing pearls, its lips receded to reveal rotten, jagged teeth. Fabric and flesh hung from it in tattered curtains, its limbs elongated, its fingers skeletal and sharp.

The moment it saw where it was, it attacked.

It hurled itself at Madame Ardea with a ferocious scream. Sparks flashed and hissed as it crashed against the Ætheric barrier, but that wasn't enough to make it quit. It screamed madly, darting toward a student, only to rebound in a flash of sparks once more. Bastian was mildly relieved that the targeted kid had yelped when it came toward him.

"Now, students," Madame Ardea said. Lights flickered around her palms while she held the circle, but she didn't seem even remotely strained. "Practice your bindings. Wraiths will seek out a living host the moment they are in our world, for without one, they quickly fade back into the underworld."

The Summoners stepped forward, toward the very edges of the circle. Some chanted, while others flexed their fingers. Blue light laced around each of them and, within the circle, chains and bindings began to appear, wrapping themselves tight around the wraith. The spirit struggled and screamed. A few of the students flinched against the screeching wail, their lights flickering out momentarily.

The wraith was clearly stronger than it looked. Bastian was just grateful the thing was still contained.

"Very good," Madame Ardea said. "Now, let's see how well you do at banishing it in the real world. Do not—and I repeat, *do not*—let it escape. If it manages to possess one of you, it will be a long night for all of us, and I've heard the cooks are serving pot pie for dinner."

Bastian looked to Harold momentarily. *She doesn't mean, she can't—*

The circle winked out in a hiss of sparks.

The moment it did, Madame Ardea's gaze snared on Bastian and his friends. She wiped her hands and strode over, completely oblivious to the vengeful spirit that screamed and struggled against its bonds behind her, or the students who struggled just as hard to keep it contained.

"What are you three doing here?" she asked. "Harold, you should know better than to interrupt an advanced class."

The wraith screamed and a student was flung across the room behind her; the girl was caught by a pair of skeletal arms on the wall and lowered gently back down. The student immediately ran back to the circle, lights flashing around her wrists.

Madame Ardea didn't spare the girl a glance.

"Bastian was summoned to the field last night," Harold said.

Despite the steel in her eyes, Madame Ardea seemed taken aback. She examined Bastian with an unreadable gaze, while behind her two more students were flung to the side. One of them didn't get back up.

"Quite unusual," she finally said.

"And dangerous," Robyn said. "He nearly died. Can't you make it so he isn't summoned?"

"The magic of the Doors is tied to the very fabric of Gallowgate, and is a force not even I can change. It is clear you survived the encounter, for which we are all undoubtedly thankful—"

"He was targeted," Harold cut in. "The spirit that chased him here was there. We all saw it."

Madame Ardea's eyebrows furrowed.

"Are you sure?"

Bastian nodded. "It was . . . it was the shadowman. The ghost that got past my aunt's wards."

"Impossible," she said. "Your aunt banished that ghost weeks ago."

Behind her, another kid yelled as they were tossed to the side. The wraith raged as more and more ropes wrapped around it.

"I said *keep that thing contained!*" Ardea yelled, not looking away from the three of them.

Harold stammered. "But we saw—"

"It is not uncommon for spirits to take on the form of that which we fear most. Think of the common phantasm, Harold. Surely you remember the basics."

"It wasn't a phantasm," Harold said.

"I assure you, it is nothing to worry about. Now go to dinner, the three of you."

She made to turn, but Harold grabbed the sleeve of her robe.

Her icy glare should have been enough to turn him to stone, but he didn't let go.

"That wasn't all," Harold said. "The ghost we were sent there to hunt, it . . . it dragged Bastian into the underworld."

If Bastian hadn't been paying careful attention, he wouldn't have noticed the flicker in Madame Ardea's eyes.

The note of fear.

"That is impossible," she said firmly. "To pass the First Veil is to die. You must have been mistaken."

I know what I saw, Bastian wanted to say. But maybe she was right? Maybe he'd made it up? Maybe it *was* shock?

"Don't you think—" Harold began.

A Summoner screamed behind Madame Ardea.

Light flashed, and with a wail of triumph the ropes around the wraith burst into shreds. The wraith lunged straight toward Madame Ardea's back.

She didn't look around. She didn't even blink.

She just raised her hand and snapped her fingers right as the wraith clawed at her back.

The wraith exploded in a puff of blue smoke and sparks that hissed harmlessly to the tiles.

Bastian cowered against the wall, trying hard not to fall to his knees as Madame Ardea stared coolly at the three of them.

"*I* think," she said calmly, "that I am the rectress of Gallowgate, and can presume to know more about the nature of the dead and the underworld than even you, Harold." She looked to Bastian, and once more he noticed the flicker of uncertainty behind her eyes, try as she might to hide it. "It is not uncommon for young Æthercists to mistake what they have seen in their first hunts. Fear does terrible things to the mind. What *is* certain is that to have one's soul split from their body is to be separated from life itself. Had that happened, Bastian would not be with us. And since he is neither a shade nor a ghoul"—she placed a hand on his shoulder, as if confirming his solidity—"it would appear the former is the most likely. Now, if you will excuse me."

She turned back to the class in a billow of robes.

"Students," she declared to the Summoners, many of whom were struggling to get to their feet, or in tears, "who can tell me what went wrong?"

"Come on," Harold said. He turned and led them back out of the Bone Chapel.

It was only when they were back up the cliff and safe from the wraith and prying ears that any of them spoke.

"Maybe she was right," Bastian ventured. "I *was* scared, and confused, and—"

"No," Harold said. He looked darkly over his shoulder to the chapel. "You weren't mistaking anything. Neither were Robyn and I when we saw the shadowman. That was no phantasm, and we *saw* your eyes turn purple." He took a deep breath. "She's lying to us. I don't know why. But it looks like we're on our own."

29

Bastian, Harold, and Robyn spent weeks trying to find something—anything—that would illuminate what the shadowman was, or what had allowed Bastian to enter the underworld and come back.

They'd found nothing.

But their failures were momentarily pushed from their thoughts when they woke the morning of All Hallows Eve. The air was infused with a scent that was rather unusual for a room that usually smelled like plants and dirt and stale socks.

"Did you order a pumpkin spice latte?" Bastian asked groggily as he got up.

"Huh?" Harold mumbled.

Bastian got out of bed and walked over to the fireplace. A great iron cauldron sat bubbling green smoke in the flames, and a half-dozen jack-o'-lanterns grinned and glimmered on the table in front of it. Smaller cauldrons spilled candy all over the table, and—sure enough—two skull-shaped goblets of spiced pumpkin coffee sat, perfectly warmed, among the glimmering wrappers.

"Just wait until you see the rest of the place," Harold said as he shoved a handful of candy in his pocket.

The entire manor had been decorated overnight, turning the place into a Gothic wonderland.

Even more so than it had been before.

Jack-o'-lanterns of all shapes and sizes—from small and grinning to huge and hideous—adorned every flat surface, lining the halls and piled high on tables, their inner flames flickering green and orange. They cackled as students passed, or wailed ominously. Extra skulls and bones were stacked everywhere, skeletons wandering down the halls or leaping out from darkened doorways. Bats fluttered overhead, darting through massive spiderwebs that draped over the rafters. And thick, low-lying fog curled down every hall, rippling as hidden beasts scurried underneath.

Harold leaned closer to a skull, which moaned ominously, and reached into its mouth.

"Hey!" yelped the skull. "Ask permission first!"

"Sorry," Harold replied. Then he held up a piece of candy. "Trick-or-treat, Gallowgate style," he explained to Bastian. "There's candy hidden all over the place. The real good stuff is kept in the scariest places. Last year I got a whole load of peanut butter cups in the iron maiden they keep in the crypts. Nearly got stuck inside, but it was totally worth it." He rubbed his arms, as if remembering nearly being impaled.

Bastian laughed and snatched the candy from Harold's hand.

"Hey!" Harold yelled, but Bastian was already running toward the dining hall.

Every table there was laden with miniature pumpkins and jeweled skulls, tapered candles and spiderweb tablecloths. Winged skulls floated over the tables, singing off-key and telling bad jokes to anyone unlucky enough to be sitting beneath them—and, on occasion, dropping pieces of candy onto kids' heads, like pooing birds. Cauldrons the size of bathtubs sat around the room, each spewing different colors of fog. Even the fires had changed, their light glittering with purple and orange sparks.

Bastian and Harold took their usual spot beside Robyn.

"Happy Halloween!" she said. "Er, I mean, All Hallows Eve. Isn't this amazing?"

Bastian nodded, a huge grin on his face. Even though he was a total scaredy-cat, Halloween had always been his favorite holiday. It was the one day seeing ghosts was almost normal, the one day being weird wasn't a bad thing. He loved the costumes and decorations. And, obviously, the bucketloads of candy. His other classmates seemed just as excited as he was. Roman and Tianna were tossing candy back and forth to each other, trying to get it in their mouths. Even Finlay, at the other first-years' table, was laughing with a Mexican girl next to him named Mariana, who was wearing a plastic bat in her wavy black hair. Finlay must have felt Bastian watching, as he glanced over just then and caught Bastian's eye.

This time, he didn't look away. Just grinned a little wider, until Mariana chucked a piece of candy corn at his forehead.

After the rest of the students had settled in, Madame Ardea stood. She was dressed for the occasion, with a traditional witch's hat and curled velvet shoes and a giant wart on her nose.

Bastian wondered if there was a costume closet hidden away in some corridor. Granted, what they wore every day would have worked as a Halloween costume in his hometown.

"Good morning, students," Madame Ardea called out as the room quietened. "And blessed All Hallows Eve."

Since Harold had brought them in to confront her, Bastian had noticed Madame Ardea watching him even more intently in class. The other professors, too, seemed to be keeping a closer eye on him. Not that it had helped him any—if anything, it had just made him more self-conscious about his failures.

"As many of you know, today is All Hallows Eve. Although traditionally a day of feasting and frivolity, it is also the day when the Veil between our world and the underworld is thinnest. This is not mere folklore. Next to Midwinter, the darkest day of the year, All Hallows is the day where the dead are most active. Because of this, we expect a higher number of hauntings than usual, for which you will all be expected to prepare, despite the celebrations. To that end, all classes will be canceled for the day, and I will ask you to stay sharp. Today of all days, the outside world needs us. Today of all days, the skills you have spent all term perfecting will be put to the test. Remain ready."

"That seems kind of ominous," Robyn muttered when Madame Ardea sat down.

Trays of themed treats floated through the dining hall, giant rolls shaped like pumpkins and green scrambled eggs that wriggled and apples carved into laughing skulls. Despite the laughter around them, Harold's expression had turned grim.

"Yeah," Harold admitted as the ghosts set a tray of pastry bats in front of them. At least, Bastian hoped they were pastry—the bats' wings flapped on occasion. "Despite all this," Harold said, gesturing to the decor, "it's not the best day to be an Æthercist. The world is overrun with spirits today. Most of them are just, like, recently deceased family members or shades. But the First Veil isn't the only one that's thin. *All* the Veils are easier to cross, which means we get some deep-level ghosts to deal with. Last year—" He shuddered. "Last year a revenant came through."

"A revenant?" Bastian asked. He remembered reading about them in the Hall of the Fallen. The word had been on Harold's mother's plaque.

Bastian immediately wished he hadn't spoken, but Harold just nodded and grabbed a muffin with a candy green witch's finger poking out. When Harold bit into it, the muffin bled strawberry jam and the finger shook in an admonishing gesture.

"They're horrible," Harold said, wiping his mouth. "And almost impossible to banish. They come from beyond the Third Veil. A single, angry spirit that can inhabit a bunch of corpses at once. It's a nightmare."

"Well, let's hope we don't run into any of those today," Robyn said. She looked over at Bastian when she said it, and even though they were friends, the look was clear—there's no way he'd survive such a thing.

Harold nodded. "It killed a kid before it was finally banished. Upperclassman. A Summoner named Mattís. Awful, awful day."

Harold trailed off, and Bastian tried to focus on food. But he was no longer hungry.

If the Veils were thin and the worst of spirits could get through . . . how easy would it be for the shadowman to find him?

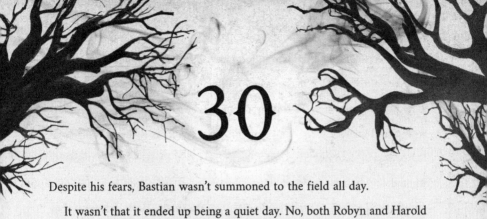

30

Despite his fears, Bastian wasn't summoned to the field all day.

It wasn't that it ended up being a quiet day. No, both Robyn and Harold were summoned. Twice. He'd even seen Finlay and Roman and a few other underclassmen get called to the field, and every time, his heart lurched with the fear that they wouldn't come back. Thankfully, they all returned. Every time, they were a little worse for wear, and clearly not interested in discussing what horrors they'd seen. But Bastian didn't hear the bells once.

Maybe Ardea had been lying about that, too—maybe she *could* keep him from being summoned to the field.

He sat in the study hall, a pot of cold tea on the table and two empty chairs facing him. An hour ago, Robyn and Harold had been summoned once more, leaving him alone with a stack of books and a pile of homework and zero desire to do any of it. It didn't matter that the titles should have been enough to excite him—*When the Dead Talk, a Necromancer's Guide; Summon Souls and Impress Your Friends!; Corpses and You: An Æthercist's Anatomy Coloring Book.*

He was bored.

Even though he didn't necessarily want to go out into the field, he felt . . . well, he felt left out. Like being picked last for a kickball team even though he was bad at kickball.

He watched a group of upperclassmen come in. Two Conjurers and an Alchemist, judging from their clothes. They were clearly just back from a hunt—there were soot stains on their faces, and the Alchemist's wheelchair was covered in mud, but they came in laughing and cracking jokes. They joined their friends amid a round of applause, and began regaling the others with grand tales of their hunt, smiling and glowing as if they'd just won a football game, and not banished a terrifying spirit. Bastian envied them. He wanted to be that confident. That powerful. But he'd been here a couple months, and still hadn't mastered more than the basics. He wondered if they would let kids like him stay on, kids who didn't seem to excel in anything.

"Third ghoul this month!" one of the returned Conjurers proclaimed.

"I swear they're getting worse this year," said a Necromancer, who until then had been staring into the jeweled eyes of a skull.

"You say that every year," said her friend, nudging her.

"Yes, but this time it's true," she replied. "The spirits . . ."

"Mind if I join you?"

Bastian jolted from his eavesdropping. Finlay stood across from him, awkwardly holding a book to his chest. His sweater was black and oversize, emblazoned with silver skulls around the collar. His messy brown hair was swept back over his ears.

Bastian was staring.

"Oh, um, sure," he replied. He moved some of the books out of the way. "Do you want some tea? I can reheat it if you want."

At least, he thought he *might* be able to—it should have been a simple Conjuring trick, but he'd only managed it once before.

"Nah, it's okay, thanks." Finlay sat down, but he didn't start reading.

"Have you . . ." Bastian began, struggling to find something to say. "Have you been summoned at all?" As though he *hadn't* been keeping worried tabs on him all day.

146

"Just once. I was paired up with a Summoner *and* a Necromancer, but we ended up just fighting off a shade. Not a big deal. You?"

Bastian shook his head. "Not yet. Still waiting."

"Well, maybe you'll be lucky and get to stay in where it's warm," Finlay said. He looked over to where the older students were telling one another stories from their worst hunts. Their laughter rang out through the hall. "Do you think it will ever feel that normal?"

"What?"

"Hunting ghosts, learning magic." Finlay looked away uncomfortably. "Some days I wake up thinking I'm back home in bed and it was all a weird dream. Sometimes I wish it *was* a weird dream."

"But you're so good at it," Bastian said. "I mean, you're already one of the best in our class."

"That doesn't mean I *want* to be," Finlay said. He looked to Bastian, and there was a note of sadness in his eyes. "Don't you ever wish your life was, you know, normal again?"

Bastian shrugged uncomfortably. "Not really. I mean . . . I dunno. I'm nowhere near as good as you, and I'll probably get kicked out by the end of the year. But here, at least, I have friends. It's nice being somewhere where seeing ghosts doesn't make you a weirdo."

"I guess," Finlay said. Bastian noticed him bite his lip. "Though I find it hard to believe you didn't have friends back home."

"I—"

But before he could finish or embarrass himself, Harold and Robyn walked in. And Robyn was dripping in green goo.

"What happened to you?" Bastian asked, suppressing a laugh.

"Kelpie," she said. "Or a ghoul possessing a dead horse and pretending to be a kelpie. Nothing quite like banishing a horse-ghost in a swamp in the middle of the night. But eyy, we got it!" She opened her arms wide. "I think that deserves a hug, don't you?"

She ran over to Bastian, who tried to fend her off with a book but failed miserably. Within moments, he was covered in foul-smelling muck. Then Harold got him from the other side, squishing him between the two of them.

"You're suffocating me!" Bastian yelped. "Finlay, help!"

Finlay laughed. "No way I'm getting in the middle of this."

Robyn broke away and looked at him.

"Oh, come on, Fin. There's more than enough muck for you!"

She took a step toward him, and he bolted from the chair. She started chasing Finlay around the study hall, causing everyone to watch and cheer them on.

Bastian couldn't stop laughing.

No. He might not have been good at being an Æthercist, but he didn't want to go back to the way it was. Not if it meant losing all of this.

31

Bastian and his friends spent the rest of the evening studying in a sugar-induced haze, interrupted only once by a group of friendly ghosts that came in with hot chocolate and sugar cookies in the shapes of pumpkins and bats. By the time midnight rolled around and they all went to bed, Bastian was yawning from the swiftly approaching sugar crash.

As he curled up in bed and listened to Harold's steady breathing from across the room, Bastian felt more content than he had since his parents' deaths. He'd spent the entire night sitting next to Finlay, sharing glances and stories and laughing as Harold regaled them all with his most fantastical alchemical explosions. Even Finlay had opened up, talking about the time he nearly wet the bed because a group of shadowy umbras appeared in his closet.

Bastian closed his eyes. Let the sugar crash roll over him. It buzzed in his veins, made him feel heavy and light at the same time. Sleep washed over him.

Almost instantly, he started to dream.

He was standing outside the door of his dormitory. He could see a million stars through the windows, the moon completely dark. And in his sleeping mind, he remembered what Professor Luscinia had said, about the dark moon increasing spiritual activity.

The moment he thought that, someone whispered his name.

It was a man's voice, distant and entreating. Bastian didn't hesitate. On the wings of his dream, he followed. The manor's hallways wavered and wobbled, stretched and shifted. But always, he heard the voice calling him forward.

His father's voice.

In no time at all, he stood in the Hall of the Fallen.

But it was not as he remembered.

In the waking world, there had been plaques torn off or missing from the walls. But here, the hall was completely covered in plaques, and some of them glowed with a faint purple light. The pile of rubble, however, was still blocking the way forward.

"*Sebastian,*" his father called out. From behind the tumbled stones.

Bastian wandered forward. At the far end of the hall, beside the stones—and beside the plaque for his mother—a silver plaque glowed bright purple. He stepped closer to it. The plaque didn't seem quite there—he could see the wall behind it, like it was a spirit of some sort. But that wasn't what made his heart leap.

It was his father's plaque.

EDGAR WIGHT

FEARED PSYCHOPOMP

WHO DELVED DEEPER THAN OTHERS DARED

"A what?" Bastian whispered, at the same time wondering, *What sort of dream is this?* He reached out and touched the plaque. It hissed under his fingers with cold electricity. Flared a fiercer purple.

Moments later, the stones began to shift.

Piece by piece, they lifted from the ground. Rearranged themselves. Reassembled.

Debris reconstructed into an archway.

A stone door assembled itself within.

And flanking the door were two stone herons. They each perched atop a human skull, and held wrought-iron lanterns in their beaks. The moment the wall was complete, the lanterns flared to life, their flames a deep, flickering violet.

Bastian stared in awe.

He also knew, in that moment, that he wasn't actually asleep.

He pinched himself, but he didn't wake up, and when he looked around the hall, the glowing purple plaques from before were missing again. The floor was cold under his bare feet, and the purple-flame lanterns somehow made the hall even colder.

Had he sleepwalked here?

Even if he had, it didn't explain how or why the door had built itself in front of him, or why his father's voice had led him here.

He considered turning around. This was strange, even by Gallowgate standards.

"*Sebastian.*"

He froze. It was his father's voice. He knew it. But how was he hearing it? According to Harold, his dad should have passed through the Final Veil ages ago.

And yet . . .

Bastian took a halting step forward.

The door opened as he neared. And as it did so, a scent washed out. Like cologne and leather, palo santo and vetiver and woodsmoke.

It smelled like his father.

He followed the scent forward, past the stone door, and into a room he knew he had never seen before, but felt entirely familiar.

Everything in Gallowgate had a particular air. A coldness that seeped into his bones, a draftiness that never went away, no matter how many fires blazed or how many layers he wrapped himself in.

But here, in this room, Bastian felt warm.

The walls were floor-to-ceiling wooden bookshelves, filled with tomes and crystal orbs and golden astronomical instruments. Gold stars glittered on the ink-dark ceiling, reflecting the light from three large fireplaces set in each wall, and iron domes filled with candles hung from the wooden rafters. A long worktable stretched along one side, covered in rolls of parchments and more strange instruments and candles, while a trio of plush leather sofas made a triangle around a coffee table on the other wall.

The floor, too, was warm wood. Inlaid with gold leaf—circles within circles, runes and stars. And at his feet, a large circle had been laid out in purple amethyst, the crystals embedded within the wood glittering magically.

Bastian took a deep breath. He knew this smell. This was how his father's study had smelled. The comforting, woody spice made him want to curl up on one of those sofas and take a nap.

"What is this place?" he whispered. He stepped into the room, looking around. Was it a private study hall? But if so, why had the way been barred by rocks? Why had it opened to *him*?

And how had he gotten here in the first place? Everything had been *glowing*. Once more, he pinched himself to see if he was sleeping. He was most definitely still awake.

"This," came a voice behind him, "is where your training truly begins."

32

Bastian leaped around to see an old man standing in front of him.

No. An old man *floating* in front of him, in the space he'd just been standing.

The man was bald, his pale skin translucent, with a long white beard that reached his knees. Somehow his skin showed no wrinkles. He was tall and slightly stooped, dressed in a simple linen tunic. His dark eyes glinted purple when they moved.

A ghost.

The man smiled.

"Not quite, young man. Not quite." He bowed deeply, his beard falling to—and *through*—the floor. "My name is Virgil."

"You can read my thoughts?" Bastian asked. Like the room, Virgil's voice was familiar, but Bastian couldn't quite place why.

"Just expressions," Virgil said. "And you look like most do the first time they see me. It is only natural, given your training, to assume I am dead. But I was never truly alive to begin with. I am a construct, an Ætheric creation designed to serve. Speaking of assumptions, am I to believe you are young Sebastian Wight?"

Bastian nodded.

"As I thought. You have your father's nose. Though your hair was quite a bit darker last I saw you. How is your father, anyway? He told me I could be expecting you soon."

Bastian's voice caught. "He was . . . he was here?" He looked around, as if expecting his dad to walk out from behind one of the bookshelves or peek from beneath a sofa.

"The last time he stepped foot in this room, you were but a boy." Virgil grinned. "At least, younger than you are now. But that doesn't answer my question. Your father said I could expect you, but you seem too young to be attending Gallowgate, unless I am much mistaken. Has he forced Madame Ardea's hand?"

"He . . . he's dead."

Just saying it was enough to bring the crime scene back to mind, the blur through his tears as he stared at his parents' bodies, soaked in blood. The dreams of their coffins. The shadowman, watching from the small crowd of mourners.

Bastian shook his head and forced the thoughts away.

"I am sorry to hear that," Virgil said. He lowered his head. "He was the brightest Psychopomp I'd ever taught."

"A what?"

"A Psychopomp. Dear boy, you aren't telling me that your father never told you of his profession?"

"I didn't know anything about any of this until I came here. I didn't know my parents were Æthercists."

"Not just *any* Æthercists," Virgil said, his eyes lighting up. "The most powerful this school had seen in centuries. Your mother was the greatest Summoner of her time, and your father . . . well, your father knew more about the underworld than even I."

"But what's a Psychopomp?" Bastian pressed. Even though he wanted to know more about his parents and what they did here, that was the easier question to ask. Every time he thought of them, tears welled up in his eyes.

"You may as well take a seat," Virgil said, gesturing to the sofas. Bastian shuffled over and sat on one, sinking down deep into the cushions. Virgil sat as well. He didn't make the slightest imprint. "I teach Descending, Sebastian. The fifth pillar of the Ætheric arts taught at Gallowgate. A Psychopomp is one who can descend through the Veils of the underworld, ferrying souls to their final rest. And, unlike all others who pass into the underworld, a Psychopomp is able to return to their living body. It is a rare skill, and one that cannot be taught. Unlike the other skills, you either have the ability to descend or you do not."

Bastian's head spun. "But there are only four pillars . . ." he began.

"Whatever do you mean?"

"They only teach four pillars here. Madame Ardea said so herself. Summoning, Conjuring, Alchemy, and Necromancy."

That gave Virgil pause. "That . . . is curious," he said. "But if Madame Ardea did not send you here for your studies, how did you arrive? I am afraid that, as a construct, I am bound to the confines of this room and the underworld—I have little notion of what happens in the mortal plane beyond."

"I don't know," Bastian said. "I was sleepwalking, I think. And I heard my father's voice."

"I thought you said your father had died?"

"He did. He was shot."

"Are you quite sure?"

The question was so soft, and yet so intrusive, Bastian felt anger flare in his chest. *Of course* he was sure—he had been there when the gun had gone off. He had been there when the ambulance had arrived. It might have been a blur in his memory, but it was there.

He just nodded.

"Interesting," Virgil said. Though it was very much *not* interesting to Bastian. "In any case, it would appear your arrival is just as much a mystery as the reasons why Descending was hidden from you. But these are questions outside of my realm. You are here to learn Descending, the most revered of the Ætheric arts. So it is there we must focus."

He gestured to a shelf on the wall. A large book floated out, a musty tome coated in black leather. It settled itself on the table in front of Bastian. *The Ferryman's Handbook*, it was titled in looping silver script. Once more, Bastian's memory stirred. He could have sworn he'd seen this book before. On his father's desk?

Trying to remember hurt.

"If you would open to chapter one," Virgil said, "we will begin with the theory of how one splits their soul from their body, in an act we call astral projection. It is a similar process to falling asleep, when your conscious thoughts drift to the world of dreams. It will be quite some time before you are ready to descend to the underworld, but once you have mastered astral projection, why—the mortal plane will be as your playground.

"Now," he said with a knowing smile. "Begin."

33

"You'll never guess where I just was!" Bastian said, running back into his bedroom. He grabbed a pillow from his bed and tossed it at Harold. "Come on, wake up!"

Harold grumbled, "Where? I was called out for a hunt in the middle of the night and you were gone. Figured you'd been summoned as well."

"No, but—come on! You have to see it for yourself."

"What is it?" Harold groaned. "I just got back . . ."

Bastian ran over and grabbed Harold's arm, yanking him out of bed. "Come. On!"

Harold was a good friend; he complained about it, but he didn't resist. He let Bastian lead him out the bedroom and down the hall, yawning all the way. Bastian knew that he himself should be exhausted, but adrenaline spiked through his veins.

After he'd read about astral projecting, Virgil had made him practice it. The first few times he'd fallen asleep, lying on his back and counting his breath, trying to let his body relax while his mind stayed awake. But there had been a moment, near the end, when he had felt it. He'd realized he was no longer lying down, but standing—floating—beside the sofa, and everything glowed with a soft purple light, much as it had when he was sleepwalking.

The excitement had woken him up, and although he'd wanted to try again, Virgil had insisted he go back to his room to get some real sleep. Not that Bastian *could* sleep. He had to share this with someone else. He had to ensure it wasn't all a dream.

They rounded the corner to the Hall of the Fallen.

The far wall was collapsed once more.

"What?" Bastian asked.

He ran forward, pressing a hand to the rocks, making sure they were real. They were.

"No, no, this isn't right. It was here!"

"You know," Harold grumped behind him, "when kids say *trick or treat*, no one actually wants to be tricked. And All Hallows was yesterday." He yawned and started to turn around. "I'm going back to bed," he grumbled.

"No, you don't understand!" Bastian grabbed one of the rocks and yanked it aside. It clattered along the tile floor . . . and more rocks slid from above to take its place. "I'm telling you, it was *here*!"

Harold paused, looked at Bastian, and asked, "Are you okay?"

Bastian wasn't okay. It wasn't just that he wanted to show this to his friend—as he knelt there, defeated, he feared that he would never find his way back.

Was the door only open on All Hallows Eve, when the Veils were thin?

Had he lost his one chance to study something he might actually be *good* at? His one chance to connect to his own family's forgotten legacy?

Tears welled in his eyes as he grabbed another stone and tossed it to the side.

Harold's hand on his shoulder made him jerk.

"Dude," Harold said. "What's going on?"

"There was a door. And a study. And there was a ghost, only it wasn't a ghost, he was a construct. And he taught a fifth branch of magic."

"Whoa whoa whoa," Harold said. "Calm down. How much sugar did you *have?*"

"It wasn't a dream!" Bastian replied. "It was real! Right behind this wall."

"Okay!" Harold raised his hands in defeat and took a step back. "I believe you. So what was this fifth pillar?"

"Descending," Bastian said. "The ability to travel through the underworld."

Harold's eyebrows rose.

"Think about it," Bastian hurriedly continued. "That night in the warehouse, you said that it was impossible to enter the underworld. But what if it wasn't? What if it was another branch of magic?"

"But Ardea said—"

"Ardea was lying," Bastian replied firmly. "Just like she lied about the shadowman. Come on, Harold. Trust me."

"I do," Harold said. "At least, I want to. But come on, Bastian. That's a little out there. I mean, why would they conceal an entire branch of magic?"

"Why would they keep this hall in disrepair when they could have conjured it back into place?" Bastian asked back.

"Fair point," Harold said.

"They're hiding something. Virgil—that's the construct—he said that my dad was a Psychopomp."

"A what?"

"Someone who can descend. And I saw my dad's plaque on the wall. Right there." He pointed to the empty space on the wall. "It's like someone tried to erase him. And Descending. I want to know why."

Silence stretched between them. Eventually, Harold yawned.

"Right," he said. "Look, I've seen stranger things in this manor than a hidden door. But it's way too early and I've had way too little sleep for us to start spinning conspiracy theories. Since it's clear you're not going to let me go back to sleep, I demand caffeine and donuts. We can figure this out when I'm more awake."

Bastian begrudgingly let himself be led out of the hallway. But he refused to let himself believe it all had been a dream.

I'll find my way back inside, he thought. *Promise.*

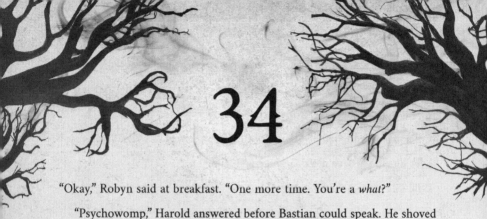

34

"Okay," Robyn said at breakfast. "One more time. You're a *what*?"

"Psychowomp," Harold answered before Bastian could speak. He shoved the rest of his donut in his mouth.

"Psycho*pomp*," Bastian replied. "And keep your voices down."

Robyn just chuckled. They were at their usual table, and even though the rest of the school had filtered in, they didn't need to worry about eavesdroppers. Everyone was too busy chatting about the hunts they'd gone on yesterday to be listening in, but Bastian still felt the pressing need for secrecy. This was too important for just anyone to overhear. Especially Andromeda, who was at the nearby table but way too close for comfort.

He just wished his friends felt the same way about privacy. Robyn was being way too loud.

"And you're sure you weren't hallucinating?" Robyn asked. "Maybe one of Harold's potions leaked in the middle of the night and sent you down the rabbit hole."

Bastian shook his head. He wanted to slam his fist on the table. Why didn't they understand how important this was? There was a whole other branch of magic. One tied to his *father*. And the entire school had hidden it from him.

Why? *Why?*

"You did say you were sleepwalking," Harold said. He, at least, had the decency to sound nervous when he suggested it. "Maybe it was all a dream?"

"It wasn't a dream. I was there. I know it."

"So why didn't you bring back any evidence?" Robyn asked. "Didn't you say there was a book?"

Bastian poked at his breakfast. The bacon jerked away angrily. "I didn't think to bring it." Truth be told, he'd been so wrapped up in astral projecting that everything after was a bit of a blur. "Why would I make this up?"

"Because," Robyn said, "you're so bad at everything else you needed to find *something* you were good at."

Bastian stuck out his tongue. "I'm not *that* bad at everything else."

"You're welcome for that," Robyn replied. "You'll get my tutor bill at the end of the year."

"The more important question is," Harold said, "if this *is* real—and I'm not saying it isn't!—why would they hide it from us? If there's a fifth branch of magic, you'd think they'd want us all to know about it."

"Virgil said that Psychopomps couldn't be trained," Bastian said. "You either are one or you're not. Maybe that's why they don't teach it."

"There's a big difference between not teaching something and hiding it," Robyn said, her face going serious. "Someone destroyed that hallway, and it's a little strange that in a school where they could literally levitate those stones back into place, they've just left it. Like they wanted to forget. Not to mention, they've scrubbed all mention of it from the library and curriculum. Heck, I've never even read about it in the books my parents had. It's like the entire Æthercist community is pretending it never existed."

Bastian suddenly understood why she'd found it so hard to believe. He kept forgetting that she'd actually grown up knowing all about this stuff. If *she'd* never heard of Descending . . .

"Why would they go to such great lengths to hide it?" Bastian wondered aloud.

Robyn shrugged. "Maybe it's dangerous?"

"Everything they teach here is dangerous," Harold said. He held up a bundle of plants from his satchel. "Half of these plants cause paralysis, and the other half could kill you if you took too much. Not to mention the fact that I nearly lost my eyebrows in Conjuring the other day. This place is definitely *safety third*."

"You nearly lost your eyebrows in Alchemy, too," Bastian muttered.

"I know what you're going to say," Robyn said, "but hear me out. Maybe you should talk to Madame Ardea—"

"What? No way."

"I'm just saying! If they went to all that trouble to wipe Descending off the face of the earth, there has to be a good reason. Maybe that *good reason* is that it's dangerous."

"But we just discussed Harold's eyebrows—"

"More dangerous than a little physical mutilation," Robyn countered. She looked at Bastian levelly. "Look. Right now, you've just been exposed to a few ghosts. But I've *seen* what happens when things go bad." She swallowed. Her eyes flickered to her hands—she still wore her fingerless gloves. She never took them off, even during meals. "Sometimes ghosts don't just attack a person. There are some spirits out there that can make a person do things. Horrible things. You know the basics, Bastian. You know that the deeper down a soul went before trying to return to the mortal plane, the worse they are. If you can go down there . . . maybe there's a risk you could bring something horrible back."

She looked him straight in the eye. "Your father was a Psychopomp. You said it yourself. What if he brought something back with him?"

Bastian stared. His gut churned. He didn't want to connect the dots.

"Think about it," she pressed. "A vengeful spirit no normal wards can stop. A spirit no one else can identify. There are ghosts down there that no Æthercist has ever encountered. Ghosts we better hope we never encounter. But maybe . . . maybe you have."

"The shadowman," Bastian breathed. What had his father's plaque read? *Who delved deeper than others dared?* What if he'd found something down there? Something that had followed him back? That might explain why it had been able to follow him, why his aunt hadn't been able to banish it.

Though it didn't explain why it was so set on coming after *him*.

His head ached when he tried to think about it. He needed more sleep.

"I don't trust people who keep secrets," Robyn continued. "And it's clear Madame Ardea is keeping at least one from you. But maybe she has a reason for it."

"Do you think she'd say anything if he asked her outright?" Harold wondered. "I mean, if Bastian knows all about this, she can't exactly pretend it doesn't exist anymore."

"You know her better than I do. If she's hiding all this to protect him, maybe she'd open up now that the cat's out of the bag."

"You forgot," Bastian said. "I can't get back in there. It was a onetime thing."

"You might be surprised," Harold said. "Like I said before . . . Gallowgate provides."

Unless you're looking for a clear answer, Bastian thought.

He just hoped that Harold was right. He was so close to learning about his family, to finding something he was good at. He wasn't going to give up now.

35

Bastian tried multiple times over the following days, but he couldn't figure out how to get back into the Psychopomp's study. He tried going in the middle of the night, wondering if it—like a few other hallways—was dependent on the time of day. He tried channeling the Æther at the fallen stones, to no effect. He even tried falling asleep in front of it, hoping maybe that would help. It just gave him a really bad kink in his neck.

Nothing had worked.

"Are you sure giving it another kick won't help?" Robyn asked.

She and Harold had camped out in the hall with him for another night of studying while he vainly tried to get past the barrier.

Bastian glared at her. He'd hoped she hadn't noticed him kicking—and stubbing his toe on—a large boulder. But he should have known better— she noticed everything.

He went over and sat down beside them.

Robyn had conjured a flame to keep out the draft that whistled in through the rafters, and Harold had brewed a large pot of tea to keep them awake.

They were only a month away from winter break, which meant midterms. If Bastian didn't get his act together soon, he risked getting thrown out at the end of the year. At least, that's what he worried would happen. He'd been too scared to ask what happened to the kids who never developed an affinity for anything.

And at this rate, he wouldn't even have Descending to fall back on.

"Try the transmutation again," Robyn said to him. "Water to fire. I know you can do it."

Bastian glared at the small iron cauldron she held out to him. He'd been trying to turn the water into fire all night. The most he'd been able to do was make it steam. Still, he made another attempt. He concentrated on the water and reached into the Æther. If he couldn't manage to get into the study, the least he could do was master the absolute basics of Conjuring.

"There's an infusion that can do that, you know," Harold said unhelpfully. He was currently weighing out a powder he'd crafted on an old scale. Oddly enough, the more powder he added, the lighter the scale became.

"He won't be able to use any Alchemy for his Conjuring midterms," Robyn snipped.

"I know," Harold said. "But he could always hide a bit in his sleeve or something. Fennick would never know."

"He'd know," Robyn replied. She sighed and went back to her own homework: She was trying to get the skull in front of her to talk. Necromancy gave very weird homework. At least this time they weren't being asked to divine the weather from rat intestines. Bastian had refused to do that on moral principle.

After a while, Bastian gave up and flopped back on the floor. He gazed up at the arched ceiling, feeling defeated.

"What happens if you fail out?" he asked. He'd been holding off asking for a while now. But maybe it was time to face the music.

"You won't," Harold said.

"But *if*," Bastian replied.

"Well . . ." Harold said. He looked to Robyn. "There are two options. You're either sent back home with the basics and left to fend for yourself, or . . ."

Bastian looked over. "Or what?"

"Or you're deemed too dangerous to progress," Robyn finished.

"What does that mean?" Bastian asked. Neither of them answered. "Harold, what does that mean?"

"It means . . . sometimes, kids come here and they want power more than they want to help. Usually, pretty easy to spot. And if they have a lot of power but no control, well, they're . . . dealt with."

"Killed," Bastian clarified, his voice cracking. "You're saying they kill kids who fail out?"

"Only the powerful ones," Robyn said soothingly. "You have *nothing* to worry about."

Harold barked out a laugh, and even Bastian chuckled.

He looked over at the ruined door. He had to get through there. He had to . . .

"I'm going to try something," Bastian said.

"Kick it with the other foot next time," Robyn said. Bastian glared at her.

He'd considered trying this before, but if he was being completely honest, he was too scared. Too scared it wouldn't work, and the whole memory would turn out to be a dream. Too scared it *would* work, and he'd get trapped or bring back a ghost or a dozen other terrible scenarios that had wormed through his head.

But he was running out of time. He had to find something he was good at.

"I'm going to try astral projecting," Bastian said. "Just . . . cover me, if anything weird happens."

Robyn's skull began to talk in Ancient Hebrew. She raised an eyebrow. "You're going to have to be a little more explicit about what constitutes *weird*." But she grew serious. "We got you."

Bastian closed his eyes and took a deep breath, settling back on the floor and trying to get comfortable. He followed his breath, in and out, acutely aware of his friends' concerned eyes on him.

He felt the tingle. A hum that vibrated through his skin. He breathed into the energy, let it build and grow. As Virgil had instructed, he envisioned the energy floating up, up . . .

When he opened his eyes, he hovered a few inches from his body, and Harold and Robyn were watching him closely. Well, watching his body. When he stood up and waved at them, they didn't notice. For a moment, he considered toying with them, because he really wanted to see if Harold would jump if he poked him. But he didn't want to risk waking up, and he had things to do.

He looked around the hall. And just like before, the plaques that had been missing were glowing purple. As he wandered past them, he noticed that they were all plaques for Psychopomps.

At the end of the hall, he paused in front of his father's. A thousand questions ran through his mind. He just hoped this would work.

Like before, he pressed his hand to the plaque.

The stones rumbled.

"Look!" Robyn said. She stood as she spoke, knocking over the cauldron of water in the process.

The water splashed over Bastian, and with a gut-wrenching jolt he was back, gasping as his eyes fluttered open. Just in time to see the doorway reassemble.

Harold helped him to his feet.

"You weren't making it up," Harold said.

"I know," Bastian replied. But he found that he was still grateful for that confirmation.

"Should we . . ?" Robyn asked.

"I think it's just for me," Bastian said. He looked to his friends. "I mean, I'm sorry, but . . ."

"No, no, it's fine," Harold interjected. "I need to head to the greenhouse, anyway."

"And I have a perfectly valid and not-awkward reason to leave as well," Robyn said with a grin. "Go learn about being a Psychowomp. We'll catch up after."

Bastian grinned. Gathered up his notebooks and supplies. And before the door could disappear, he walked into the study.

36

As December neared, snow and shadows gathered outside the walls of Gallowgate. Bastian woke to blistering winds rattling his windows more mornings than not, and the little daylight they had was swallowed in all-consuming gray clouds that never seemed to break. The school grounds were blanketed in white, disturbed only by the winds that swirled and the faint green ghostlights that flickered through the trees, or the spectral dogs that roamed after dark.

Inside the manor, however, the halls bustled with light and activity.

Every hearth fire in Gallowgate seemed to burn 24/7, and as midterms encroached, the halls were filled with frantic students practicing for exams, or returning from their time out in the field.

It seemed to Bastian, as he crept toward the Hall of the Fallen, that there were more hunts now than ever before.

Thankfully, he'd only been called to the field a few times, and even then with large groups of upperclassmen. Each time, he'd managed to stay back and watch as the skilled Summoners and crafty Conjurers put the rogue spirits in their place. He'd given up wishing he could be like them.

He knew who he was supposed to be.

He reached the crumbled hallway and—with a quick glance behind him—steadied his breath. He didn't even need to close his eyes now (a fact that had creeped Harold out the first time he saw it). Between one breath and the next, Bastian astral projected, standing a few inches to his physical body's side. With his transparent hand, he touched the plaque and slipped back into his body just as the door reassembled, and he made his way into the study.

"You are getting quite good at that, young Sebastian," Virgil said.

"It's getting easier," Bastian replied. He went over and sat on the sofa, picking up his copy of *The Ferryman's Handbook* and his notebook.

"You won't be needing those now," Virgil said. "You are ready."

Bastian's breath caught in his throat.

"Are you sure?"

Even though astral projecting came easily, he'd been hesitant to start descending. He looked down at the page he'd flipped to in the handbook. It was one of the chapters on the lower levels of the underworld. And while he'd learned everything he thought there was to know about the ghosts that dwelled in the depths in his theory class, it had turned out that there were horrors there that even old Nicodemus didn't know about.

Including the spirit on this page. A hulking, shadowy beast with the name *maleficarum*.

Bastian shuddered and shut the book.

"I'm quite sure," Virgil said, "you have memorized all the necessary wards and protection circles. You are ready to descend. Now, join me over here."

Virgil floated over to the amethyst circle inlaid in the floor.

"This is a special protection circle," Virgil said. "While other circles will only protect you in the mortal realm, this will protect you past the *Corpus Velamentum*, or the First Veil."

He gestured, and Bastian sat in the middle of the circle. Virgil guided him to lie down and close his eyes, to follow the exact same process as when he astral projected.

"But this time," Virgil said, "focus on your energy sinking *down*."

Bastian nodded, tried to quell his fear, and let himself drift.

It felt exactly like astral projecting. Only now, when he forced the energy down, he felt his skin grow cold, felt the buzzing in his bones chill to ice, grow heavy like lead.

The darkness behind his eyes shifted. Lightened.

He never opened his eyes, but soon he realized he could see. He stood in the study, but the colors had all faded out, leaving only blurred watercolor traces of the shelves and sofas of the study. The hearth stood cold and black and empty. His physical body was nowhere to be seen. The only color in the room came from the amethyst circle that glowed brightly in the floor around him.

A moment later, Virgil appeared in a shimmer of light.

"Excellent," Virgil said. "You're a natural."

Bastian smiled, but tried to keep his excitement in check. He knew that emotions would jerk him back to his body.

"Still, there is more to Descending than entering the underworld," Virgil instructed. "There is a reason it is called *The Ferryman's Handbook*, after all. In the underworld, you may use special types of Ætheric magic that are similar to the skills you have learned in the mortal realm. But the most important skill you will learn is the summoning of the River.

"As you know, the River of Death flows from the First Veil all the way to the Fourth and Final. It naturally seeks out those who have crossed the barrier between life and death. You, as a Psychopomp, can summon it. You will try this now. Just be wary not to slip. You would not be the first fledgling Psychopomp to fall into the surging waters, never to be seen again!"

He must have noticed Bastian's terrified expression.

"But fear not, dear boy. None of them had *me* as a teacher. Now, let us continue . . ."

37

Despite his early successes with descending, Bastian barely had time to practice after that first attempt. He didn't dare practice outside of the protective wards of the study, and since then, preparations for midterms had taken all of his concentration. He'd only managed to make it back to the study once before exams, and even then he'd been so tired from his late-night Necromancy session with Harold and Robyn that he just slept on the sofa for a few hours.

And as Descending was the only class without a midterm exam, it was the last thing on his mind.

"I swear my brain has turned to goo," Harold said as they trudged back from the library together.

"It wasn't before?" Robyn asked.

"Hah hah," Harold said. He yawned. "Seriously, who knew theory would be so boring?"

"Me," Robyn replied, raising her gloved hand. "Theory is *always* boring. Practice is where the fun is. Speaking of, want to get in a few more rounds of Conjuring for Fennick's exam?"

Bastian groaned.

His limbs ached from the last time they'd practiced. Robyn had thought that maybe he'd do better if his life were in danger. So she'd spent the time chucking very painful balls of ice at him and asking him to deflect them with air. It had felt like getting pelted by a paintball gun. Or so he imagined—he'd never been cool enough to go paintballing. The welts still on his skin confirmed that he was perfectly fine with that.

"Come on," Robyn said. She grabbed his arm. "If practice doesn't kill you, Fennick will for failing his exam."

"For some reason that doesn't cheer me up," Bastian said. He looked to Harold. "You coming?"

Harold shook his head. "As fun as it is to watch you get your butt handed to you, I have to go study for Summoning. Ardea's doing practical exams, and the last time I tried to banish a banshee, well . . ."

"It got loose and nearly destroyed everyone's eardrums," Robyn finished. "We remember. I still have ringing in my ears when I try and sleep."

Harold grinned sheepishly.

They parted ways, and Robyn led Bastian toward one of the inner court-yards they'd been using for practice. It was usually empty—especially at this time of year—and there were no trees, only a few tombstones. So, much less chance of Bastian blowing anything up.

The halls were filled with students cramming for their next exam. Bastian passed by Finlay and Andromeda, who sat at a table with a pack of oracle cards in front of them, clearly trying to commune with a spirit for Necromancy.

Finlay smiled at Bastian when they locked eyes, and Bastian gave a little wave before feeling his face blush furiously. Andromeda just glared at him.

"I don't know why he hangs out with her," Robyn mused when they were out of earshot. "Maybe he has a crush. I mean, she's attractive in that mean-girl-rip-your-heart-out sort of way, but maybe he likes that. He seems pretty sweet. Cute, too, wouldn't you agree?"

Bastian's blush just deepened. Robyn chuckled and didn't say anything else.

The courtyard was miraculously empty. Probably because it was really cold; Bastian immediately wished he'd grabbed a thicker coat. The snow was trampled and churned to mud, and there were melted remains of a snowman that had clearly been used for fireball practice.

"Poor snowman," Robyn said, nudging a charred carrot that had once been its nose.

"Just so long as I don't look like that by the end of this," Bastian said.

"I make no promises. But I'll try to go easy on you. Now, speaking of fireballs . . ."

She held her hand in front of her, palm up, and a curl of flame formed between her fingertips. It shifted from orange to purple to green, making the snow glow eerily.

"Show-off," Bastian muttered.

"This is on the exam," Robyn said. "Heard so from a third-year. Now come on, show me what you've got."

"Just don't attack me again," Bastian mumbled.

He reached out to the Æther, as he'd practiced a hundred times before. He twisted the otherworldly energy between his fingers, forced it to materialize to his will.

A faint flicker appeared in his hand.

He concentrated harder.

The light grew stronger, warmer. His numb fingers tingled as heat filled them and his blood returned.

"You're doing great!" Robyn said. She let her own fire die out, watching him work intently.

He focused on changing the flame's color. Just a simple twist of Æther . . .

The firelight flickered in the courtyard, cast shuddering shadows in the dull gray light.

The flame slowly turned green . . .

From the corner of his eye, he saw one shadow in particular elongate.

At first, he didn't think anything of it—a trick of the light, or maybe a resident ghost coming to watch.

But as the light shifted from green to purple, the shadow stretched up behind Robyn, who was transfixed by Bastian's work. She didn't see the ghost rising behind her, its hands tipped with talons, its eyes vacant spaces in shadow.

An umbra.

Bastian didn't think.

He flung the fireball at the spirit.

Robyn flinched away with a yell as the fireball shot over her shoulder. A second later, the fireball splashed over the umbra in a blazing blast of light. It screamed a high-pitched whine, but Bastian didn't let go of the flame. He made the fire burn brighter, until the whole courtyard glowed like a summer day in Spain. The umbra screamed once more, but the shadow didn't come back.

Umbras were spirits from beyond the First Veil, spirits who lived in shadows and preyed on the warmth and life of their victims. Without a shadow to flee into, the spirit was forced back into the underworld. Bastian held the light like that for a few more breaths, until the adrenaline coursing in his veins died down. When his panic faded, so too did the power. The flame winked out, and they were plunged back into a near-darkness that felt even colder than before.

"Thanks," Robyn said, staring at the patch of melted snow where the umbra had just been. "That was quick thinking."

Bastian just nodded. His hands shook, and his heart beat way too loud and too fast.

"What was it doing in here?" Robyn asked.

She didn't seem particularly worried about nearly being attacked by a ghost. Then again, umbras didn't usually kill right away—they preferred to latch on to their victims and drain them over months or years, eventually killing them or driving them mad.

"I don't know," Bastian said. "It shouldn't have been able to get past the wards."

Robyn bit her lip. "Maybe it followed a kid back from the Doors. There've been more hauntings than usual, lately."

"I don't think that's possible," Bastian said.

"Yeah. Neither do I."

They stood there in silence for a few moments. Bastian knew they were both thinking the same thing: They should tell Madame Ardea. But ever since he'd started practicing Descending, he'd tried to avoid appearing on her radar. He worried that she would somehow know what he was doing. And that she'd find a way to force him to stop.

"I guess that's proof you won't fail Conjuring," Robyn said. "If only Fennick were here to see it."

Deep in the manor, the bells signaling their next exam began to chime.

"Guess there's only one way to find out," Bastian said.

Together, they headed toward the Conjuring tower, the steaming remains of the impossible umbra still hissing behind them.

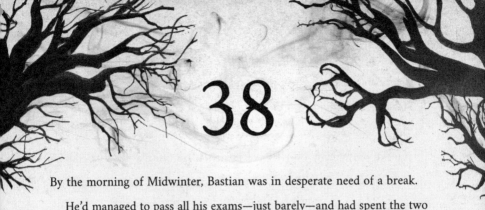

38

By the morning of Midwinter, Bastian was in desperate need of a break.

He'd managed to pass all his exams—just barely—and had spent the two days after in a haze of sleeping and peeling himself out of bed for meals before huddling back under his covers and watching the snow drift down outside while the fire crackled in the fireplace. He wasn't sick, but he'd never felt more exhausted in all his life.

Thankfully, they now had two weeks off. He'd had the option of going back to see Aunt Dahlia, but he just kept picturing the shadowman breaking in again, and any thoughts of holiday cheer vanished. So he'd opted to stay here, where it was safer for both of them.

Here, where no one would force him to get up. Or so he thought.

Harold leaped on his bed at the crack of dawn, calling out at the top of his lungs, *"Presents!"*

Bastian groaned, but he opened his eyes and threw a pillow at Harold, who deflected it easily.

Sure enough, just like on All Hallows Eve, the room had been decorated overnight.

Sparkling silver garlands draped between the rafters, crystalline spiders slowly scuttling across them, and a spindly pine tree sat in a cauldron before the fireplace. More spiders spun delicate strands of garland over its branches, while red baubles in the shapes of skulls glittered from the light of a handful of will-o'-the-wisps that danced lazily through the boughs.

A dozen or so presents sat beneath it, wrapped in silver-and-black paper in stripes and patterns of cobwebs and skulls and bats.

"Does it ever bother you that the ghosts just come in unannounced and set things up like this while we're sleeping?" Bastian asked.

Harold was already over by the presents. He lifted a plate of cookies and a mug with a pyramid of whipped cream on top. He was sporting a whipped cream mustache.

"So long as they bring presents and hot chocolate? Not one bit."

Bastian made his way over, a blanket draped over his shoulders, and settled himself in front of the fire. There was another mug of hot chocolate for him, and . . .

"Who sent all these?" he asked.

Half of the presents under the tree bore his name, but he didn't recognize the handwriting on the name tags. They were all in a looping, curling script. Save for one, which was the familiar chicken scratch of Aunt Dahlia.

He reached for that first, while Harold explained.

"Don't know who sends most of them," he admitted. "I started getting them the first year I was here. I think it's the school ghosts. They feel . . . well, they feel sorry for those of us without families. I mean, it's the most common reason kids come here."

"Oh," Bastian said. He was halfway through unwrapping his present, but now it felt rude. He noticed that all of Harold's gifts were addressed in that ghostly script.

"It's okay!" Harold said. "Seriously. My parents have been gone so long, I don't even really remember them." He nodded to the present in Bastian's hands. "Go on, don't let that ruin the gift. I'm guessing that's from your aunt. What did she send you?"

Bastian finished unwrapping and discovered a beautiful leather-bound sketchbook. It was thicker than any of his textbooks, and the cover was a swirling design of Celtic knotwork and delicate leaves. Aunt Dahlia had also sent a set of really nice markers and felt-tip pens—which would be a huge improvement over the bone quills they usually used in class—and a card. His hand trembled when he opened it.

Little bird-

I miss you dearly, and hope this holiday season is filled with love and laughter. I know I don't write-I haven't wanted to distract you from your studies!-but I've heard you've made plenty of new friends to keep you company. I'm so proud of you!

The summer can't come soon enough.

All my love,

Dahlia

Bastian set the note inside the sketchbook. He felt . . . well, he felt a little disappointed. He hadn't heard from Aunt Dahlia since coming here. And sure, he hadn't written either, but he'd just thought that maybe she'd explain everything when she finally *did* write. She'd tell him why his parents made her keep this place hidden. Why there had never been any mention of who they were and what they'd done with their lives. Maybe she'd even bring up Descending.

Instead, it felt like a card she might send to a distant nephew. Full of love, but not much explanation.

He took a drink of hot chocolate and focused on the rest of the gifts.

The ghosts had gotten him a new pack of oracle cards and a genuine crystal ball in the shape of a skull, as well as a fancy wool peacoat with the Gallowgate crest on its breast, and a few hand-knit sweaters and scarves in purple and gray. Harold had gotten some sweaters as well, his in brown and earthy green. And a shiny new plague doctor mask—this one with a lot fewer burn marks.

"So that's what all those possessed knitting needles were doing," Bastian figured as he tried on a sweater. He'd seen a dozen or so knitting needles knitting in the corners of the library and study hall late at night. He'd never looked closer to see what they were working on; he'd just figured the ghosts were bored.

Dressed in their new sweaters and stuffed with cookies, they slowly trudged down the halls to breakfast.

Thick garlands of fresh evergreen draped overhead, illuminated with candles and floating will-o'-the-wisps. Spiderwebs in metallic thread glittered over every window, turning the gray morning light into a rainbow shimmer. Multicolored bats hung from ruby-encrusted chandeliers, while owls in elf hats peered out from the alcoves. Snow drifted down from the ceiling, magically enchanted not to melt and forming drifts along the edges of the hall, while more lights flickered within.

Even the undead denizens of the manor were dressed for the occasion. Skeletons walked past in full Santa outfits, while the skulls lining a few windowsills had ornaments in their eyes. Passing ghosts flickered between red and green, and Bastian swore he saw a herd of ghostly reindeer out on the lawn. A quartet of friendly banshees floated past, singing carols slightly off-key but still hypnotically, while a group of entranced first-years followed dazedly behind them.

Even though everyone had the option of going home, the halls were still bustling with students. It looked like *everyone*—even the upperclassmen—had gotten at least one knit piece of clothing. The laughter and decorations were enough to help Bastian forget about missing a morning of opening presents and listening to carols with Aunt Dahlia.

Massive pine trees were spaced along the walls of the dining hall. Some were covered in green needles, while others were barren and frosted white. Each had a unique decorating scheme. ("There's a competition among the skeletons," Harold explained. "The best tree decorator gets a trip to Fiji.") One tree was draped in living bats. Another was covered in lacelike spiderwebs. One levitated a foot off the ground, spinning slowly while spectral lights floated through the branches. The fireplaces burned red and green, and even the stained-glass windows had gotten into the spirit. The reapers held staves with wreaths on the end, and the portrait at the far end of the hall was now a leering face of Krampus.

Harold and Bastian spotted Robyn at their usual table. And she wasn't alone.

"Happy Midwinter!" she said, leaping off her chair and wrapping them both in big hugs.

Finlay stood up awkwardly beside her. He looked cute in the slightly oversize sweater, his hair mussed from sleep and his glasses a little lopsided.

"Happy holidays," Finlay said. Harold stepped over and wrapped him in a bear hug. Finlay squirmed, but when Harold let go, the smaller boy was smiling.

In what was probably the most awkward moment of his life, Bastian stepped forward and gave Finlay a half hug, half pat on the back. He blushed furiously when they stepped apart.

Finlay was beet red, too, fighting a grin.

Once they sat down, the ghosts brought out their food. Finlay sat beside Bastian. Bastian didn't think he'd ever been so conscious of how close someone was to him in his life. It made him giddy and sweaty at the same time.

As everyone started eating, Madame Ardea stood. She, too, was dressed for the day, in rich red robes trimmed in white. She looked like Mrs. Claus.

"Happy Midwinter," she called out. "On this, the darkest day of the year, we are reminded of the importance of family. Of trust." Bastian swore her eyes settled on him for a moment when she said it. "And we are also reminded of the importance of celebration. You have all done splendidly on your exams, and we look forward to another semester of expanding your knowledge. First-years, especially, have much to look forward to. As your studies progress, your professors will be watching keenly to match you to your future specialization. The Naming of the Guard will be here in a blink!

"But . . . enough about school. Today, we have a very special event for you all. Back by popular demand, Gallowgate will once more be hosting its annual snowbeast competition, and we hope to see all of you there this afternoon."

The hall burst into excited applause and chatter from the upperclass-men. Finlay looked to Bastian, confusion plain on his face.

"What's so exciting about building a snow . . . beast?" Finlay asked.

Bastian shrugged. Because it sounded like Ardea had announced they were taking part in the Super Bowl. Even Robyn looked confused.

"Oh, you'll see," Harold said with a huge grin.

39

That afternoon, Bastian followed Harold and Robyn and the others out into the soft, knee-deep snow that had fallen overnight. Billows of powdery white lay in drifts against the tombstones, while icicles dripped like talons from the boughs of the evergreens and scraggly black oaks. Even the lake had frozen over, making a white blanket that stretched out into the moors beyond. Unlike the last few days, the air was perfectly still. It made Bastian think the whole scene had been magically induced.

It looked like a holiday card—a holiday card set in a graveyard, with a few skeletons in elf hats tossing skulls and snowballs between the tombstones.

They made their way through the thick trees and tombstones and out to the wooden path he'd taken that first eventful day here. But they weren't going to the moorlands or the waiting Door beyond.

No, a great patch of snow had been cleared on the lake, easily the size of a football field. Its boundaries were marked with cauldrons of blue-and-white flame, and groups of students huddled near the heat, many of them with their own floating balls of fire near their hands.

Despite the bite in the air, Bastian was warmer than he had been in some time. He—like everyone else on the field—was wearing a full black snowsuit, which had magically materialized at the foot of his bed when he'd returned from lunch. It made it hard to tell the upperclassmen from the first-years. But he had no trouble spotting Finlay, who stood next to one of the cauldrons with a rust-red beanie squashed down on his hair and a red blush to his cheeks.

Sadly, he was also standing next to Andromeda, which meant Bastian and his friends stayed well away. Instead, they joined Roman and another first-year named Thaddeus next to a cauldron of blue flame.

"Any clue what this is about?" Thaddeus asked. He was a small, quiet Korean boy who seemed to have a knack for Necromancy. Bastian rarely heard him speak, and when he did, it was usually because he was channeling a spirit. It was strange to hear his normal voice.

"It's hard to explain," Harold said. "But trust me, you've never seen anything like it."

They didn't have long to wait.

After the final students straggled in, Professor Fennick strode out into the middle of the field. He was the only one out here not wearing a snowsuit. Instead, he was in his usual ripped leather and denim. Bastian didn't know how he wasn't freezing. Then again, Fennick always seemed on the urge of exploding—maybe that rage was enough to keep him warm.

"Right, then," Fennick called out. "For you newbies, the game is simple. Everyone picks a team of three. There are three rounds. First is construction. The team with the most intricate creation and with the fastest construction time is awarded the most points. Second round is animation—how well you bind your spirit to the creation, how you articulate it, et cetera. But in the end, this is a death match. After the initial two rounds of judging, the fight commences, and the team with the last snowbeast standing wins.

"During the fight, there are four rules. One, you can use any skill to build the snowbeast, but you cannot bind any nonwilling entity to it. As per usual, the staff spirits have volunteered to take part. Two, once the spirit is bonded, there is to be no interference from the human teammates. The snowbeast is on their own once the death match begins. Three, you must utilize and display all four of the Ætheric arts in the creation of your snowbeast, though how and when is up to you. Extra points will be awarded for artistic flair. And four—and this is the most important—the snowbeasts are only to attack each other. If I get the slightest whiff that any of you are trying to do something malicious, you'll be out of this school faster than you can say *abominable*. Understood?"

Everyone nodded vigorously. Even Bastian, though he had no idea what was going on.

"Take your places," Professor Fennick said. Harold and Robyn and Bastian stepped away from the cauldron, and Thaddeus and Roman joined Mariana a few feet away. "On the count of three. One."

"What exactly are we doing?" Bastian asked.

"Building a snowbeast!" Harold replied, cracking his knuckles.

"*Two.*"

Bastian looked to Robyn.

"Do *you* know what's going on?"

"Not yet," she said, an excited light in her eyes. "But I'm starting to get an idea."

"*Three!*"

Snow exploded in the pristine field, as Bastian's classmates began to conjure.

"We should make a giant spider!" Harold said. "Bigger isn't always better—the last three seasons it was a small, fast snowbeast that won. The best tactic is to take out your opponents as quickly as possible."

"Snow spider, got it," Robyn said. "I'll start on the body."

"I'll work on the claws. It needs some good, solid ice claws, I think," Harold said. "Maybe half-spider, half-crab?"

"Sounds sick," Robyn said.

"What am I supposed to do?" Bastian asked.

"Stand there and look pretty," Robyn said with a wink.

Then she gestured her gloved hands in front of her and got to work.

Bastian was only mildly offended, because it was clear the magic she and his classmates were working was way beyond his abilities. Snow billowed around her, swirling around her fingers in serpentine spirals and coalescing into a glimmering pillar that stretched a full story high.

Harold fumbled through his satchel and pulled out a few vials of multi-colored liquid. One by one, he unstoppered them and tipped them onto the snow, muttering incantations under his breath. The snow erupted and crystalized where the potions hit, growing like a fast-motion tree. Within seconds, five sharp talons of ice clawed up from the ground.

"How long have you been planning this?" Bastian asked. Because it was clear Harold had come prepared—Alchemic concoctions were very particular. It's not like everyone just carried around claws-out-of-snow infusions all the time.

Harold grinned. "Since, um, last June, I think." Then he started on the next claw, and Bastian stepped back to watch.

For a moment, he'd thought that there was no way what Robyn was building was small—already, the snow spider's eight legs stretched two stories tall, each of them covered in glittering icicle spikes. She was just now siphoning snow up toward the body, which was at least the size of a VW Bus.

But, looking around, yes. Their spider *was* on the small side.

In one corner of the field, a cyclopean giant reared up against the sky, a good four stories tall, with boulders for hands and its eye a disk of pale blue ice as wide as Bastian was tall.

Another team had created a dragon the size of a garage, complete with glittering spines of green ice and sharp icicle teeth and delicate crystalline wings that stretched high, high above.

There was a serpent coiled on the far side, its teeth like javelins. A monstrous yeti-like creature with bristling fur and an alligator maw for a face. Even a giant teddy bear made of snow . . . though the wicked fangs materializing from its lips made it anything but cuddly.

When Bastian looked back to their snow spider, it seemed dainty by comparison.

"Get ready," Harold said, nudging him.

"For what?"

"Once she's done with the body, you'll need to bind a spirit to it so it can pick up its claws."

"Nearly . . . there!" Robyn called victoriously. She clapped and stared up at her creation. It was huge. And beautiful, in a terrifying sort of way.

Across the field, the giant snake had started to move. They were already behind!

"Your turn," Robyn said. "Hurry!"

Bastian nodded. With a deep breath, he reached out to the Æther and cast a large summoning circle around the spider—one of the few Summoning tricks he had mastered. Instantly, he heard a small voice beside him as one of the house spirits offered to be bound to the snow spider. Technically, binding a spirit to an object was pretty advanced work. But he knew the theory, and since the spirit was willing, it was a lot easier than he had expected.

With a flash of Æther, the spirit joined with the snow spider. Pale blue light washed over it, a glimmer of power as the summoning circle collapsed in on itself, the magic complete. Light flickered in the spider's eyes. It shook its monstrous head, sending puffs of snow over them, and looked down at the three of them. And yes, Bastian knew that the ghost was friendly, but there was something inherently terrifying about staring up at a hulking spider with jagged pincers and glittering, lifeless eyes.

Robyn cupped her hands to her mouth. "Hey, we've got some claws for you down here!"

Harold stepped aside as the spider dislodged its legs from the ground and picked up the two massive claws Harold had created. It clicked them menacingly.

"We've totally got this," Harold said.

Then, across the field, someone screamed.

40

"NOT YET!" roared Professor Fennick, darting across the field toward the offending team. "I SAID NOT YET!"

Thunder rumbled, vibrating the ground. But it wasn't thunder at all—across the field, the giant teddy bear had roared to life, smashing its fists to the ice and sending the kids who'd created it flying.

"Control it!" Professor Fennick yelled to the students. But it was clear the creation was far outside of their control. The bear swung at them, just barely missing as they dodged and screamed in terror.

Blue light flashed around Professor Fennick's hands, and great glowing manacles appeared around the bear's wrists and legs. The monster roared. For a brief moment, Bastian felt a spark of relief—the creature was bound; there was no way it could break free. But with another roar, the bear lashed out its arms, and the manacles shattered into a million glowing icicles.

Fennick skidded to a halt in front of the bear, a great billow of fire swirling in front of him before he came to a full stop. With a yell, he threw the enormous fireball at the bear, hitting it square in the chest. The fireball burned straight through, leaving a hole that hissed and melted. Seconds later, the melting ice re-formed.

If anything, the attack only enraged the beast.

The bear howled and lunged toward Fennick as the professor conjured another fireball. The manacles around the bear's legs snapped, vanishing into stardust as it raced toward Professor Fennick.

Professor Fennick cast the fireball, and the world seemed to fall into slow motion.

The fireball ripped through the beast, but didn't slow it down. Another step, and the bear swung at Fennick. Fennick yelled out in pain as he was flung high into the air and far past Bastian and his friends. He skidded across the ice, finally stopping in a drift of snow.

He didn't get back up.

Bastian wasn't certain why he did it, but the moment it was clear that Professor Fennick was hurt, he sprang into action. He ran out onto the ice toward his fallen professor, while behind him, the field erupted into screams and chaos. He didn't look back.

Halfway across the ice, a different sort of chill washed over him. Distantly, he knew he'd passed through the wards surrounding the manor, but it was too late to worry about that now.

He fell to his knees beside Fennick. The teacher wasn't moving, but Bastian could see the puffs of his breath in the cold air. Blood trickled down a gash in his forehead—if he lived, he'd have another scar to add to his collection.

If he lived.

Fear crept through Bastian. He was alone out here, and he didn't have any of Harold's healing herbs. He needed help.

He turned around to call to his friends. But they were clearly distracted.

The field was a flurry of thrashing creatures and flashes of light as the snow creatures and students battled vainly against the rogue bear. Bastian couldn't make out his friends in the billows of snow that obscured everything but the hulking shapes towering and fighting above it all.

But he could tell, even from here, that his friends were losing.

The bear roared in victory as it snapped the head off the snake that had wrapped around it. Then, it stuck the head on its own shoulder.

The serpent head shuddered, then its eyes burned white and its fangs lengthened.

The bear wasn't just attacking its foes—it was devouring them. Making them a part of it.

Getting stronger.

Professor Fennick coughed, and Bastian looked back to see fresh red sprayed across the snow.

"It's going to be okay," Bastian said. "I'll get you back to the manor, I'll—"

"Is he alive?" someone called out.

Bastian quickly looked over his shoulder to see Finlay racing toward them, huffing as he shuffled through the deep snow.

"I think so," Bastian replied. "But he's really hurt. I think his legs are broken. We need to get him back inside, but I can't—"

"Here," Finlay said. He knelt down beside Bastian. "I'll conjure a stretcher from the ice. We can carry him back together."

He twitched his fingers, and a sheet of snow beside Professor Fennick glossed and solidified into a makeshift stretcher. Together, they awkwardly lifted Fennick onto it. He groaned when they set him down.

"We have to hurry," Bastian began. But before they could lift the stretcher, the ground rumbled. Cracked.

They looked over to see the monstrous bear breaking from the flurry of warring beasts. Except now, it looked nothing like the creepy teddy bear from before.

It had taken on pieces of its opponents, and in the process, it had become a truly monstrous creation. It now had three heads—one a serpent, one a bear, and one a cyclops. Five arms stuck out at odd angles from its body. Two of them, Bastian noticed with a grimace, were from his own spider.

Fireballs and Ætheric chains lashed toward it, but they bounced off its hardened ice skin as it ran straight toward Bastian, Finlay, and Fennick.

Bastian and Finlay glanced at each other. There was no way they could outrun it, especially not if they were carrying Professor Fennick.

Finlay stepped in front of the professor, blocking him from the beast that barreled toward them.

Bastian stepped up beside him.

"I'm not going down without a fight," Finlay said. Fire flickered at his fingertips.

Bastian tried to calm his frantic heart as the beast bore down on them. He reached for the Æther, formed the symbols for binding and banishing in his mind, even though he knew his paltry magic wouldn't stand a chance. Not if everyone else had failed.

The beast bore down on them. Finlay cast his fireballs, targeting the ice at the beast's feet. Snow burst in a hiss of steam, but it didn't slow the beast down at all. It was on them in moments.

It snatched Finlay up with one clawed hand and raised him high in the air. The alligator head opened its mouth wide.

Finlay screamed.

Something in Bastian snapped. He raced toward the monster.

Leaped toward one of its legs.

And the moment he latched on, he closed his eyes and descended.

41

The world shifted.

Snow and sky blurred, until only a dark smudge of trees marked a horizon that was as gray above as it was below. Nothing stirred out here.

Nothing, save for the monstrous green ghost that Bastian had latched on to.

The ghost reared up above him. Unlike the more humanoid shades or banshees he'd encountered, this was a mishmash of parts. Like the poltergeist, but even worse. It had three arms that crooked at odd angles, its legs the size of tree trunks. There was a snapping mouth where its torso should have been, with a serpentine tail or tongue lashing out through the teeth. It had five heads, some human and screaming silently, others animal, and still others unlike anything living he'd seen before.

And he was positive that the ghost shifted with every passing heartbeat, twitching and changing form. As if it were remembering what it was meant to be.

That's when he knew he was facing a revenant—a monstrous spirit from beyond the Third Veil, a ghost with the ability to animate and possess multiple corpses at once. Which explained how it had compiled a new body of broken snowbeast parts.

The ghost kicked, and Bastian was sent flying. He skidded on the ground and stumbled to his feet. It didn't hurt, but he felt his connection to his body quiver—he knew if he was killed here, his body would also die. He had to work fast.

As the revenant roared and lumbered toward him, Bastian summoned the River.

It felt different, now, practicing outside the safety of the study's protection circle.

As the brackish waters of the River rose around his ankles, it felt wilder, stronger. Harder to control.

Still, he reached for it, pulled it up into this, the *terra sine forma*, the world without form: the first layer of the underworld.

Black hissing water surged around the revenant, and where the water touched, the green light of its body seemed to dim as the River sucked away at its life force.

Bastian didn't look down: He knew, if he checked, he would find that his own translucent ankles had blanched as the River tried to take him, too, away.

The revenant roared. One of its arms transformed, turned from talon to tentacle, and it lashed it forward, wrapping around Bastian's body.

It lifted Bastian high in the air as he pulled the River ever higher. When he was at eye level with the monstrous beast, the revenant spoke.

"*He will reward us for this,*" it said, its voice both young and old, masculine and feminine and everything in between, switching with every consonant. "*With you as our offering, we will taste sweet life again.*"

One of the malformed maws opened, and a ropelike tongue snaked out, caressing Bastian's cheek. He cried out in pain—the tongue seared where it touched like burning iron. He tried to force down the pain. If he reacted, he'd snap back to his body.

And so long as the revenant touched him, he risked bringing the spirit back . . . and potentially letting it into his body in the process. The last thing he wanted was to become possessed by this horror.

"Who?" he managed. "Who is looking for me?"

The monster just laughed.

"*Come. We will show you.*"

It began to walk. Not upstream, toward life and the mortal world. But downstream toward the Second Veil, the *Harmonius Velamentum*, where Bastian would lose the ability to speak.

Bastian squirmed against the revenant's grasp. He couldn't risk passing the next Veil. He'd never gone so far, and Virgil had warned that it got harder to return the deeper one went.

He called to the River, but even though it responded, even though it rose to the revenant's waist, it wasn't enough to dislodge the monster or set Bastian free. The revenant was too strong, too full of life.

And while Bastian would grow weaker the farther down into the under-world he went, the revenant would only get stronger.

The world before him shifted. The horizon darkened. As they walked toward where the River ran, he saw only a wall of misty, encroaching dark-ness. The Veil.

Bastian tried to remember his teachings. Virgil hadn't taught him how to fight off ghosts yet, but he knew the basics. He knew, too, that his normal Ætheric magic wouldn't work down here. There were no mortal elements to conjure, and summoning only worked in the mortal world.

But he was a Psychopomp.

Death was his domain.

He reached out to the Æther and twisted its undead twin through his fingertips. Purple light sparked around his hands, glimmering on the raging black River just feet below him. It wasn't enough to bind or harm the beast, but it would be enough to surprise it.

He stabbed the energy forward, a purple lance that shattered into one of the revenant's heads. Where purple light hit, the green ghost vanished.

The revenant howled in anger and dropped Bastian into the River.

It didn't feel like falling into water. Not really.

It felt like slipping into mist made manifest, a hissing, electric surge that ran around and *through* him, a stream of energy, neither mass nor matter, a tide tugging relentlessly toward oblivion. He felt it rip through him, felt it draw out everything that made him human, felt it leech away his soul. And for a brief, terrifying moment, as the waters engulfed him, he almost let it. Almost let himself slip downstream, almost fell prey to the siren song of the River: *Give in, give up, let go.* But then he thrashed his way to the water's surface.

He saw the revenant farther upstream, raging about as it looked for Bastian, who had floated away unseen.

Bastian took his brief advantage. The River, after all, was his to command.

He reached toward the tide and—without truly knowing *how*—sent a ripple through the water. A ripple that surged forward, rapidly becoming a towering wave that crashed against the revenant.

It toppled under the wave, fell into the raging tides.

Bastian grabbed for the Æther, forced the waters around him to subside, so he stood on dry land. And as he watched the revenant fight its way back to the surface, Bastian lashed out with his magic again.

Purple bands arced around the revenant's arms, binding them to its body, forcing it back under the waves. He sent other manacles around the revenant's legs.

The revenant howled in rage.

While downstream, from the Second Veil, came an altogether different howl.

The shadowman had found him.

Panic raced through Bastian even as the revenant was swept downstream, thrashing wildly past the spindly form of the shadowman. The shadowman stood tall above the waves, two arms arced overhead and two clasped behind its back. The serene porcelain face snared Bastian to the spot.

The shadowman looked so calm. So *victorious* even as his minion slipped past the Second Veil, thrashing through the mist and disappearing into darkness. The shadowman didn't give the revenant a second glance.

The shadowman stalked closer, trudging through the River as though it didn't affect him. In fact, the River almost seemed to make him *stronger*, as though the very source of death gave him strength.

Bastian began struggling backward, toward the First Veil, toward life. He let the River fade away, until it was nothing but a small trickle around his ankles. The shadowman stalked on.

"You can run, Sebastian!" the shadowman called out. *"But what will you do when I come for your friends? I have seen them, as I have seen you. What will you do when I send the very hordes of Death after everyone you love?"*

Bastian reached toward the strand connecting him to his body. The shadowman was only a few dozen yards away, and he knew that his magic wouldn't help him—the shadowman wouldn't be tricked like the mindless revenant.

"The dead awaken," the shadowman said. *"And the dead follow me. It would be better if you came to me willingly, Sebastian. I will have you in the end. As I was always meant to have you."*

The shadowman reached out his hand, and for a moment the gesture almost looked welcoming—the open palm, the warm smile on his ceramic face.

Then the face began to split.

Bastian yanked hard on the thread connecting him to his body. Forced himself back into the world of the living.

Cold snapped around him, along with a burst like thunder and the stinging spray of snow as it exploded around him.

He spluttered and staggered back. The snow monster dissolved in a cloud of powder, and Finlay fell safely into a pile of snow.

Instantly, Bastian ran over and helped him out.

"How did you do that?" Finlay asked, wiping snow from his face.

Bastian looked to the mound of snow and ice—all that remained of the snow monster. Barely seconds seemed to have passed since he entered the underworld. Near the field, his classmates had begun to run toward them.

"I have no idea," Bastian lied. "Come on, let's get Professor Fennick back."

They were still outside the wards of the manor, and the shadowman was on his trail.

He didn't feel safe until he and Finlay had carried Professor Fennick back through the wards, until they were surrounded by classmates, and one of the remaining snowbeasts picked up the stretcher in its paws to carry the professor back. Bastian tried to smile as his classmates cheered and asked him questions. He couldn't focus on them. Not until they were back inside the wards.

He kept looking over his shoulder at an ink-dark stain blotting the horizon.

He knew it wasn't just an old gnarled tree.

He knew the shadowman was watching.

42

Word spread fast after the snow monster's defeat.

No one had seen what, *exactly*, had happened—not even Finlay. All they'd seen was Bastian standing triumphant, haloed in purple, while the snow monster burst into a cloud of sparks and snow. There were plenty of rumors—Bastian had bound the spirit to the depths of the lake, had conjured some sort of otherworldly Ætheric explosion, had some secret word of power delivered by his studies in Necromancy, or had a special blend of herbs he stole from Harold's Alchemy kits. None were close to the truth.

And Bastian fully intended to keep it that way.

Overnight, he was no longer just another first-year wandering slightly lost and confused through the halls.

He'd become a celebrity. And he hated to admit just how much—after years of being actively ignored or humiliated—he enjoyed it.

The holidays passed in a haze of lounging around the study hall playing board games, or trudging through the forest scavenging for rare winter-blooming herbs, or joining his classmates in snowball fights that left everyone frozen and wet and shivering in front of the fires, while ghosts swept in with hot chocolate and warm towels. He went to bed every night exhausted and content, in a way he hadn't felt in, well, ever.

"What do you think?" Harold asked. They were both in their beds, Bastian with a comic book (he had no idea where the ghosts got them, or how, but he was grateful for the ever-changing stack in the library) and Harold with a spread of notebooks and imposing alchemical texts.

Bastian looked over to see his friend holding up a diagram. He squinted.

"What is it?" Bastian asked.

He could make out a humanoid shape, and a bunch of symbols and arrows and transmogrification charts he didn't understand, all in Harold's neat, orderly handwriting.

"A homunculus," Harold replied. "It's basically a miniature human. I'm thinking of trying to make one for my project next year."

"Aren't you getting a little ahead of yourself?" Bastian asked. "I mean, we haven't even had the Naming yet."

Harold shrugged. "I like being prepared."

Bastian looked over the bookshelves and tables of their room. Even though Harold had initially moved all his stuff to his side of the room, it had slowly crept back over Bastian's things, like the ivy plant slowly taking over the wall.

"I noticed," Bastian said with a smirk. "So what does a homunculus do?"

"Anything!" Harold said. "It's basically like a miniature servant. It'll do whatever you want."

"Because that worked out *so well* for Dr. Frankenstein."

"That was a story."

"You say that like you don't believe stories have anything real to teach!"

"Says the kid reading comic books," Harold said.

"They're educational."

"They're filled with muscly superheroes in tight clothes."

Bastian blushed, but Harold didn't say anything else.

"I'll have you know," Bastian replied, "these are story-based comics and not at all about superheroes."

"I mean, you do you," Harold said. "But don't come for me when I bring up my mini-Harold."

"Please don't call it that."

"Better than mini-Bastian. Sounds like some sort of kitchen appliance."

Bastian laughed and threw a pillow at Harold. Harold yelped and threw one back. But before they could get into a full-fledged war, there was a knock at the door.

They both looked at each other. It was late—who would be coming by at this hour?

Bastian slipped out of bed and opened it.

Madame Ardea stood before him, wearing fluffy robes and with her gray hair unbound. She looked like a kindly grandmother, though the expression on her face was troubled.

"Sebastian," she said. "Please, come with me."

Harold began to get out of bed.

"*Just* Sebastian, please, Harold," she interrupted.

Harold grumbled and pulled up the covers, while Madame Ardea led Bastian out the door.

She didn't say anything as she led him down the hall.

It was the last night of winter break, and a few stragglers who'd gone home for the holidays trudged through the halls, leaving wet footprints as they lugged their bags back to their rooms, the cleaning ghosts muttering angrily as they mopped up the mess. A few of the kids waved at Bastian as he passed, though only when Madame Ardea's back was to them.

Had *everyone* in the school heard about what happened on the ice? He glanced to Madame Ardea. Is that what this was about?

He almost asked, but there was a look on her face that kept him silent. She didn't look angry. She looked . . . worried.

Madame Ardea led him through twisting back halls and up a set of spiral stairs that looked vaguely familiar. Then he realized, when they reached the top, that she had led him to her office.

She opened the door for him and gestured inside.

His heart stopped when he stepped in.

Aunt Dahlia sat in one of the leather wingback chairs.

And she was covered in blood.

43

Bastian raced over to his aunt and dropped by her side.

Her eyes were closed, and thick red blood was smeared over her face and hands.

"Is she—?" he asked.

"She's alive," Madame Ardea said. She closed the door gently and swept over to Aunt Dahlia's side. She rested her palm on Aunt Dahlia's forehead. Pale blue light glowed under Madame Ardea's fingertips, rippling over Aunt Dahlia's skin. "She sleeps. She had a very difficult night."

"What happened to her?"

"I was hoping you might tell me that."

Bastian looked at her in disbelief. She went over to her chair and sat down, watching him levelly.

"What do you mean?" Bastian asked. "I would never—I couldn't—I've been here the whole time!"

"I am not accusing you of harming your aunt," Ardea said, raising her hand. Her palm was coated with Aunt Dahlia's blood. "But when you first stepped foot here, I requested that you tell me if anything strange happened during your studies." She raised an eyebrow. "Tell me, Sebastian—has anything unusual occurred in recent days?"

Bastian's throat went dry. He would have killed for some of Harold's tea right now. He kept looking at Aunt Dahlia, as if reassuring himself that she was still there, and still breathing. There were tiny cuts all over her face and hands.

"A poltergeist attacked her in the supermarket," Madame Ardea finally said. "It caught her unawares. Apparently it blew out a couple windows, which explains the cuts. But it doesn't explain how or why a poltergeist would attack a fully trained Æthercist in broad daylight, in public. The undead know not to attack our own. Especially not one with a reputation such as your aunt's."

"Nor," Madame Ardea continued, "does it explain why she immediately came here, asking if you were still okay."

What will you do when I send the very hordes of Death after everyone you love? the shadowman had asked.

Was that it? Was he targeting Bastian's family? Well . . . Aunt Dahlia was the only person he had left.

Bastian opened his mouth. But he couldn't tell her about Descending. He *knew* if he mentioned it, she would forbid his studying it. And he couldn't stop. Not now—not when he'd found something he was good at, something that could *help*.

"There was a revenant," he said. He knew she knew about it—she was the rectress, after all.

"And you defeated it," she said. "How?"

He looked to his aunt.

"She will be okay," Madame Ardea said, noticing his concern. "She is healed and recovering. When she wakes, she will be good as new. Now tell me, Sebastian: How did a first-year like you banish a revenant? I have seen your Summoning skills. They are lackluster at best."

He almost felt offended. Almost.

"I don't know," Bastian lied. He looked to his aunt, hoping that way Madame Ardea wouldn't see the admission in his eyes. "I just . . . I don't know. I think it was weakened by everyone else, and Finlay attacked it, too. Maybe you should ask him."

"I did," Madame Ardea said. "The night of the attack. But he doesn't remember much of what happened, either."

"What does it matter?" Bastian asked. They were talking about all this like his aunt wasn't sitting, covered in blood, in the chair beside him. "We banished it. What does that have to do with my aunt being hurt?"

"Because the revenant was summoned on school grounds," Madame Ardea said softly. "Which should have been impossible. And now, one of our best Æthercists was targeted by a spirit that should have fled from the mere mention of her name. And you, Sebastian, are linked to both incidents."

Bastian swallowed.

"It was the shadowman," he whispered.

"The shadowman?"

"The ghost that chased me here . . ."

He saw her eyes tighten. She sighed.

"My dear boy, whatever chased you here was taken care of by your aunt. And you were attacked here by a revenant, while she was attacked by a poltergeist. No, Sebastian. There is no such thing as a shadowman."

She was lying. He knew she was lying. But why?

The fact that she was, though, decided it for him. If she was keeping secrets, so would he. His aunt was being attacked because of the shadowman, not because he was training as a Psychopomp in secret.

He just stared at his aunt. Guilt writhed in his chest. This was because of him; he knew it.

But what he didn't know—what no one would tell him—was *why*.

"What's going to happen to her?" he asked.

"She will recover here," Madame Ardea said. "And when she is ready, she will return home. No doubt she will wish to speak with you before she goes." She leaned forward and looked at him intently. "Once more, Sebastian—are you *sure* nothing abnormal has occurred in your time here? Nothing at all?"

Bastian shook his head. *She knows.* But he wasn't going to say anything.

If his aunt was being targeted because of him, if the shadowman was attacking the people he cared about, he had to get stronger. And Descending was the only skill he'd started to master here.

With it, he'd taken down a revenant. And he had barely trained. Surely he could use it to banish the shadowman as well?

If Madame Ardea wouldn't help him by telling him what the shadowman was, he'd have to help himself.

"To bed with you, then," Madame Ardea said. "Classes resume tomorrow, and you will need to redouble your studies. My fellow professors and I are concerned that you haven't yet shown an affinity for any of the pillars."

He looked down. *I have. You just don't know it.*

"I'll study," he said.

"Good," she replied. "Because you will have a new Conjuring professor tomorrow, and I want you to make a good impression."

"Is Professor Fennick okay?" Bastian asked.

"Oh, he's fine. A broken arm, a few bruises. All already healed. But I would never admit to saying this, Sebastian: Professor Fennick is the biggest baby I've ever had teach in these halls."

Despite everything, Bastian managed a grin.

Then he kissed his fingertips and pressed them to Aunt Dahlia's forehead. Her eyelids didn't even flutter. *I'm sorry this happened. But I'll study harder.*

I will protect you. No matter what.

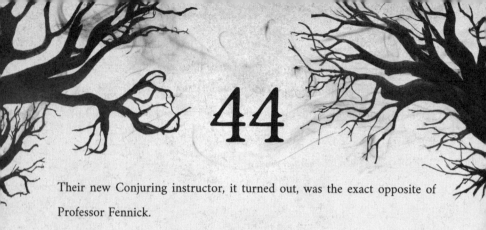

44

Their new Conjuring instructor, it turned out, was the exact opposite of Professor Fennick.

Madame Muriel was an elderly white woman with short gray hair and tiny wire-framed glasses. She wore a pastel floral dress complete with a knit cardigan and a half-dozen shawls, as well as a chunky necklace of agate and amethyst that seemed to pull her down into a pronounced stoop. She looked like she was almost on death's doorstep herself. Her voice wavered when she spoke, and she leaned on her cane like it was the only thing holding her up.

Madame Muriel had set them all to Conjuring sprouts from dormant seeds. Which turned out to be a lot harder than Bastian expected. They were all grouped around circular standing tables, seeds spread across the gnarled wood. Even Robyn seemed to have a hard time—she kept poking the seed with her finger, as if that might help speed it along. She flicked it too hard, and it rolled off the edge. She grumbled and got down to find it. They were each only given one seed on which to practice.

"I wonder how she even made it up the stairs to the tower," Andromeda mused loudly. She, too, had been having a hard time making the seed grow. She was great at destructive magic, but this seemed beyond her reach.

Only Harold had managed to succeed. A tiny pale green shoot was struggling out of his seed like a tiny worm. He coaxed it gently while the rest of the kids around the table giggled at Andromeda's joke.

Madame Muriel smacked her cane on the table, sending seeds flying.

Harold groaned as his seedling vanished between the flagstones.

"Detention," she snapped.

"What?" Andromeda groaned.

"You heard me. All four of you. Except you, Harold dear—you weren't laughing at her horrible joke."

Bastian was about to open his mouth, but a stern look from Madame Muriel made him shut it. *He* hadn't laughed, either. At least, nothing more than a smirk. The woman turned around and stalked over to the other side of the class.

"First day back," Robyn said, glaring at Andromeda, "and you land us in detention."

"I didn't think the old bird could hear," Andromeda said.

"Shh," Finlay retorted. "You're going to make it worse."

"I wonder what detention even looks like in a place like this," Andromeda mused. She didn't seem to care either way. "It can't be worse than going out into the field."

"You'd be surprised," Harold said.

He refused to say anything else.

Bastian was grumpy for the rest of the day. Not just because of the detention, but because it meant he wouldn't be able to make it to Descending.

Virgil had called off classes for winter break as well, stating that even Psychopomps needed a break from the dead on occasion. Bastian was itching to get back to practice. He didn't feel comfortable doing anything beyond some simple astral projecting, especially not after what had happened on the lake. He had a thousand questions he wanted to ask Virgil, and because of Andromeda, it would have to wait another night.

The only light in his otherwise dark day was getting to see Aunt Dahlia. She was resting in the nurse's wing, but she'd opened her eyes briefly and given him a hug, before the resident physician—a banshee in nurse's scrubs—ushered him out, saying his aunt needed rest.

As far as the detention was concerned, he wasn't certain what to expect, and Harold hadn't helped ease his fears; by the end of the day, he fully expected to be thrown into the dungeons or something. Which was why, when a ghost delivered a small roll of parchment with his fate at dinner, he was almost relieved.

"Cleaning duty?" he asked.

Robyn unrolled her own parchment. "Same," she said. She looked to Finlay. "What did you get?"

"Weeding," he said.

Harold whistled.

"What?" Finlay asked. "That doesn't sound too bad."

Harold looked at him. "You know the section of the greenhouses with all the thorny, poisonous plants that Professor Pliny won't let us go near?"

Finlay's face fell. "Yeah?"

"Yeah," Harold said. "Make sure you wear good gloves. And don't touch your eyes. Like, ever. And shower a lot tonight. I have some herbs that should neutralize any toxins that get on you . . ." He started rummaging around in his satchel, and pulled out a tiny vial.

"You have everything in there, don't you?" Robyn asked.

He shrugged as he handed the vial of pearly-white powder to Finlay. "When you've had as many accidents as I've had, you learn to come prepared."

After dinner, Bastian and Robyn wandered into the kitchens, where their parchments had told them to go.

A ghostly servant handed them each a mop and a bucket, and pointed to the main entry hall. Which—since the recent weather had turned rainy, making the snow into a muddy slop—was completely covered in muck. Bastian and Robyn groaned.

Then they set about cleaning.

"I don't know how the ghosts do it," Bastian said, tackling a large spot near the door. The mud on the flagstones he could get, but how were they supposed to clean the crimson rug that stretched from the opening to the fountain of Willow?

"Well, no bodies to get tired, I guess, and an eternity to spend," Robyn said.

"Are they, like . . . stuck here?" Bastian asked. "Like, bound to be servants?"

She looked at him. "What? Not at all. Most of them are spirits that had been aided in life by an Æthercist. They're all here by choice, usually to pay back our help. It's not, like, a real servitude thing."

"Gotcha," Bastian replied. It made him feel a bit better. About the ghosts. Not about the mud, because right then a group of alchemists came in from gathering plants in the forest, trailing mud and plant bits over his freshly mopped floor.

"You missed a spot," Robyn said.

He nearly threw the water bucket at her.

When the study hall was done, the ghost reappeared. But rather than take their mops, it just gestured for them to follow and guided them into the halls leading to the greenhouses. Which, like the entrance hall, were completely filthy.

"You gotta be kidding me," Robyn complained. "It's nearly ten, and we still have homework to do."

The ghost shrugged in a clear *not my problem* sort of way, and vanished.

"I don't know if I can take much more of this," Robyn said, slopping her mop back in the bucket.

"I wish we could just, like, wave a wand and make this all disappear," Bastian said. He squinted his eyes in concentration and raised the dripping mop, swishing it around and making magical *pew pew* noises.

Robyn giggled. "You look ridiculous," she said.

"I always look ridiculous," Bastian replied. "You get used to it when you've got hair like this."

"How did that happen?" Robyn asked. "Because if you're, like, bleaching it or something, you gotta let me know your secret. My roots always show after a day or two."

Bastian dropped the mop. "It happened after my parents were killed," he said. He was honestly surprised at how calmly he said it.

"Shock?"

"That's what the doctors said." Bastian forced himself to grin. "Maybe I can steal some of your hair dye. I think I'd look good in pink."

"What, this?" she asked, running a hand through her pink-streaked hair. "This is *all* natural."

He laughed, but stopped when he saw someone coming down the hall. He and Robyn both went back to their work.

As the figure got closer, Bastian realized he didn't recognize the guy. He was an adult, though something about him seemed off. He couldn't quite place it, but whatever. He was pretty nondescript. Bastian looked away, and quickly forgot what the man looked like. A second later, he forgot the man had been there at all.

He didn't think anything of it. Until he smelled the effluvium.

Robyn noticed at the same moment.

Before he'd even dropped his mop, Robyn reached out with her fingers crooked. Blue light sparked around the intruder's wrists and ankles, binding him in place.

He snarled. But Robyn's bindings held strong.

"What is it?" Bastian asked.

He took a step closer to the ghost—because it *was* a ghost. He could see the courtyard through the spirit's body. But try as he might, every time he attempted to look at the spirit, his gaze just slipped aside. Like his brain was trying to tell his eyes that there was nothing there at all.

"A ghost," Robyn said. She stepped closer, squinting hard to get a good look at the spirit. "Spirits from beyond the Second Veil. They look pretty much like they did in real life, but there's a magic to them that makes it hard to look at them straight on. They're able to hide in plain sight and don't make a sound unless they want to. Which makes them perfect assassins."

"What?"

She looked to him. "Rogue Æthercists sometimes summon them and send them after their victims. Or they're summoned by some quack mystic who uses an oracle board one too many times. But you . . ." She looked to the ghost. "What are you doing here? There's no way you accidentally wandered into the halls. Who sent you?"

The ghost sneered. He had a rough face, his cheeks sunken and covered in stubble. One eye was missing and shadowed, bleeding black goo. It made the sneer even more gruesome—when Bastian could look at it, that was.

"*He knows who sent me,*" the ghost said. "*And I won't be the last. You aren't safe here, Æthercists. Soon the halls of Gallowgate will run crimson with your blood.*"

"Blah blah blah. If you aren't going to tell us anything useful," Robyn said with a sigh.

She gestured with her other hand. The ghost yelled out, and the bindings around his limbs dragged him back down into the underworld.

Once the ghost was gone, Bastian and Robyn stood there in silence, both of them breathing heavily. Clearly, she hadn't been as calm and collected as she'd been letting on.

She looked to him.

"The shadowman?" she whispered.

He nodded. "I think so."

"But how? Nothing should be able to get past the wards."

Bastian had no idea.

45

They mopped until midnight, when a ghost (one *not* out to kill them) came and relieved them of their duties.

Even though they were both exhausted, they didn't go to bed right away. Instead, they trudged into the dining hall. They grabbed some mugs and hot chocolate from a carafe, as well as some sugar cookies, and sat beside one of the few burning fires.

For a while, they ate in silence. They hadn't really spoken much after the ghost attacked. There was always someone walking down the hall, which meant they were always on edge—wondering if they were about to be overheard . . . or attacked.

"Should we tell Madame Ardea?" Robyn asked. "That's the second time we've been targeted by a ghost on school grounds. Well, that *you* have been targeted."

Bastian bit his lip. "Third," he confessed. "The revenant was after me, too."

"Why?" Robyn asked. "I mean, no offense, but you don't seem all that special to me."

Bastian snorted. "Thanks."

"I'm just saying! You're a normal first-year. Unless . . . You don't think it's because you're a Psychowomp, do you?"

Bastian just shook his head. "Psycho*pomp*."

"Really that doesn't sound any better. But seriously. They were wiped clean from the records. Maybe that's why. Maybe you're being targeted because of what you can do."

"Maybe . . ." he said. It was the only logical explanation. Because she was right—he wasn't exactly the shining star of Gallowgate. Until the revenant had attacked, no one beyond the other first-years had even known his name. "But you said ghosts were summoned by Æthercists."

"That's what I've read," she said. "Do you have any enemies?"

"Billy Horwarth," he said. "But he's not the spirit-summoning type."

"More the throw-a-football-at-your-face type, I take it?"

He nodded.

Robyn grabbed for a cookie in the center of the table, but knocked her mug of hot chocolate over in the process. Cocoa splashed over her hands, and she grumbled under her breath. She grabbed some napkins and began to wipe off her gloves.

"Why don't you ever take those off?" Bastian asked. He'd seen a bunch of Conjurer kids wearing gloves, but theirs were enhanced with runestones and precious metals that aided their work. Robyn's were just simple leather.

For the first time since he'd known her, Robyn looked uneasy.

"Well, I suppose it's only fair, since you told me your scars . . ."

She slowly peeled off her gloves.

Her palms were covered in poorly healed burns.

Bastian winced.

"I told you my parents were Æthercists, yeah?" she asked. She didn't look him in the eye. She just stared at her gloves, her hands palm up on the table between them.

"Yeah."

"Well . . . my mother wasn't the, um, easiest person to get along with. She made enemies. Lots of them. And one night . . . one night, there was a fire. I still don't know what caused it, but it wasn't natural. We were in bed—I shared my room with my little brother, Jacob. He's a year younger than me. So we were asleep, and my parents were watching TV, and then out of nowhere, the whole house caught on fire. All at once. I've never seen anything like it." Her eyes had a far-off cast to them, and Bastian knew that she was seeing it all over again. He almost reached out to take her hand, but he had a feeling that would make things worse.

"I grabbed my brother and we managed to escape by jumping out the window. We went out to the front yard like we were taught to. You know— have a meeting place, wait there until help came. And we stood there and watched as the house burned. And no help came, and my parents didn't come out. Finally, I heard my dad calling out. I ran to the house and the front door burst open and he was there, trying to drag out my mother. He yelled at me to get away but I didn't listen. I went to grab her legs but a beam was falling so I tried to catch it. It nearly crushed me. And my mom . . . she conjured some air, just enough to move the beam aside. And we all made it out, but I was burned. She died in the hospital a few hours later."

"I'm so sorry," Bastian said.

Robyn swallowed.

"Thanks," she said. There were tears in her eyes, which she quickly wiped away. "I wear the gloves because I don't want people asking. I could have had someone heal the scars—heck, I'm sure Harold has something, even—but I want to remember. I want to remember what happens when you're too slow, when you rely on others to save you. People get hurt. People die."

Bastian thought of Aunt Dahlia sitting up in the nurse's wing. He opened his mouth to say something, when he caught sight of movement.

Finlay stood in the entrance, and he looked horrible.

Robyn sniffed and quickly pulled on her gloves.

"What happened to you?" she asked, her voice gruffer than usual.

"Harold wasn't kidding," Finlay said. He walked over awkwardly, gingerly, and it was easy to see why.

He was covered, head to foot, in boils.

"Dang, boy! Did you jump into those nettles or what?"

Finlay winced. "Andromeda got it worse. We were pruning some poison oak, and a ghost thought it would be real funny to possess the vines and have them attack us."

Bastian and Robyn shared a glance. *Maybe it wasn't a joke?*

"Come on," Bastian said. "I bet Harold's in our room. He was working on some new infusion. I'm sure he has something to help."

Finlay turned and let Bastian and Robyn lead him onward.

As they walked, Robyn leaned in and whispered. "Just don't tell anyone, okay? I don't want their pity."

Bastian glanced at her. "I think people are too scared of you to pity you."

"Good. Let's keep it that way. Or I'll give them another reason to be scared of me."

"What are you guys talking about?" Finlay asked.

"Just debating which of us is going to have to give you a sponge bath," she said.

Finlay looked like he was about to faint.

"Kidding!" Robyn said. She turned to Bastian and winked.

46

It felt like Bastian blinked and a week went by.

The rains outside hadn't slackened, and the grounds were a sodden mess. Which just made the drafts in the hallways colder, and the damp in his bones a chill he could never quite warm. Bastian was just grateful that they were no longer on cleaning duty.

It was late, and even though the term had just started, he was already exhausted. It seemed like all their professors had doubled their course loads in an attempt to ready them for the Naming of the Guard. He passed by a group of upperclassmen walking down the hall. They waved to him as they passed.

"How's it going, Bastian?" one of them—an older Conjurer boy with brown skin and long black hair—asked. He wore spiked leather gloves and a painted bomber jacket. Bastian had no idea who he was, or how he knew Bastian's name. His tongue wrapped itself up in his mouth.

"Um, good," Bastian said.

The guy grinned. Bastian was certain his chest was burning.

"That's good," the boy said. "Off to banish another revenant?"

Bastian blushed. "No. Just studying."

"Well, next time you do, let us know. We want to see how you did it. I'm Alejandro, by the way."

He reached out and took Bastian's hand.

"We just got back from a hunt," Alejandro went on. "Nearly lost it, too. Three poltergeists and a phantasm. Can you imagine?"

"They're getting worse," said one of the alchemist girls. Her plague mask hung off a peg on her wheelchair, beside a few satchels of herbs. "Seriously. Term just started and I've already been called out five times. I don't know how they expect us to study if we're always in the field."

"But you don't have to worry about that, do you?" Alejandro asked with a grin.

Bastian had no clue what to say.

"Well," Alejandro said. "See you around, Bastian."

They turned and meandered down the hall, laughing and discussing tactics, leaving Bastian standing there, staring after them. *They knew my name,* he thought.

Shaky and light at the same time, he continued on. But as he got closer to his destination, the excitement within him faded, replaced with a slow dread. He walked past a hall of grandfather clocks that chimed for various natural disasters and down a corridor filled with flickering torches held in coiled brass serpents, toward the nurse's wing.

Aunt Dahlia lay in a bed at the far end of the hall. Fireplaces cast warm light over the open room. It was cozy, almost, filled with tall plants and white candles and windows overlooking the lake. Aunt Dahlia opened her eyes when he came in. The nurse was thankfully nowhere to be seen.

"Sebastian," Aunt Dahlia said. He gave her an awkward hug and sat down on the chair beside her bed. She was covered in bandages, but she looked a lot better than she had a few days ago. "How are classes?"

"Okay," he said. "How are you feeling?"

"Better. Much better. Nurse Joanne says I'll be ready to return home in a day or two."

"That's good."

Before, he and Aunt Dahlia had been able to talk about anything. Everything. But now, as he sat there, he felt like he was talking to a stranger. He knew it wasn't just because she had changed in his eyes, but because he had changed in his own.

"I heard what you did on the ice," Aunt Dahlia said. She smiled, then winced at the pain. "Your mother would have been so proud. She was an amazing Summoner, herself. She taught here before Madame Ardea, did you know that? Madame Ardea was just in charge of running the school then. But once your mother passed away, well, Ardea had to step in, although we knew no one could ever truly replace your mom."

Bastian's throat went dry. He took a deep breath. "Why did no one tell me about them? Why didn't *they* tell me about this?" He gestured to the school.

"Because, little bird, we wanted to protect you. You've learned by now that being an Æthercist is not an easy path. No one wanted you to have to walk it. We thought, if we could shield you . . ."

"You don't know what it was like," he said, suddenly grumpy. "Everyone made fun of me for it. Everyone thought I was freak. If I had known what I was, what was happening . . ." *I wouldn't have felt so alone. I wouldn't have hurt all the time.*

She reached out and put a hand on his arm. He realized, then, that he was crying.

"I'm sorry for what you went through," she said. "But we thought it was for the best. We really did."

"I want to know about my father," he said. His voice was gruff when he said it.

Aunt Dahlia didn't answer right away.

"What do you want to know?" she whispered.

"What was he?"

"I don't know what you mean."

"My mom was a Summoner. What was my dad? No one will tell me, and I can't find his name in the Hall of the Fallen."

He knew the answer. But he had to hear her say it. He had to have someone living confirm what he knew—because then he could ask questions without them being suspicious.

"He was a Conjurer, dear," she said after a moment. "One of the best. Why, he even worked with your friend Harold's father. They were inseparable."

Bastian couldn't look at her. Why was she lying? Though the part about Harold's father sounded true enough.

Bastian sniffed. Another question crossed his mind. Not holding back, he asked it out loud.

"How did they die?"

Aunt Dahlia seemed surprised. "Why would you ask that?" she whispered. "You were there, Sebastian."

Bastian swallowed hard. He remembered. He mostly remembered. But when he closed his eyes and tried to bring back the details, they were blurry. Everything was blurry, like the first level of the underworld.

"But if they were so powerful . . ."

"Even powerful people can be hurt, or taken by surprise," Aunt Dahlia said softly. "I mean, look what happened to me! And I'm the most powerful Æthercist my side of the Mississippi."

Bastian forced himself to smile. She touched his arm.

"I know you want to make sense of things," she said. "But some things just don't make sense, no matter how hard we try to make them. Bad things happen, Sebastian. Very bad things. The best that we can do is try to prevent them, to protect those we love. And to not beat ourselves up when we fail."

He knew, in a way, that she was also talking about herself.

"You're right," he said. He looked at her and tried to smile. "I should let you rest."

He stood and gave her another hug.

"I love you, Sebastian," she said as he walked out of the room.

"I love you, too," he said.

And he meant it, Really, he did.

But he also knew that she was lying to him. Lying to him about his father, and who knew what else. Just like Madame Ardea was lying about the shadowman.

He knew, somehow, he had to figure out the truth.

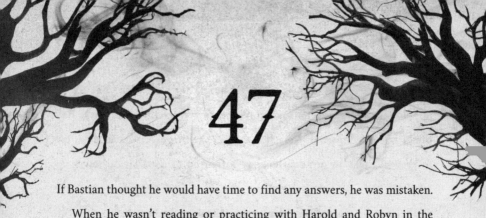

47

If Bastian thought he would have time to find any answers, he was mistaken.

When he wasn't reading or practicing with Harold and Robyn in the library or Alchemy labs, he was in the Psychopomp's study, practicing wards and bindings that would aid him in the underworld.

When he told Virgil about the revenant, rather than being excited for Bastian's quick thinking and victory, Virgil instead doubled down on the need for safety and protection.

"There is no point doing this work if you are going to get yourself killed," Virgil said.

Bastian hadn't mentioned the shadowman. He didn't want Virgil to stop teaching him for fear he was being hunted, not when he was finally excelling at something.

Because for all the new precautions, all the new defensive studies, Virgil still pushed him harder than any other professor there. Harder even than Madame Muriel. Virgil had already sent Bastian down past the Second Veil, a place where even he couldn't follow. The journey always left him frozen and drained. More often than not, on those nights, Bastian just passed out in the study beside the fire, rather than plod back to his room at a stupid time in the morning. Which is why Bastian had started bringing clothes and books with him to the study. He didn't want anyone to get suspicious.

Tonight, though, was different.

"That was very good," Virgil said. "Very good indeed. That should protect you well past the Second Veil, so long as you stand within it."

Bastian grinned. He stood within a protection circle he had just cast himself. Purple light shimmered around him, and runes and sigils danced and sparked in the air. He felt its power flooding through his veins.

"Can I descend?" Bastian asked.

He wanted to explore the *terra sine sano*, the land without sound. When he'd first stepped foot there, he had found himself in a flooded, murky world of dark trees and utter silence. He'd only been there a moment before Virgil had yanked him back out by kicking—quite forcefully, for an immaterial construct—his mortal leg.

"Not tonight, Sebastian," Virgil said.

"Why not?"

"Because the moon is dark and the Veil is thin. The more time you spend in the underworld, the more your presence becomes known. And expected. Never forget that you are still a living force—the dead will feel your vitality, will hunger for it and seek it like a moth to a flame. The deeper you go, the more that life force stands out. It is best not to tempt fate on a night like this. One never knows what forces might malinger there in the lower realms."

I have an idea, Bastian thought. He was about to press it, to convince Virgil to let him try, anyway, just for a moment, when a yawn escaped his lips.

"And if you are tired," Virgil said for the thousandth time, "you risk losing yourself entirely. Descending requires precise focus, Sebastian. The forces of the underworld may be yours to command, but they are still wild, merciless things—they will rip you apart the moment your concentration slips."

Bastian sighed and waved his hand across the circle; it fizzled out in a series of sparks, the runes winking and falling like stardust.

"Tomorrow?"

"If you rest tonight," Virgil said. "And in your own room, please. You snore. And although I do not need sleep, I have grown quite used to my peace and quiet."

Bastian gathered his things and plodded back through the halls. It wasn't too late, though night lay thick outside the windows, and the drafty hallways echoed with the wails of the dead. Which, really, wasn't all that unusual. It kind of went with the territory.

What was strange was getting back to his room and finding Robyn sitting outside his door.

"What's up?" he asked.

She looked up from the book she was reading.

"Oh, it's you," she said.

"Um, thanks?"

"No, I mean, I was waiting for Harold. He was supposed to help me with some Alchemy homework, but he said he had to gather some plants out in the woods first. He said he'd meet me back here. But that was almost an hour ago. Have you seen him?"

"No," Bastian said. "But I'll help you look for him. Maybe he got lost."

"He knows those woods better than anyone," Robyn said.

Maybe he hurt his ankle or something?

Bastian grabbed his coat, and together they hurried outside.

It was a beautiful, clear night. With no moon in the sky, Bastian felt like he could see every single star in the galaxy. Countless dots of light shone above, almost as bright as a full moon.

"I don't think I've ever seen so many stars, before," Bastian whispered.

"Me neither," Robyn replied.

Then, in the distance, they heard a cry.

He and Robyn looked at each other. "*Harold.*"

They ran off down the lawn and toward the forest that covered this side of the island. Gnarled bare trees and stoic evergreens pierced the night. He and Robyn cast their merelights the moment they passed under the branches. Instantly, sharp shadows twitched around them. Bastian felt his skin crawl.

"Harold!" Robyn yelled out, trudging toward where they'd heard him cry out. The ground was covered in tombstones, mounds of lingering snow, and twisted roots. Even though they hurried, it was slow and precarious going.

"*Help!*" Harold called out.

"What is he doing all the way out here?" Robyn asked.

"I don't know," Bastian replied.

They carefully made their way through the undergrowth, trying not to trip and twist their own ankles.

"Harold, are you okay?" Robyn called out again.

Her voice seemed to get swallowed up in the forest. Bastian almost wished she'd stop shouting.

It felt like there were a thousand unseen eyes on them. And although he knew the forest was filled with ghosts . . . these eyes didn't seem to be the benevolent kind.

"Robyn," Bastian whispered, "look how dark it is."

"It's night, Bastian. What do you expect?"

"But look!" He pointed into the deep shadows farther in. "When was the last time you *didn't* see will-o'-the-wisps floating around, or even some ghost hounds?"

Robyn hesitated. "Maybe they're at a party?"

Harold called out again. He sounded in pain.

"We can worry about that later," Robyn said. "Come on."

They hurried on, calling out to Harold, who kept calling back in turn.

But his voice never seemed to get any closer. And Bastian swore, at times, it almost sounded like someone else.

It's just the woods getting to you, he thought.

"Harold, where *are* you?" Robyn called. "What happened?"

"I'm over here!" Harold cried. And maybe it was Bastian's imagination, but he could have sworn the voice was a little more to the left than it was before. And it had a strange warble to it. As though Harold were underwater.

Robyn cast another merelight out into the branches, toward the voice. But it didn't illuminate anything.

"I'm going to kill him when we find him," Robyn muttered. Then, louder, "Light a spark or something so we can find you!"

"I'm over here!" Harold called again. His voice was *definitely* strange.

"Robyn . . ." Bastian muttered, grabbing her arm. "Robyn, I don't think that's—"

Light flared in the darkness.

And it wasn't Harold lighting the spark.

The spirit that appeared before them was pale green and translucent, glowing brighter than the missing moon. Its face was unearthly in its beauty—androgynous, with long white hair and tattered robes and delicate long fingers. Its mouth, however, was far from beautiful—a bleeding slash of black across its jaw. The effluvium wafting from it was overpowering, but rather than making Bastian flinch back and cover his nose, it seemed to draw him closer.

"Stupid children," the banshee said. "To have come so very far, when so very alone."

Its voice was neither young or old. It was a mix of everything, switching tone and timbre, sometimes sounding like Harold, or Madame Ardea, or even Bastian himself.

The banshee floated forward, giggling to itself. In a distant part of his mind, Bastian knew that banshees were powerful spirits from beyond the Second Veil, knew that they lost their voice in the underworld, but could steal the voices of their victims to make up for it. Did that mean it had already killed Harold?

But that fear, that dread, was distant and muffled. Because a banshee was as alluring as it was terrifying. Like the sirens of myth, they could lure anyone to their death with a simple sound.

Right then, Bastian couldn't have turned to flee or fought even if he wanted to. And he didn't want to. Even though he knew he should.

"But such beautiful voices you have," the banshee continued. "Such beautiful voices to add to my collection. Do you like it?"

The banshee's blackened lips stretched wide in a smile. When it spoke again, it wasn't its voice, but Harold's.

"Help! Please! I'm stuck, I'm over here!"

The banshee cackled.

"What did you do to him?" Robyn managed.

"Nothing. Yet. Heard him, though. Through the woods. Always mumbling, mumbling. Once I have your voices, precious ones, I will lure and steal his, too."

"You can't—" Bastian began. The banshee turned to him, and Bastian's voice cut off.

"Ahh, you are a special one," the banshee cooed, gliding closer. "So special, and so wanted. But he won't mind if I take your voice first. No, he won't mind that at all." It reached out and caressed Bastian's cheek. The touch burned like ice. "Sing for me, sweet child. Sing, and be mine."

The banshee leaned in closer, its pale moon eyes boring into Bastian's mind. The world began to slip away as the banshee opened its mouth, as Bastian felt his throat burn, and a scream escaped his lips, spiraling down the banshee's own throat.

"Hey!" someone yelled in the far-distant nothingness.

Light flashed, and Bastian fell to the ground. His vision refused to come back—everything was blurred, smoky.

No, it *was* smoke. Incense smoke. And behind him, lifting him up, was Harold. The real Harold.

Bastian blinked and rubbed his neck. When he tried to thank him, to ask what happened, he found he couldn't. His voice was gone. Panic raced through him.

"It's okay," Harold said, noticing Bastian's wide eyes. He lifted up his plague mask. "It'll pass. It didn't get your voice. But you're going to have a sore throat for a few days."

"What happened?" Robyn asked. "We thought you—"

"I got sidetracked," Harold said. "I was going to go to the forest, but then Professor Pliny wanted me to double-check Roman's transmutation chart, and it took a lot longer than expected. I dropped by my room but you weren't there. So I came out here, and heard you thrashing around . . ."

"It's a good thing you did," Robyn said. "That thing nearly killed us. *How* did it nearly kill us? It shouldn't be able to get past the wards."

Harold didn't answer. He looked around the dark woods. The smudge bomb he'd thrown was dissipating, now just a low fog on the ground. The banshee was nowhere to be seen.

"Let's get back to the manor," he said. "I'll make you some tea for your throat, Bastian. And then I think we need to talk to Madame Ardea."

They stumbled their way back through the woods. With the banshee gone, they saw a few will-o'-the-wisps darting about the branches, and more than once Bastian heard a spectral dog howl.

Oddly, it was comforting.

"Why does this only happen when I'm with you?" Robyn asked when the manor was back in sight.

Bastian was glad he couldn't speak. He didn't think she'd want the answer.

The shadowman. This is all because of the shadowman.

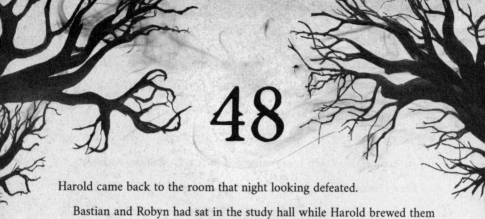

48

Harold came back to the room that night looking defeated.

Bastian and Robyn had sat in the study hall while Harold brewed them tea, and then Harold offered to go find Madame Ardea himself and tell her what happened.

It apparently didn't go well.

"She didn't believe me," Harold said. He flopped down on his bed.

"What?" Bastian managed to croak. "Why?"

Just those two words were enough to make him wince from the burn in his throat. But at least he could speak somewhat.

"She said it was our imagination," Harold replied. "Or a resident ghost playing a trick. But that was no harmless trick. I know a banshee when I see one."

Harold pulled off his shoes and began to change for bed.

"Something strange is going on," he said. "And I'm starting to think if we don't learn why Madame Ardea's keeping secrets, it's going to get us all killed."

There was one person, it seemed, that Madame Ardea had done a good job of keeping alive.

When they made their way to Conjuring later that week, Bastian was surprised to see it wasn't Madame Muriel standing at the desk, or even Professor Fennick pacing angrily back and forth.

Aunt Dahlia stood there, wearing her usual clashing paisley and floral prints and a chunky red necklace around her neck. Her wounds were healed entirely, and if she looked more tired than usual—well, who among them didn't?

She smiled warmly at him when he entered, but she didn't sweep him up in a hug. He was grateful—even though he'd gained a bit of popularity, he knew that would have made everyone in class laugh at him.

"Welcome, everyone," Aunt Dahlia said. "My name is Dahlia Noble. But you may call me Professor Dahlia. I will be taking over for Madame Muriel, until Professor Fennick is feeling better."

"*Such* a crybaby," Harold whispered. "It sounded like your aunt had worse injuries than he did!"

"Now," Aunt Dahlia said, "as I know your previous professors focused more on practice than theory, we are going to switch gears today. Please open your textbooks to the section on precious metals. We're going to begin learning about the elemental properties of various materials, and how they—in addition to specific runes and sigils—can amplify your Conjuring work. Some of you might wonder if this is a little too close to Alchemy for this class, but as you will find as you progress in your studies, our fields tend to overlap."

"I like her already," Harold said.

They started following along, while his aunt wrote down the various metals and their properties on a chalkboard. Robyn leaned over. "Where's Andromeda?" she whispered.

Bastian looked over to where Andromeda usually sat beside Finlay. The seat was empty. Finlay glanced his way, and Bastian quickly looked back to his notes.

"Maybe she was sent to the field," he replied.

Robyn just muttered something and went back to taking notes.

Love his aunt though he did, it was *very* hard to stay awake during her class. Especially after his sleepless night last night. He forced down yawns the entire class, and had to continually shake himself awake when the text started to blur.

By the time class was over, he wasn't the only one who looked like a zombie. This was the most theory they'd learned in Conjuring ever.

As his classmates shuffled down into the main building, Bastian went over to his aunt, who was wiping off the chalkboard and preparing for her next class.

"You're still here," he said. It was almost a question.

She laughed. "You sound disappointed, little bird."

"I'm not!" he said. "I'm just . . . surprised, I guess. I thought you'd want to go home. Aren't your students there missing you?"

"Oh, they'll be fine. They won't miss me one bit. Besides, Madame Muriel despises teaching. The moment she learned I was mobile again she basically forced Ardea to make me take up her post. And since Fennick *still* hasn't left his bed . . ." She rolled her eyes. Then she looked more seriously at Bastian and said, "I hope it doesn't make you uncomfortable, having me as a teacher."

"No. It's just . . ."

But he didn't get the chance to finish his sentence.

From the hall below, someone started screaming.

Aunt Dahlia went rigid. "Wait here," she said, darting toward the staircase.

Bastian hesitated only for a moment before following.

At the bottom of the stairs, a small crowd had gathered.

"Out of the way!" Aunt Dahlia said, shooing the kids aside.

The kids parted. Bastian paused on the stairs, looking on in shock.

Andromeda lay in the middle of the floor in a pool of blood, crying wildly.

She was missing her left arm.

49

Bastian sat with Harold and Robyn in a tower just off the study hall. There was only space for a few cushions and a floating fire between them, and windows circled all around, looking out over the shadowed grounds. The room itself was apparently a secret—Harold had found the ladder behind a painting of Nostradamus a few years back—which meant they had it all to themselves, with no chance of being overheard. Not that anyone was paying attention to them, anyway. All anyone could talk about was Andromeda.

"Do you think she's going to be okay?" Robyn asked. "I mean, she's a horrible human being, but no one deserves *that*."

"She'll be okay," Harold reassured her. "It's not the worst injury I've seen Nurse Joanne fix up. Last year—"

"I don't want to know," Bastian interrupted.

It was bad enough that he saw Andromeda every time he closed his eyes. His aunt's face had blanched white when she saw Andromeda lying there, right before she sprang into action. He'd never seen her look that scared before, not even when facing the shadowman.

Harold swallowed and nodded and didn't say anything.

"But what *happened*?" Robyn asked.

"No one knows," Harold replied. "She was sent into the field alone. Which is rare, especially for a first-year."

"That shouldn't be allowed," Robyn said.

"And Bastian shouldn't have been sent out in his first month," Harold said. He sighed. "I've lived here most of my life. And I've never experienced anything like this. Something is wrong."

Even though neither of them looked his way, Bastian felt like their eyes were boring through him.

"It's the shadowman," he whispered.

"But how?" Robyn asked. "That's just one ghost."

"He said he would send others after me. And after everyone I cared about." Bastian hesitated. "I think that's how ghosts are breaking through the wards. He's helping them break through; maybe he's too big to get in, and he has to send lesser spirits after me. You've seen it yourself—we're getting called into the field more than ever before. And Andromeda got hurt."

"If you're saying this is all because of you—" Harold began.

"That's precisely what I'm saying," Bastian said. "Look, it makes sense, doesn't it? The shadowman is after me, and he's doing whatever he can to get me. Even if that means hurting my friends."

"Andromeda was never your friend," Robyn pointed out.

"But the shadowman wouldn't know that," Bastian retorted. He took a deep breath. "I think . . . I think it would be best if you just stopped hanging out with me. It would be safer."

Robyn and Harold stared at him for a while. Then Robyn laughed.

"That was the worst attempt at a breakup I've ever heard," she said. "Try again."

"I'm serious!"

"So are we," Harold said. "Even if what you're saying is true—and I'm not saying it is!—we're stronger as a group. That's why Æthercists are sent into the field in teams. None of us can do this on our own. We're your friends. We aren't going to abandon you."

"But what happened to Andromeda—"

"Might not have had anything to do with you. I told you before, Bastian: This is dangerous work. Kids get hurt. Some kids get killed. I've seen it myself. And that was way before you ever came here."

"But—"

"No," Robyn said. "Stop. We aren't abandoning you, and you aren't pushing us away, so give it up. Now, can we please focus on our homework? If I don't manage to get one good message from the underworld, Professor Luscinia is going to fail me. Hey, actually, maybe you can just go down there for me and talk to a spirit on my behalf."

Bastian just looked at her. Why couldn't she take this seriously? Why could neither of them see what sort of danger they were in? If the shadow-man ever got them . . .

Robyn let the facade drop, just for a moment.

She reached over and took his arm.

"I know you're worried about us. And it's noble and all. But you don't get to make this choice for us, okay?"

He felt tears burn in the back of his eyes.

He focused on the divination cards in front of them, tried to push down the ache that grew inside him. Not just fear for losing his friends, but realizing that for the first time in his life, he had friends he was afraid to lose. Friends who were willing to stick out unspeakable horrors for him, without worrying about their own safety.

Despite everything, in that moment, he felt more loved than he had in years.

Harold handed him a tissue.

"You're crying on the cards," Harold said. "And these are handmade. You'll smudge the ink."

Bastian sniffed and managed to laugh.

Robyn and Harold focused back on the assignment. But as Bastian sat there, watching them work, a new thought struck him.

Aunt Dahlia.

The shadowman had threatened to harm everyone he cared about. What if she wasn't staying here to take Madame Muriel's position? What if it was because the shadowman had nearly gotten her, and Gallowgate was the only safe place left?

Except now, it seemed, it wasn't nearly as safe as anyone once thought.

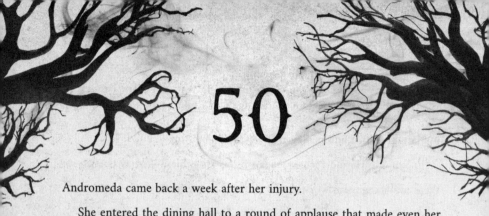

50

Andromeda came back a week after her injury.

She entered the dining hall to a round of applause that made even her blush. She sat down at her usual table and was immediately surrounded, everyone asking her how she was, or—more often than not—asking what it was that did it to her. Finlay was immediately by her side, helping load her plate with food.

"It was a wraith," she said clearly. She picked up a mug and brought it to her lips. It shook slightly. Bastian wondered if she'd been left-handed. "But I took it down with me."

"A *wraith?*" a Conjurer asked. "That's incredible!"

"Girl loses an arm and she's back in a week," Robyn muttered. "Fennick twists an ankle and he's out a month. The next time he calls us weak, I swear . . ."

But Bastian wasn't focusing on her. He was watching Andromeda. She kept looking over to him, and the glare in her eyes scared him more than the shadowman.

He felt her eyes on him all through breakfast. And when they were getting up to go to Summoning, he found out why.

She pulled him aside. Harold looked at them, but Bastian urged him to go on.

"I'm glad you're back," Bastian told Andromeda.

"What did you do?" she seethed.

He'd seen her angry before, but not like this. Her fingers dug into his arm painfully, and her eyes were wide and wild.

"I don't—"

"It was asking for *you*," she said. "It demanded I take it to *you*."

"What?"

"The wraith!" she yelled. A few ghosts clearing plates looked over in alarm. "Before it did *this*," she said, gesturing to the leather wrap over her shoulder. "It told me this was a message, Bastian. That this was just the beginning. So I will ask you one. Final. Time: What did you do?"

"Nothing, I am sure," Professor Luscinia said behind them.

Bastian had never been so happy to see the enigmatic professor before. She swept up beside them in an elegant black dress.

"Whatever is the matter here?" Professor Luscinia asked calmly.

For a moment, Bastian feared Andromeda would say something. But she just let go of his arm and stalked away. Bastian stood there, watching her go.

"I wouldn't worry about her," Professor Luscinia said. "Grief and pain make us do terrible things."

"Thanks, Professor," Bastian said. "I . . . I should get to Summoning."

Professor Luscinia bit her lip. She looked around, but save for the serving ghosts, the dining hall was empty.

"I beg you to be careful, Sebastian," she said in a whisper.

Bastian felt his blood go cold. "Professor?"

"There have been rumblings in the underworld. A storm brews, Sebastian. We all feel it. And that storm, I fear, swirls around you."

"I don't understand."

"Neither do I," she replied. "But remember that we fight for the living. Always for the living. When the darkness comes, we must be the light."

She squeezed his shoulder gently.

"Just be careful down there," Professor Luscinia said. "I am a speaker for the dead, Sebastian. They have told me they've seen you where no mortals can tread. Just like your father before you. But that world is not meant for the living. No matter how appealing its secrets may be. At some point . . . at some point, even though you return to your body . . . at some point, there is no true coming back. Your parents learned that the hard way."

A bell rang deeper in the manor.

"Off to class with you," she said.

He nodded and shuffled toward Summoning.

She knew he could descend. Just as she knew his father could.

But what secrets was she talking about?

And why did she seem so scared?

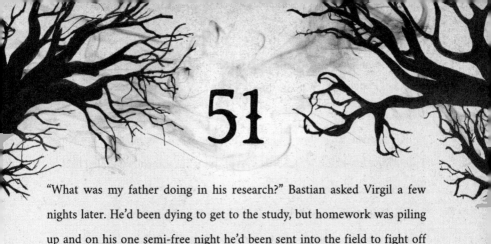

51

"What was my father doing in his research?" Bastian asked Virgil a few nights later. He'd been dying to get to the study, but homework was piling up and on his one semi-free night he'd been sent into the field to fight off a shade.

"Good evening to you, too, young Sebastian," Virgil said.

"My father," Bastian said. "What was he doing? His plaque said he *delved deeper than others dared*. What does that mean?"

Ever since his conversation with Professor Luscinia, he couldn't get the question out of his mind. His dad had been the last Psychopomp to study at Gallowgate. After him, all memory of the skill had been intentionally wiped out. And that whole *your parents learned the hard way* thing—was his dad somehow the *reason* Psychopomps were no more?

"What your father did in his spare time is beyond my knowledge, I'm afraid. As I have told you time and time again, my sight is constrained to here."

"But he was *here*," Bastian said. "I know he came here when I was a kid. I know he was still practicing and studying, even when he wasn't a student."

How else could he explain the familiarity of this place? The fact that the very scent of the study made him think of his father?

"I am sorry, Sebastian, but I don't—"

"Don't say you don't know!" Bastian threw one of the pillows from the sofa. It landed in a fireplace by accident and quickly burst into pungent flames.

He flopped back down on the couch and put his head in his hands. Everything felt like it was falling apart. And it all, somehow, circled back to him. And the shadowman. Always, the shadowman.

Virgil sat down beside him. He couldn't do anything to comfort Bastian, being immaterial and all, but his presence helped a little.

"Sorry," Bastian said. "It's just . . ."

"Why don't we try going a little deeper tonight?" Virgil said.

Bastian looked to him. "Really?" He would have thought Virgil would tell him to take the night off, since he was clearly distressed.

"Really," Virgil said. "Perhaps it will help distance you from your emotions a bit. You still remember the wards I taught you earlier?"

Bastian nodded.

"Good. Because once you pass the *Memorius Velamentum*, you will start to forget who you are, and why you are there. The wards will help keep those memories intact. For a time. A quick in and out should do nicely. Nothing sets the mind right like a new horizon, after all."

Bastian wanted to press Virgil, but he could tell the construct was telling the truth. After all, Virgil wasn't human—he didn't have a motive to lie or hide things from Bastian. If Virgil didn't know what his dad was trying to do . . . he had to find someone who did. And the only people here who knew clearly wouldn't talk.

Bastian nodded and went over to the protection circle embedded in the floor. He took a deep breath and tried to calm his racing thoughts, reached out to the Æther. Purple light flared around him as the amethysts in the floor sparked to life. He drew the sigils and wards in the air with his finger, leaving trails of sparking light behind it. When he was done, he lay on the wooden floor and calmed his mind.

It was so much easier now.

Between one breath and the next, he descended.

First, he felt the world slip away as he passed through the First Veil, the *Corpus Velamentum*. He saw the study blur and fade, but he kept reaching down, sending his soul even farther. Past the *Harmonius Velamentum*, the Second Veil. Instantly, he felt the great and terrible silence stretching within and without him. It was unsettling. There wasn't even a ringing in his ears from the silence. Just . . . nothing. All that surrounded him was black trees and a marshy gray mist, the sky the palest off-white.

But he pressed further. He reached toward the Third Veil, the *Memorius Velamentum*. He felt it draw closer. The trees bled and spread like ink in milk, the whiteness spilling over as he grew heavier and lighter at the same time.

Nearly there.

With a jolt, he was back, and his head was splitting in two from a terrible clanging.

"What was that?" he yelped, sitting upright. The circle dissolved in an explosion of sparks.

Virgil looked at him in confusion.

"What is what, dear boy?"

Then Bastian realized what the ringing was.

The bells.

He was being sent into the field. Again.

He groaned.

"I have to go," he said. "The bells."

Virgil nodded gravely. "Yes, you don't want to ignore their summons. You are welcome to come back and practice once more, should your endeavor be swift."

Given the way the week was going, Bastian highly doubted that would be the case.

He grabbed his satchel and coat and headed out the door, into the Hall of the Fallen. His footsteps felt uneasy. After being jolted so suddenly out of the underworld, he felt like he wasn't all there. Like being woken up unexpectedly from a deep sleep. He was only a few steps past the rubble that once more lay strewn behind him when he ran into Finlay.

"What are you doing here?" Finlay asked. He didn't slow down.

"Um . . . I'm heading into the field," Bastian replied. Which, they both know, didn't answer the question.

"Me too," Finlay said. They began walking together. "Good thing you're coming with. Last time I was sent out I nearly got my butt handed to me by a phantasm. Should be fine with you around, though."

Even though Bastian was frustrated and tired, even though all he'd wanted to do was practice his descending and try to learn more about his father, Finlay's words made him glow. Even if they were based on a lie.

"I'm glad you're coming with, too," Bastian said.

Finlay smiled.

52

They stood in the courtyard of the Doors as rain misted down around them. Bastian wondered who else would be sent into the field. But a few moments after their arrival, they heard a creak as a Door on the far side of the courtyard opened. This one was pale blue, with a starburst windowpane; it almost looked like the door on Aunt Dahlia's front porch.

"After you," Finlay said, gesturing Bastian forward. Bastian forced down his fear—even now, he hated going on these hunts, hated having to fight the dead. Partly because, since he couldn't descend with others around, he was so bad at it. And partly because, yes, he was still afraid of the dark.

Especially since he now knew that there *were* monsters hiding there.

Bastian conjured his own merelight and stepped through the door. The light flickered above his hand. He still felt woozy, and Finlay's closeness didn't help.

He found himself in a hallway. Clearly, this was someone's house: Smiling family photos lined one wall, while a kid's crayon artwork lined the other.

Finlay stepped in behind him, the Door vanishing from sight.

"I don't sense anything, do you?" Finlay whispered.

Bastian shook his head. He didn't smell any effluvium, and the house was unnaturally quiet. They began walking forward, peering into the empty rooms—in all their hunts, it had always been to empty places. Even the houses were vacant. Bastian wondered if that was part of the magic of the Doors, only sending them in when the inhabitants weren't around.

He saw a kid's room, covered in toys, the bed unmade and filled with stuffed animals.

In the parents' room, the bedspread was tight and the photos on the bureau were perfectly arranged. He wanted nothing more than to head over to the bed and flop down. He needed to sleep. For a year. But he couldn't, not now. There was a ghost to catch.

A staircase leading down to the main floor waited at the other end. Bastian sent the light forward, but there was nothing. Not even the wind whistled outside. It felt like they were the only living things for miles around.

Something isn't right, Bastian thought. His skin crawled. There should have been a ghost by now, some sort of horror for them to banish.

They reached the top of the stairs, and when Bastian took the first, creaking step, someone called out from below.

"Who's there?!"

Bastian froze.

He looked to Finlay, whose eyes were wide.

The house wasn't empty, after all.

Bastian gestured backward, and Finlay took a quick, faltering step, but it was too late. The lights flicked on, and a man stepped out at the bottom of the stairs. He was middle-aged, white, with messy black hair and an exhausted look to his tired eyes. When he saw them, rather than looking surprised, he looked furious.

"What are you doing here?" he growled.

"We, um," Bastian began. The merelight flickered out.

"This house is mine," the man yelled. "Do you hear me? MINE!"

He roared the last word, and as he did so his jaw split open, his mouth stretching impossibly wide, revealing rows of serrated teeth.

"Phantasm!" Finlay yelled.

Blue lights flashed around Finlay's fingertips as he tried to bind the spirit that began running extraordinarily fast up the stairs. Bastian's own instincts were slow and blurry. He leaped backward in shock, knocking into Finlay in the process. The bindings around the phantasm shattered.

Finlay yanked Bastian back, into the hall. The phantasm roared past, but he didn't stop at the landing. He ran *through* the upstairs wall, vanishing in a ripple of green light.

Silence.

Finlay helped Bastian up.

"Are you okay?" Finlay asked.

"Fine . . . just . . . really out of it." His head was swimming. *This is not the time!* he thought angrily to himself. But he couldn't snap out of it.

He felt . . . not all there.

There wasn't time to process. A second later, blood started to drip down the walls.

"What . . . ?" Finlay gasped. He stepped into the center of the hall, as blood had quickly started to pool at their feet.

"What's going on? Phantasms can't do this. Can they?"

Phantasms could change their appearance, but he hadn't heard anything about them making the walls drip blood.

"Maybe it isn't real," Finlay said. "Maybe it's an illusion."

Bastian, still in a dream state, reached out to touch the dripping red goo that ran behind the photos.

Before he could, the picture frames rattled and slammed. He yelped and leaped back.

"This definitely isn't just a phantasm," Finlay said. "This is poltergeist activity."

"Two ghosts?"

"Must be," Finlay said. "I'll cast a summoning circle. Maybe we can draw one out and snare it."

Bastian nodded, and Finlay began his work. Blue lights swirled around Finlay's fingertips as a circle sliced itself along the floor in front of them. The rattling of the picture frames grew louder, and a few began to float off the walls. Toys began to crawl out of the bedroom, dolls and bears and figurines, scratching toward them.

Æthercists weren't supposed to leave a trace if they could help it, so Bastian couldn't melt them with fire. Instead, he conjured a gust of air that knocked a few of the toys back into the bedroom, and slammed the door shut.

"It's working!" Finlay said. "I think I've got the poltergeist!"

Bastian looked over to see green smoke swirling in the circle as Finlay drew the ghost out. The rattling frames grew louder, angrier, and screaming faces appeared in the dripping blood walls as the poltergeist vainly tried to fight back.

That just left . . .

"GET OUT!" roared the phantasm's voice behind them.

Bastian jolted around. The phantasm stretched its arms out to the sides of the hall, looming inexplicably large, its white face elongated and cracked, its jaw snapped and stretched, its eyes shadowed and rolling. With a terrible roar, it lumbered toward them.

Bastian stumbled back in fright, knocking into Finlay again.

Blue light flashed as Finlay's circle imploded, and the poltergeist raced free with a victorious scream.

"Careful!" Finlay yelped. Before Bastian could apologize, the phantasm was on them.

Bastian tried to conjure a fireball. Really, he did.

But the moment he reached for the Æther again, a deep exhaustion rolled over him.

He felt himself slip.

Felt the world fall away.

The hall melted into grayscale, blurred at the edge, and the towering phantasm changed shape, became less a man and more a stick figure with gaping eyes, a crooked mouth, and talons ready to rip Bastian's soul in two.

Bastian didn't have time to wonder how he'd ended up in the first layer of the underworld.

As he stood there, the black River flooded down the hall, churning against Bastian's ankles and knocking the phantasm down. The hall and the River seemed to stretch out for eternity, becoming a distant black smear that Bastian knew was the Second Veil. Why had the River come unbidden? Why was it already churning so furiously?

The phantasm screamed as the River rushed around it.

It wasn't the only one screaming.

Behind him, quickly falling to the River's clutches, the transparent form of Finlay thrashed in the waves.

Panic raced through Bastian, a surge he had to temper lest he snap back to his body.

Finlay fell under the water. Bastian had no choice but to dive in after him.

Churning black electric water beat against him. He could barely see in the darkness, but he *could* see the faint glow of Finlay's spirit. Virgil was right—down here, life force radiated like a sun. Though for Finlay, that sun was quickly fading.

Bastian struggled forward, trying to will the River to push him toward his friend, or Finlay toward him. He almost forgot about the phantasm.

Until it grabbed him by the scruff of his neck and yanked him out of the River.

"*You will be his,*" the phantasm raged.

But Bastian wasn't focusing on the spirit—he watched in terror as Finlay's form surged past him, tumbling and tossed in the waves. As his diminishing glow rushed downstream, toward the Second Veil.

"Finlay!" Bastian screamed. This couldn't be happening. He had to act fast, before the phantasm regained its footing or Bastian lost his . . . and lost Finlay in the process.

Anger and fear turned to action.

Power pulsed in his veins as he snapped glowing purple bindings around the phantasm's wrists and ankles. The spirit immediately dropped him into the waves, but now that Bastian was holding on to the power, the River didn't pull him away. The River obeyed him.

He reached out with one part of his awareness and forced the River to subside around Finlay. The River struggled. It didn't want to give up the delicious life that had fallen so easily into it. But Bastian's will was stronger.

While the water eddied around Finlay, Bastian struck the phantasm down with a surge of Æther. The spirit wailed as it fell beneath the waves. It struggled up, just once.

"*He will find you, Sebastian! And you will wish you came to him willingly!*"

Bastian hurled his power with all his might. The phantasm sank beneath the roaring waves and, in a matter of moments, slipped beyond the Second Veil.

Bastian barely paid that any attention. As the River subsided around him, he sloshed through the black froth, forcing his way to Finlay, who lay shivering in a tight ball. Even as Bastian knelt beside him, he could see the vitality draining from his friend with every moment.

Even without the River leeching at him, Finlay didn't have long. The living weren't meant to stay here, after all.

Bastian didn't know what he was doing. Not really. But Psychopomps were called ferrymen for a reason. He grabbed Finlay's shoulder and reached out to the First Veil with his mind, tugging at the cord between him and his body.

The underworld melted away, the land of the living washing over them in a warm wave.

But they weren't safe. Not yet.

The poltergeist still raged, blood dripping down the walls and picture frames lunging toward them.

Finlay was curled on the floor, unable or unwilling to move but miraculously alive, and Bastian had had more than enough of spirits trying to hurt him and his friends.

He reached to the Æther and cast forth his bindings. Blue lights flared around the poltergeist. Rage or desperation or both fueled Bastian's magic, and with a quick twist of power he banished the poltergeist back to the underworld.

Instantly, the picture frames clattered to the carpet, and the blood vanished from the walls.

Bastian knelt by Finlay. His head spun from the movement, and if he hadn't been intending to drop to his knees in the first place, his sudden vertigo and energy loss would have forced it.

"Are you okay?" Bastian managed. He reached out for Finlay's shoulder.

The moment his fingers touched, Finlay jerked back.

Finlay's skin was cold and pale, but his eyes were sharp. Wide.

Terrified.

"What are you?" Finlay asked, curling tighter into himself.

"I—" Bastian began.

He never got a chance to finish or explain.

The Door appeared back in the wall beside them, and Finlay scrambled through.

By the time Bastian wobbled back up to standing, the room spinning deliriously, and made it into the courtyard, Finlay was nowhere to be seen.

53

By breakfast the next day, everyone had heard what happened in the field.

Or rather, everyone had heard a *version* of what had happened in the field.

"Did you know they're saying you became possessed and tried to rip his head off?" Robyn said as she sat down.

"No," Bastian replied. "I hadn't heard that one, thanks."

He hunched over his plate, his hunger forgotten. He could have sworn that everyone in the dining hall was looking at him, could have sworn that every whispered conversation was about him. The trouble was, the paranoia was probably right.

He'd barely slept that night—he couldn't stop thinking about the fear in Finlay's eyes. He'd looked more afraid of Bastian than he had been of the ghosts.

"Better than what some of the skeletons were gossiping," Harold said. "They say you actually tried to kill Finlay of your own free will. But don't listen to them. They have loose tongues."

"They don't have tongues at all," Robyn pointed out.

Bastian gave a half-hearted laugh.

It didn't matter what people said. They all knew some variation of the truth: Finlay had fallen into the underworld, and Bastian had pulled him back. Bastian still didn't know exactly how it had happened. Had Finlay been too close when he had descended, and been dragged down by proxy?

Had it been some unknown magic of the ghosts or Finlay's own magic gone wrong?

He wanted to believe it was the spirits, but he knew in his gut that it had been him. He'd nearly killed Finlay. Maybe he *was* a danger—a *liability*—like Andromeda had said.

He wondered if it was the type of danger that wouldn't get him expelled, but would get him executed.

He glanced around the room, positive everyone was glancing at or talking about him. Finlay wasn't the only one looking at him like he was different. Like he was dangerous.

His stomach gave an unhelpful lurch.

It was exactly like being back in his old school.

"Just give it a few days," Harold said, trying to be helpful. "You know how it is. Someone will break up with someone else, or someone will become possessed, and you'll be old news."

"I just have to make it that long," Bastian said.

He glanced across the cafeteria, to where Finlay sat at Andromeda's side. Finlay looked over to him, and the same terrified look crossed his face before he turned away. Bastian couldn't blame him. If *he'd* been dragged to the underworld against his will and nearly lost in the River of Death, he'd be scared as well.

Bastian just hated that Finlay felt that fear toward *him*.

"Stop being dramatic," Robyn said. "If I fell apart every time kids started spreading mean rumors about me, I never would have made it this far."

"I guess, it's just—"

"Bastian, a word, if you will."

His words froze in his throat as Madame Ardea spoke.

He didn't need to look at her to know that she knew everything.

He shakily rose and followed her out of the dining hall. This time, she didn't take him to her study. Instead, she brought him into a side corridor, this one a hall of antique mirrors in gilded frames. Most reflected the person passing by, but a few reflected spirits trapped within. She paused beside one of them; the spectre inside banged her fists silently against the glass. Trapping a spirit inside an object was a type of banishing they hadn't been taught yet. But it seemed like the worst sort of punishment.

And as he stood under Madame Ardea's scrutiny, that is exactly what he expected.

"How long have you been descending?" she asked.

She was so forthright, so blunt, he didn't know how to speak.

"A while," he finally said.

"Well," she replied. "From this day forth, I strictly forbid it. I have no idea *how* you even came about it, but as you have no doubt learned, it is terribly dangerous. There are reasons we don't teach it here, Sebastian. It has claimed more lives than any other pillar of magic, and I won't have it claiming yours or anyone else's."

Bastian looked down at his toes. He didn't just feel ashamed. He felt angry. And the more he stood there under her gaze, the more it boiled up to the surface.

"But why?" he asked. "Why did you keep this from me?" He glanced up at her. "You knew I could do it, didn't you? That's why you asked me to tell you if anything strange ever happened. Why wouldn't you tell me? Or teach me what I could do?"

"Because you never should have known about it in the first place! After your father . . ." She cut off.

263

"What about my father?"

"Nothing," she said. "He is not important." She took a deep breath, and when she spoke again her voice was colder. "You will not descend again, Sebastian. More than you know is at stake. If I so much as hear about you stepping a toe into the underworld, you will be expelled immediately. Have I made myself clear?"

He swallowed his anger.

She knew. She knew all along and she refused to tell me. She's been lying this whole time, and she still is, and she has the nerve to blame me for it all!

"Yes, Madame Ardea," he said.

"Good," she replied. "Now run along to your studies. You need to apply yourself, Sebastian. Should you fail the Naming, there is nothing I or anyone else can do to keep you here."

"I will," he replied.

I'll apply myself, he thought. *I'll apply myself to learning what you're keeping from me, and why.*

And he knew just how he was going to do it.

54

Just getting through the day was easier said than done.

Bastian's classmates whispered about him in the halls, pointing at him when they thought his back was turned and avoiding him in class and at meals. His teachers, too, seemed to know what had transpired. They all stared at him a little too long, a little too intently—his aunt, especially, watched him worriedly, as if she was terrified he'd descend in the middle of class.

When Bastian walked by the Hall of the Fallen on his way to class, he saw that two skeletons had been stationed there as guards; their glowing green eyes followed him as he walked past. One of them even had a sword. His heart sank at the sight. The study had been his one remaining connection to his father, and that had been taken away. Madame Ardea hadn't been kidding about preventing him from studying any further.

The worst, however, was Finlay. Whenever they passed each other, or managed to make eye contact, Finlay would scurry away. Bastian knew that whatever friendship they'd made was shattered, and it would never be rebuilt. Not because of anything Bastian had done. But because of what he was.

That hurt worst of all.

The only thing getting him through the day was his plan. It was a tiny spark, but he held on to it with all his might. It got him through the stares and the whispers and the silent meals. When he'd finished dinner and Harold invited him to the Alchemy labs to help with his homework, Bastian refused.

"I think I'm going to go to bed," he said.

He looked up to the head table, where Aunt Dahlia was whispering something to Madame Ardea. They both looked at him. He quickly looked away. And when he glanced back, they were leaving.

"Already?"

Bastian just shrugged.

"Okay . . . well, let me know if you need anything."

Bastian nodded and watched his two remaining friends head off together. Then he hurried back to his room and locked the door.

What he was about to do was immoral. But he was desperate. If Madame Ardea wasn't going to tell him the answers he needed, he had to take matters into his own hands.

He lay down on his bed and shut his eyes. Tried to block out the ache in his heart.

When his breathing slowed, he astral projected.

Within seconds he was floating above his bed. But there was no time to linger. As Virgil had taught, he focused his attention on where he wanted to go.

Without moving, without a whoosh of wind, his bedroom blurred. When his vision cleared, he was floating in Madame Ardea's study.

Madame Ardea sat behind her massive desk, the fire roaring behind her as a cold wind rattled the windows. He couldn't feel the heat or the cold. He couldn't feel anything at all. Madame Ardea's desk was littered in gems and skulls and arcane geometric graphs. And in the armchair he had first sat in what felt like years ago was Aunt Dahlia.

Even though Bastian knew they couldn't see him—he was just an invisible spirit, after all—he still edged to the very corner of a bookshelf, just out of their eyesight. Just in case.

"—hide this anymore," Aunt Dahlia said.

"It clearly *isn't* hidden," Madame Ardea said. "As should be remarkably obvious, given the circumstances. The question is, what are we to do about it?"

"We should tell him the truth," Aunt Dahlia replied.

"And go against your sister's dying wish? No, Dahlia. I will not do that."

"He doesn't need to know everything. He just needs to know how to defend himself. How to fight back. The wards I placed on him only work in the mortal world. If he descends again . . ."

"He won't," Madame Ardea said. "I have spoken with him. He knows it is forbidden."

Aunt Dahlia's eyes glinted. "You don't know Sebastian as well as I do. He can be headstrong."

"Just like his father," Ardea completed. "Which is another reason we must keep him in the dark."

"What will you do if it comes for him again? The maleficarum can track him anywhere, even here."

"Gallowgate's wards will keep it out."

"Like it's kept out the other spirits?" Aunt Dahlia arched an eyebrow. "We've all seen it, Ardea. The wards of Gallowgate are crumbling. We have to train Sebastian to fight back."

"And risk history repeating itself?" Madame Ardea's eyes took on a distant, haunted look. "You weren't there, Dahlia. You don't know the horrors I witnessed."

"I saw enough," Aunt Dahlia replied curtly. "I *lost* enough. I lost more than most."

"And that is why we cannot risk losing any more. So many Æthercists died that day, Dahlia. We must rebuild. But we must rebuild using the skills we have, and not the curse that dragged us here in the first place."

"But what about Sebastian?"

"We both know there is only one way to stop a maleficarum, Dahlia. No matter what we do, there is only ever one outcome. The last seven years have shown us as much."

"So, what? You intend to do nothing?"

"I intend to give him every tool at Gallowgate's disposal to defend himself. *Without* inviting the complete destruction of everything we've rebuilt in the process."

"I'm not willing to give up."

"Neither am I, dear. But teaching him to descend would be offering him up on a silver platter. You said it yourself—his protective wards only work when he is in the mortal world. Down there, he has no hope of surviving. Here, at least, we can give him the proper tools to defend himself, without putting anyone else at risk."

Aunt Dahlia looked like she wanted to fight. But the light in Madame Ardea's eyes said she refused to back down.

"So be it," Aunt Dahlia said. "But if he dies . . ."

"We all die, Dahlia. It's how we live that counts."

Aunt Dahlia glared and stood. Bastian sank back against the bookshelf and disappeared into the tomes.

"And Dahlia?" Madame Ardea said when his aunt reached the door.

Aunt Dahlia paused and turned back.

"I think it is time your contract here was terminated. Fennick has been chomping at the bit to return, and the man is a force of nature when he wants to be."

"I'll be gone at the end of the week."

"No," Ardea said. "I think it is best if you leave tonight."

"But I—"

"I can't risk you breaking what I have tried so hard to rebuild. I gave you the opportunity to be with him after your recovery. That should be enough."

Aunt Dahlia opened her mouth.

"Good night, Dahlia," Madame Ardea said. "Willow will escort you home."

She gestured, and a swirl of blue appeared in the corner.

Before Willow could materialize, Bastian snapped back to his body. Mortals might not be able to see him when astral projecting, but other spirits could.

He lay in bed, staring at the ceiling, his heart racing over everything he'd heard.

But rather than an answer, all he had was questions, and the terrible feeling that he did not want to know the truths waiting on the other side.

55

Harold had been mostly right: After a few days, Bastian stopped noticing the whispers of his classmates, and the wide berth they gave him in the halls. Maybe it was because they moved on—he wasn't paying enough attention to know or even care. He barely noticed them at all.

All he could think about was what Madame Ardea and Aunt Dahlia had been discussing in the study. He never even got a chance to try and intercept Aunt Dahlia before she left. The moment he got back to his body and ran out the door, she was already gone, her room and office empty. She didn't even leave him a note; he wondered if Willow or Madame Ardea had prevented even that.

He was alone. And with everyone in the school still avoiding him, that abandonment felt even worse.

Well. He wasn't *entirely* alone.

"Say it again," Robyn said.

"Mah-leh-fi-care-oom," Bastian intoned.

They sat at a table in the back of the library, surrounded by stacks of books: *Denizens of Death*; *101 Ghosts and Ghouls*; *The Æthercist's Guide to the Undead*; *A Mofte Compleat Compendium of Corpfes*. He and Harold and Robyn had combed through them all, but there wasn't mention of a maleficarum anywhere. He knew he'd read it somewhere, though. He just couldn't remember where.

Not for the first time, he wished Gallowgate had working internet.

"And you're *sure* you heard them correctly?" Harold asked.

Bastian glared at him.

Harold raised his hands in surrender. "Just checking," he said, and went back to skimming the giant textbook in front of him.

"You know," Robyn said, "you're going to have a hundred percent fewer friends if you keep up that mopey attitude."

She was giving him *a look*, and he knew if he said anything he'd just make it worse.

"Sorry," he said.

"Much better," she replied. Then she sighed and leaned back from her book, rubbing her eyes. "So we know this creature is after you. And we know it isn't in *any* of the books on spirits we've looked at. Was there anything else?"

He shook his head. He saw movement on the other side of the library. When he looked up, he saw Finlay darting away between the shelves. Finlay still hadn't spoken to him since their hunt together. Bastian wanted to explain, but Finlay was never alone. He was always with Andromeda now.

"We'll find something," Harold said. He lowered his voice. "Have you talked to Virgil? Maybe he knows."

"No," Bastian said. "I can't get into the study when astral projecting. I've tried. It's warded. And Ardea has a guard out front all the time now. I can't get close." He sighed. "Besides, when I told him about the shadowman before, he said he didn't know of any spirit like it."

"But maybe the name would ring a bell," Harold suggested. Then he relented. "Not that it matters, if you can't reach him."

Robyn's eyes lit up.

"That's it!" she said. "I don't know why I didn't think of it before!"

"What?" Bastian asked.

"If the living won't help us find the answers, we can ask the dead!"

"Of course!" Harold said.

"I don't think Necromancy is going to help," Bastian argued. "Have any of us even been able to do more than get a ghost to say hello?"

Necromancy wasn't their best subject, not by a long shot. The dead just did *not* want to talk to them.

"You never know," Robyn ventured. "It's worth a try. You said the shadowman was sending other ghosts after you, right? Well, maybe one of them can tell us what he is, and how to defeat him."

"It can't hurt," Harold said.

Bastian was already gathering his things. "Let's go," he said.

He just hoped Harold was right.

The crypts were always damp and dark and cold, but that was even more amplified at night.

Bastian, Robyn, and Harold trudged past sarcophagi whose inhabitants snored loudly or grumbled at being disturbed by the trio's passing. The only illumination came from the pale white merelights floating about their hands, making everything down here even more otherworldly.

Finally, they reached an empty crypt (the others were filled with skeletons playing cards, and a group of friendly poltergeists in rehearsal for their metal band) at the far end of the hall and settled in.

This room was smaller than the crypt they usually had class in—barely the size of a bathroom, with a single concrete casket in the center of the room that had a few white candles melted on its lid. The three kids squished in around it, trying to get comfortable. Harold pulled a few new candles from his satchel and set them on the casket. Robyn lit them with a flick of her wrist. It was easier to perform Necromancy if it was your sole focus—even trying to keep a merelight lit would be enough to deter it. None of them wanted to be down here in the pitch dark.

"So what are we going to try?" Harold asked. "Oracle cards or carromancy or . . . hmm, I think I have some runes in here somewhere."

"The last time you did carromancy you somehow made the candle explode and got wax and blood all over the room," Bastian said. "And I don't think oracle cards or runes are gonna be any help, unless there's a specific card for *ghost that won't leave Bastian alone*."

"We could try channeling," Robyn suggested.

They both looked at her.

Channeling was advanced Necromancy work. It basically involved allowing a spirit to take over your body so it could speak through you. It was dangerous, for very obvious reasons.

"Robyn—" Harold began, but she cut him off.

"Look, I'll do it," she said. "I've read up on it. And I . . . I might have tried it before, once or twice. My mom was a Necromancer."

"Are you sure?" Bastian asked. "I don't want you getting hurt because of me."

"I won't be." Robyn cracked her knuckles. "Just slap me if the ghost gets out of hand. That usually does the trick."

"You're joking, right?" Harold asked.

"One way to find out."

She closed her eyes and took a deep breath, slowing her breathing on the exhale.

Bastian and Harold exchanged glances, then turned all their attention to her.

For a while, there was just the distant sound of the practicing ghosts and Robyn's steady breathing.

Then the candles on the casket flickered. Guttered.

And went out.

They were cast into darkness, and before Harold could relight the candles, twin points of white glowed in the dark.

Robyn's eyes.

She croaked and moaned as she inhaled.

Harold quickly lit the candles. Robyn's eye sockets were ringed with black veins, and her limbs were crooked to the sides at odd angles, like a broken marionette.

"R . . . Robyn?" Harold asked.

Her head snapped to him.

"*Not . . . Robyn . . .*" Robyn said. Her voice was deep, masculine, and it sounded like it crawled out from the bottom of a well.

Harold looked to Bastian. It was now or never.

Bastian cleared his throat. He nearly lost his voice when Robyn's gaze jerked to him.

"I want to know about a ghost. It's called a maleficarum."

The ghost inhabiting Robyn screamed. She rose up from sitting, arching back and clawing her hands. She didn't drop back to her knees, but stayed in that awful position while she spoke.

"*We do not speak of him,*" she wheezed. "*We dare not cross him.*"

"You have to tell me!" Bastian said. "I command you! How do we kill it?"

"*Cannot . . . be killed . . .*" she replied, struggling against herself, struggling against Bastian's command.

"There has to be a way," Bastian said. "All ghosts can be banished."

"Not . . . a ghost . . . Not . . . truly."

"How do we banish it?" Bastian demanded.

"Nothing . . . can banish . . . a maleficarum," the ghost groaned. *"Unless . . ."*

Through the words, Bastian could hear Robyn crying in pain.

"Bastian," Harold whispered, putting a hand on Bastian's shoulder. "That's enough."

"Unless what?" Bastian demanded. "Tell me, *unless what?*"

Robyn screamed out. She rose to her tiptoes, tears streaming down her face. Clearly, the ghost did not want to answer. But it didn't have a choice.

"Only death will banish a maleficarum. The death of its Summoner . . . or the death . . . of its prey."

"That's enough!" Harold called out.

There was a flash of blue light as he yanked the spirit from Robyn's body and sent it back to the underworld. Robyn crumpled against the wall. Bastian was there in a heartbeat to catch her.

"You pushed her too far," Harold said darkly. He stepped over with a damp rag and some smelling salts. Bastian patted the sweat from her forehead with a rag, while Harold wafted the tube of salts under her nose.

A second later, her eyes shot open and she jumped up.

"Ugh, what is that, your old socks?" she said. She sniffed. "Why am I crying? What happened? Did we learn how to banish it?"

"Yeah," Harold said, looking over to Bastian. "We did."

56

It was hard to be around his friends after that.

Hard to be in their presence when he knew that he was the reason they were potentially in danger. When he knew that the only way to *prevent* that danger was to offer himself up to the shadowman.

"You're not doing it, Bastian," Harold said.

A week had passed since their discovery in the crypts. A week of constant rain and gray clouds that seemed to mirror Bastian's mood. He couldn't stop thinking about what the spirit had said. Couldn't stop wondering if maybe giving himself up was the best option. Which was making it very hard to focus on the Alchemy homework they were supposed to be completing.

"Definitely not," Robyn said. "If we have to make it through finals and the Naming, you are, too. Even if I have to drag your sorry spirit to the final ceremony."

Bastian chuckled, but his heart wasn't in it. He didn't want to give up, either. But he had no clue who would have sent the shadowman after him, or why. Which meant only one option.

He had to keep everyone safe.

"Hey," Harold said. He reached across the table and took Bastian's wrist. "We aren't giving up. There has to be another way. There's *always* another way. And you know your aunt and Madame Ardea are looking for solutions, too. We just need more time."

"But what if there are other attacks?" Bastian asked. In that one week, he'd encountered two more spectres in the halls of Gallowgate, and had nearly been pulverized by a poltergeist on his last outing to the field.

He hadn't used or practiced Descending since overhearing his aunt and Ardea, though. If that made him vulnerable to the shadowman, he couldn't risk it. Especially not with his friends around.

"Then we fight them off," Robyn said. "That's kind of what we're here to do."

Bastian grumbled. There was no use fighting with them. He'd already tried.

"I've almost perfected a concealment charm for you," Harold said. Bastian looked at him—Harold had never mentioned such a thing before. "I've, um, been working on it in secret. A bit of extra credit, you know. Professor Pliny says it should be able to ward you from any type of spirit. It's based on some old Greek myths; I just have to wait a few more days for the infusion of bay and hellebore to steep completely, and then some minor transmutations, and then we're set!"

Robyn just stared at him, wide-eyed. "I only understood half of what you said," she said.

"And that's why you need to keep studying," Harold replied, pointing to her open textbook. "Come on, turn to page seventy-four, the chapter on—"

But he didn't finish his sentence, because right then a terrible, deafening clang rang through Bastian's ears. And, judging from the yelp from Harold and Robyn, they heard it, too.

They all looked at each other.

"All three of us," Robyn said. "Aww, the Three Musketeers, together once more."

She leaped up. Bastian couldn't tell if she was excited that they were all finally on a hunt together after that one at the beginning of the year, or if she was just excited to get an excuse to stop studying.

"Come on, boys," she said, slinging on her jacket and grabbing a few things from her rucksack. "A-banishing we will go!"

"You know," Harold said to Bastian, grabbing his plague mask and satchel, "she really does enjoy this too much."

"I don't insult you for loving dirt so much," Robyn said.

"Yes, you do," Harold said. "All. The. Time."

Bastian grinned. Right then, their shared excitement was enough to push the dark thoughts from his mind.

He wasn't willing to give up friends like these. And if that meant fighting something that couldn't be killed, he'd do it.

"Oh no," Robyn muttered when they stepped into the courtyard.

The Doors lay ringed before them in the late-night gloom, illuminated by the merelights cast by none other than Finlay and Andromeda. Finlay actually flinched back when he saw Bastian, taking a slight step behind Andromeda. It made Bastian's heart ache. He wanted nothing more than to go over and tell Finlay that the last thing he intended was to hurt or scare him, but he didn't have a chance.

He also knew it was a lie: Even if he didn't mean it, he was a target, and the people around him would inevitably get hurt.

Just like that, his fragile optimism from before was snubbed out, all by the fear in Finlay's eyes.

"Great," Andromeda said when Bastian and his friends stepped out. "Just great."

"Trust me, princess," Robyn said, "we like this even less than you."

Andromeda just glowered and took a step forward, her fist clenched.

"Now, now," Harold said. "There's no use fighting amongst ourselves."

"Shut it, Harold," Robyn said. "We aren't fighting. Just a friendly bit of banter. Right, Andromeda?"

Andromeda narrowed her eyes. "Right." She looked over to Bastian. "So, Freak Show, what fresh horrors are going to come after you tonight?"

It was like a punch to his gut. *Freak Show.* No one had called him that since his last school. He looked over to Finlay, almost hoping for some sort of backup, hoping that Finlay would defend him as he had all those months ago. Finlay just looked to his feet.

Robyn stepped up beside Bastian, flares of fire spiraling around her clenched fists, but before a fight could break out, a Door creaked open.

"Um, guys," Harold said nervously. They all looked over to him. "I've never seen that Door open before."

This one was worn gray wood, the planks busted and beaten, with a weathered skull and crossbones in the center. It looked like the door to an abandoned graveyard shed. And when it opened, dark shadows pooled out before it in a soupy fog.

"That's not a good sign," Robyn whispered.

"Scared?" Andromeda asked.

Robyn scoffed.

Because although the Doors always opened somewhere new, they had a sort of theme. The pristine white one tended to open to modern homes, the blue to basements, the worn wood to abandoned places like forests, and the rusted metal ones to factories and the like. It wasn't exact, but it was something, some way to guess at what nightmares they might be facing on the other side.

This, however, was a mystery that none of them wanted to crack.

"I've never been on a hunt with five people, either," Harold said.

"Well," Andromeda said, shoulders back and chin up. "There are only four *useful* people here. We'll just see if all five of us come back."

Without another word, she gestured to Finlay and, merelights trailing above them, she stepped into the Door, disappearing from sight. Finlay looked over his shoulder to Bastian, just for a moment. His expression was unreadable—apologetic for Andromeda? Regret over avoiding him?

Then he looked away and stepped into the dark.

"You know, we could just leave her in there," Robyn said.

The bells clanged, making her wince.

"Just for a few minutes!" Robyn yelled to the courtyard. "Just as a joke." Another clang, and she shuddered. "You bells have no sense of humor."

She strode through the Door.

Bastian and Harold looked to each other. Harold pulled down his plague mask; in its glass eyes, Bastian saw his own terrified, tired expression reflected back.

We'll just see if all five of us come back.

It sounded less like a challenge, and more like a promise.

With a nod, he and Harold stepped through the Door.

57

Bastian stepped out into a graveyard.

But not just any graveyard. This wasn't the picturesque landscape with rolling hills and budding cherry trees. No. This looked like a graveyard you'd see outside of Dracula's castle.

Harsh wind and rain whipped and whistled through the cracked and aged tombstones that littered the hillside, while behind, waves crashed against the cliffs. The kids stood high up on the jagged cliff edge: graveyard before them, furious ocean below them. No trees. No distant lights of human habitation. Just the driving rain and deep darkness and hungry coast. Even their merelights couldn't pierce far into the darkness. Bastian shivered against the wind that sliced through his coat and soaked his clothes.

Though if he were being honest, it wasn't from the cold.

"Pretty, isn't it?" Robyn yelled out. Four merelights circled around her head. She was grinning, but the lights shuddered just a bit, betraying her agitation.

"Quiet!" Andromeda warned. "I thought I saw something."

She shot one of her merelights out and over the graveyard, making sharp shadows dance. But there was nothing. Andromeda cast the light in a jagged path between the graves, trying to find what they were meant to be hunting. Bastian could have sworn he saw something shuffling out there, but the moment he saw it the light was gone.

Here, on the cliff's edge, he felt horribly exposed and trapped at the same time.

"There!" Bastian called out. Right as Andromeda called out, pointing in the opposite direction.

Bastian could barely make out the shapes shambling through the graveyard, but he knew there was more than one. Potentially a lot more than one.

With the cliffs behind them, they were effectively surrounded.

"We should cast a circle," Harold suggested.

"On it," Robyn said.

But Finlay, who apparently didn't hear over the roar of the wind, raised his hands just as Robyn did.

Lights flared around each of them as they cast their circles at the same time. Twin arcs of light flashed around them, colliding in an explosion of sparks.

Bastian shielded his eyes against the dizzying light. Harold stumbled against him, calling out as he toppled over.

There was a bang, and another flash, and smoke billowed out as one of Harold's smudge bombs misfired. Bastian yelped and bumped into someone else, who shoved him away with a grunt. Bastian stumbled forward, bursting through the fog just as his vision began to clear.

Right in the path of the enemy.

The corpse in front of him reeked of rot, with great chunks of flesh falling from its face, revealing rotten teeth and a drooping tongue and white eyes. Bastian bit back a scream that wanted to be vomit and stumbled back into the fog, just as Finlay yelled out "Ghouls!" and more flames erupted in the graveyard.

Bastian's gut twisted. Ghouls were spirits from past the Third Veil, from the *terra sine memoria*. Stripped of their bodies and voice and memories, they shambled back to the mortal world with only one drive: to remain in life by whatever means necessary. They were able to reanimate corpses, able to leap between dead bodies faster than a blink as they desperately did anything to stay in the mortal world. As they desperately clawed for any spark of life they could find.

And that meant finding the freshest corpse they could.

Like Bastian and his friends.

"Burn the corpses!" Andromeda yelled from somewhere in the fog.

Fires broke out over the tombstones, dancing through the cemetery in red and orange patches of filtered light. Bastian tried to conjure his own flames, but he didn't want to catch any of his companions on fire. He took a hesitant step backward and bumped into Harold, who was fumbling around in his satchel and pulling out various vials and smudge bombs.

A cold wind sliced around them, forcing away the fog . . . and revealing just how very in trouble they were.

Dozens of ghouls moved through the graveyard while Finlay and Andromeda and Robyn fended them off with bursts of fire.

One reared up from the tombstone beside Bastian and Harold. Harold yelled and tossed the smudge bomb. The ghoul screamed in anger as the bomb exploded at its feet. In the swirling mass of fog, and without a mask like Harold, Bastian was blinded and fumbling. He had no other choice; he covered his mouth with his arm and ran.

He conjured a small flame between his fingers when he burst from the smoke and threw it toward another nearby ghoul. The ghoul's rotted flesh hissed and sizzled, but the flame wasn't enough to destroy it. Not like the flames that his comrades were tossing about behind him.

Fear lodged in Bastian's throat as he scrambled up a small hill, away from the melee and bursts of fire and smoke.

The ghoul trailed behind him, faster now, its fetid lungs rattling his name.

"*Sebastiannnnn.*"

The word sent fresh chills down Bastian's skin.

Ghouls weren't supposed to be able to speak.

Bastian ran faster. And when he reached the hilltop, he realized he had reached the cliff's edge. Waves crashed far below, and lightning flickered over the water. *That storm, I fear, swirls around you,* Professor Luscinia had said.

Bastian turned to face the ghoul. It was alone, thankfully. But he knew the others would be close behind.

The ghoul stopped its pursuit only a few feet away. It didn't lunge for him, didn't try to rip off his head. Instead, its dislocated jaw twisted in the semblance of a smile.

"*You are ours, now,*" it groaned. Bastian could see its wheezing black lungs through its ribs. "*We will call to him. He will reward us. He will set us free.*"

It tilted its head back and opened its mouth, releasing a spine-tingling wail.

Every hair on Bastian's body stood up in fear, every cell within him shuddering with a knowledge as deep as blood. If the shadowman came here, they would all die.

He knew simply destroying the corpse would send the spirit inside it to another, and another, until it was banished or it had summoned the shadowman. Just as Bastian knew he wasn't powerful enough to banish the ghoul traditionally.

There was only one way. Even though it meant doing the one thing he knew he shouldn't.

Without time to form a protection circle, he ran forward and leaped into the ghoul. The moment he hit that putrid bag of flesh, he descended.

The world faded to gray and white. The hill spread below him in a fog, filled with sparks of green light that marked the other ghouls fighting his friends. Strangely, the pale gray sky flickered with lightning. He didn't think the world without form could have, well, weather and form.

The vile, decaying green mass that Bastian clung to cackled, even as Bastian reached out and called to the River.

"You call to him as surely as I, Sebastian," the ghoul jeered. *"He will have you. Oh, he will have you. You cannot run from us forever."*

"I'm not running," Bastian said. "Not anymore."

The roar of the River filled his ears as it cascaded up over the cliff in a rush of hissing, raging black. It foamed around his feet, wrapped up over his ankles, and yanked against his very soul. And the soul of the ghoul.

Bastian shoved the ghoul away from him, just as he reached for the Æther and twisted purple coils around the ghoul's body. The ghoul cried out, but not in anger. It stumbled against the tide, its head still above the surging waves that rose around Bastian in a flood.

"He who leads the dead will rule the living!" the ghoul cackled. *"He comes! He comes, and none can stand in his way!"*

Lightning flashed overhead.

The ghoul finally succumbed to the raging River.

Bastian stood there, looking frantically around the landscape. But there was no ink blot of blackness, no insidious cackle, no smear of porcelain

285

white. The lack of the shadowman was almost more terrifying than his presence. Bastian stood there, waiting for the River to dispatch the ghoul, feeling that with every second he stood there, he fell deeper and deeper into a trap.

Finally, Bastian felt the ghoul sink back past the Second Veil. He let go of the bindings and reached back for his body. The mortal world returned to him in a freezing snap. He fell to the ground, the ghoul still twined in his arms, and gagged. Something rotten had gotten in his mouth. He rolled away and retched.

"Are you trying to hug them to death now?" Harold asked.

Bastian looked up just briefly enough to see Harold staggering up the hill. The flashes of light had calmed behind him.

"Here, I think I have some peppermint in here. It should help," Harold said, reaching into his pack.

"The others . . ." Bastian managed.

"Are mopping up the stragglers. They got 'em all."

He handed Bastian a few crumpled leaves.

"Chew," Harold said. Bastian did so. It didn't get the taste of rotten flesh out of his mouth, but it helped cover it. Slightly.

The others began walking up the hill. Bastian pushed himself up; they were too far away to see if they were hurt, but at least they were all still alive.

"We gotta go," he said.

"What? What's wrong?" Harold asked.

"The shadowman."

"Is he here?" Harold asked, his voice breaking.

Bastian glanced around. His comrades were trudging up the hill, battle-worn but victorious. Low fog from the smudge bombs rippled between the tombstones and fallen corpses.

"No," Bastian said. "No, he isn't."

At least, not yet.

58

"Whoa," Robyn said when she neared them. "Did you psychowomp that?" She gestured to the corpse.

"What is she talking about?" Andromeda asked.

"Long story," Bastian replied. He looked to Finlay, who was staring at the ghoul with fear in his eyes. Bastian knew the sight just brought him back to when he was almost lost to the underworld. "Come on, we have to go."

Andromeda stayed put. "Go where? The Door isn't here yet . . . though the ghouls have all been banished." She said the last bit accusingly, as if he had something to do with the Door's lateness.

In a way, he knew, he did. Bastian wanted to throw up again, but this time from nerves more than the foul taste in his mouth.

Where was the shadowman?

Where was the Door back?

"This doesn't feel right," Bastian said. "That was too easy."

"Hah! Says the one who ran and hid while we took care of the rest," Andromeda said.

"No," Bastian said. "This is a trap."

Robyn immediately snapped to attention.

"The shadowman?" she asked.

"The *what*?" Finlay asked. He'd finally torn his eyes away from the ghoul at Bastian's feet, and looked around nervously.

"Evil spirit that's stalking Bastian," Robyn clarified. "No one's been able to banish it. Not even the adults."

Finlay's eyes went wide. Even Andromeda seemed to take it seriously.

"But the battle's over?" she said, though it was definitely a question.

"*Oh, children,*" came a terrifying, snarling voice. The shadowman congealed from the shadows, his porcelain face a white moon in the dim merelight, his four arms folded almost casually behind his back. "*Our battle is only just beginning.*"

"Run!" Bastian yelled.

"Where?" Robyn asked. Because the Door still hadn't appeared, and for a horrible moment Bastian wondered if maybe it wouldn't. Maybe this had been a trap all along.

"*There is no use running, Sebastian,*" the shadowman said. "*Death waits for no one, and your death has been so, so long in the making. You may have fooled me once, but I will not be fooled again.*"

He spread two of his arms wide, welcoming.

"*Come, embrace your fate. No one else needs to die because of you.*" He looked to Finlay. Finlay stepped back and cowered beside Bastian. If Bastian wasn't so set on what he was about to do, he would have been slightly grateful that Finlay was no longer so scared of him. At least, less scared of him than he was of the monster before them.

Before Bastian could accept the shadowman's offer, Harold stepped in front of him.

"He's not going anywhere," Harold said.

"Harold, don't—" Bastian began, trying to move Harold aside.

"Yeah," Robyn said. She stepped up beside Harold, flames burning in her hands. "You'll have to get through us first."

It would have been touching, if not for the fact that Bastian knew without a doubt that his friends didn't stand a chance. Besides, the shadowman was right. He *was* done running. He *was* done letting others get hurt because of him. He wasn't willing to go down without a fight.

But it was his fight, and his alone. He wouldn't let anyone else fight it for him. Not anymore.

"Guys—"

Before he could finish his protest, a fireball shot toward the shadowman. Not from Robyn, but from Finlay.

Bastian watched in horror as the flames billowed up and around the shadowman in a blinding inferno . . . and the shadowman stepped out of it, completely untouched.

"*Very well,*" the shadowman said with a pleased chuckle. "*If you wish to play, we will play.*"

Fast as a whip, the shadowman scuttled forward, suddenly spiderlike. His porcelain face split down the middle, revealing his long, snaking tongue.

"Run!" Bastian yelled again. He grabbed Robyn's and Harold's hands to pull them away. Finlay and Andromeda were already careening down the hill at full speed, tossing fireballs and Ætheric bindings at the shadowman as they ran. Blue lights and streaks of fire illuminated the night. Graves exploded in bursts of stone and dirt.

The shadowman darted between the blasts effortlessly.

His tongue lashed out and smashed into a tombstone right by Robyn's head. She ducked as the tombstone exploded and sent her own fireball back, but the shadowman had already gone, darting off lightning fast to lunge toward Harold.

Harold tossed a handful of smudge bombs at it, sending up clouds of purple and blue and pink smoke. The shadowman leaped from the haze, landing on a tombstone a dozen yards away, right in front of Finlay and Andromeda.

Andromeda screamed in fear and anger, and lashed forward with her hand. The rain around her transformed into shards of ice that shot like deadly daggers toward the shadowman. It just laughed and *twisted* its body, becoming nothing but shadow for a brief moment, just long enough for the shards to pass through it.

"You'll have to do better than that, stupid children," the shadowman taunted, lashing out his tongue. Finlay pushed Andromeda to the side—the tongue slashed against the ground right between them.

Bastian's heart burned. Once more, his friends—and even his enemy!— were fighting for him. While he ran around, unable to conjure a single fireball, unable to summon a single binding chain.

He knew his only strength lay in the underworld, but before he could even try, Harold called out.

"Over there!"

He pointed, and there, between two tombstones, right at the edge of the cliff, was the Door.

Finlay and Andromeda darted toward it, casting bursts of fire and ice behind them as they ran. Bastian and Robyn and Harold weren't far behind.

Bastian glanced over his shoulder.

The shadowman wasn't running after them.

He perched on the tombstone, watching. And for some reason, Bastian got the horrible feeling that he was smiling.

Andromeda and Finlay reached the Door. They leaped through.

"*I grow tired of your running, Sebastian,*" the shadowman said. "*It is time for you to come to me.*"

Heart pounding, Bastian and his friends reached the Door. Robyn leaped through first, and Harold pushed Bastian through.

Bastian landed in the courtyard beside his friends and turned back.

Just in time to see Harold appear in the doorframe.

Just in time to see the shadowman's tongue lash *through* Harold's chest.

Harold's eyes went wide in shock.

The tongue snapped back, through the Door, and Harold toppled forward, into Bastian's lap.

The Door slammed shut.

Harold didn't get up.

59

"Harold?" Bastian yelled, patting the side of Harold's face. "Harold, wake up!"

But Harold didn't move, even when Bastian shook him and cried out for help. Andromeda paced back and forth babbling questions that no one was listening to, like *What was that what happened is he okay?*

Robyn dropped down to Bastian's side and began rooting around through Harold's satchel.

"He has to have something in here," she said, tears in her eyes. Bastian's own vision was swimming as she pulled out vials and smudge bombs. He glanced around the courtyard; Finlay was no longer there. But he didn't have time to process that. Robyn pulled out a vial of smelling salts and wafted it under Harold's nose.

He didn't stir.

"Is he still breathing?" Andromeda asked.

Robyn hovered the vial beneath Harold's nose—it frosted slightly. He was alive. But only just barely.

"Why isn't he waking up, then? If he's alive, why isn't he waking up?" Andromeda's voice had risen to a fever pitch.

Bastian couldn't move, couldn't speak. He just sat there with Harold's head in his lap, feeling the dark world close down around him. *It's time for you to come to me.*

The shadowman had taken Harold.

He had done the one thing that would ensure Bastian would follow. The one thing to ensure that only Bastian could help.

The shadowman had Harold's soul trapped in the underworld.

Robyn continued rooting around Harold's satchel, but Bastian knew it wouldn't do any good. He had to descend.

"Stand aside," came Madame Ardea's voice.

Bastian looked behind him to see Madame Ardea and Finlay striding into the courtyard.

Robyn and Andromeda leapt back, but Bastian didn't leave Harold's side. Harold hadn't left his. *This is all my fault . . .*

Madame Ardea knelt at Harold's side and placed her hands at his temples. Faint blue light swirled from her palms, rippling over Harold's frozen face. Hope bubbled in the back of Bastian's chest, a tiny spark in the overwhelming sadness.

He wanted to believe she could fix him. She was a master of Summoning. Maybe she could pull his soul back. Maybe she could save him. But Bastian knew deep down she couldn't.

Only he could go where others could not.

The seconds stretched like hours. Harold didn't stir. Only his chest moved, slowly rising and falling.

Finally, with a huff of frustration, Madame Ardea sat back. "Finlay, please run to the laboratories. Find Professor Pliny and tell him we have a depossession on our hands. Andromeda, go find Nurse Joanne and tell her the same."

Andromeda and Finlay hurried off, leaving only Robyn and Bastian at Harold's side. Madame Ardea stood and gestured. Light swirled around

Harold, and he lifted gently off the ground. His arms trailed at his sides, and his legs hung limp.

He looked dead.

"Is he going to be okay?" a distraught Bastian asked Madame Ardea.

She didn't answer right away. She stepped over and placed a gentle hand on Harold's floating forehead. She looked at Harold like he was her own son.

When she finally faced Bastian, her face was stoic, but he saw the rage and sadness battling behind her eyes.

"You will tell me everything that has happened," she said. "Every. Single. Thing. His very soul depends on it."

❧☠❧

Bastian sat by the fire in his bedroom, a quilt over his shoulders and an untouched mug of tea on the table before him.

Every time he looked at the tea, he wanted to start crying all over again. Because Harold didn't brew it. Harold wasn't there.

His body was in the same bed Aunt Dahlia had occupied, surrounded by herbs and crystals and smoldering incense, while Nurse Joanne hovered over him, administering every tonic and infusion in her and Professor Pliny's storehouse.

His body was there.

But his soul was trapped, according to Madame Ardea, somewhere deep in the underworld. She'd also expressly forbidden Bastian from taking action.

You will only make it worse, she said. *You would only be giving the creature what it wants.*

But Bastian had already made this worse. He made everything worse. Aunt Dahlia had been hurt because he'd moved in with her. Andromeda had lost her arm just for knowing him. Finlay had nearly been lost to the underworld because of him, and Harold *had* been trapped in the underworld because of him. And he wondered, with a horrible twist of guilt, if his parents had died because of him. Had *they* gotten in the way of the shadowman, tried to keep him from killing Bastian? He remembered the conversation between his aunt and Madame Ardea. *There can only be one outcome. The last seven years have shown us as much.* They'd died seven years ago.

Had that been his fault, too?

"You can't do this to yourself, Bastian," Robyn said. She perched on the other chair, arms around her knees and a strangely soft expression in her face. She'd barely said anything since coming back from the field. "It's not your fault."

He didn't look at her. He just stared into the flames. It *was* his fault, though. And he knew that no matter what Ardea or the others tried, they weren't going to be able to get Harold back. It was like she said, what felt like years ago—*no one comes back from the underworld.* At least, not unless they were aided by a Psychopomp like Bastian. He could bring Harold back with him.

Or, if the shadowman wanted him so badly, he could trade places.

"You heard what the shadowman said," Bastian croaked. "He did this so I wouldn't run away anymore. He did this because of me. Harold is going to die because . . ." He choked on the words. "He's going to die because of me."

"He's not going to die," Robyn said firmly. "Madame Ardea and the others—"

"Can't do anything!" Bastian yelled. "I'm the only one who can help him. You know that, Robyn. I . . . I have to go down there. I have to get him back."

Robyn didn't say anything. Not for a long time.

Finally, she sighed.

"I know," she said, a new resolve in her eyes. "But we can't do it here."

60

Bastian tried to fight her on it, tried to get her to back down. But this was Robyn. When she set her mind to something, she did it.

Together, they crept through the halls of Gallowgate. Bastian had expected everyone to be on high alert, for the halls to be filled with patrolling ghosts and sentry skeletons and huddles of shocked and whispering students. But the passages they crept through were eerily silent.

Had no one heard of what happened on their hunt?

They left through an exit next to the greenhouses—the main study hall was too risky, even at this time of night—and the scent of herbs and dirt just made another pang rip through Bastian's heart. It smelled like Harold.

I'll bring you back, Bastian promised. *No matter what.*

The grounds, too, were oddly still. A few will-o'-the-wisps danced through the woods as they hurried down the cobbled path to the shore, but that was it.

"This feels so strange," Robyn said when they reached the iron archway leading to the walkway across the lake. "Doesn't it?"

It did. It had been only a few months since Bastian had run under this gate, running from the very creature that he was now running *toward.* He took one last look up at the manor. The high arched roofs, the twisted turrets and towers, the glimmering stained-glass windows . . . it all looked more familiar, more like home, than Aunt Dahlia's house ever had.

He wondered if he would ever see it again.

Before he could change his mind, he stepped under the archway.

Cold rippled over him as they passed through the wards.

When he looked back up to the manor, it was nothing but derelict ruins.

Mist curled in as they ran across the walkway, their footsteps echoing in the otherwise-silent air. Halfway across, Bastian froze.

"Do you hear that?" he asked.

There were other footsteps in the mist. Footsteps running toward them.

"It's coming from the manor," Robyn whispered.

Given the number of terrible ghosts they'd had to fight within Gallowgate's walls, the thought wasn't assuring. Bastian summoned a small ball of blue that he could cast as a binding, while Robyn conjured twin flames.

The fog swirled. Bastian's heart pounded in his ears.

And right when he was about to cast the bindings, the murky shape in the gloom solidified.

Bastian didn't know whether to sigh in relief or stay on guard.

"What are you doing out here?" he asked.

Finlay looked down to his feet.

"I, um . . . I saw you two running down here. I figured you were trying to go face that thing. That shadowman. And I wanted to try and help."

"After you've given him the cold shoulder the last few weeks?" Robyn asked.

Finlay looked to Bastian, then away again. In that one look, Bastian saw the clear plea in his eyes: *Forgive me.*

"I was scared," Finlay admitted. "I . . . I didn't know what—"

"It's okay," Bastian interjected. "Really. I would have done the same if it had happened to me." *The first time I fell into the underworld, I ran out of my school screaming.* "If anything, I should be apologizing to you. I didn't mean to take you into the underworld. I didn't even know that I could."

Finlay met his eyes again. Bastian's heart fluttered. Finlay opened his mouth to say something, but Robyn cut him off.

"This is cute and all, but we really don't have time for this," she said. "We also don't need anyone else getting hurt. You should go back inside."

Finlay shook his head. "No. I'm not going to let you do this on your own."

"If the shadowman comes after us, you'll be killed," Bastian said. He was torn—part of him really didn't want Finlay to put himself in danger. The rest of him really wanted him around.

"I'm one of the best Summoners in our class," Finlay said, drawing his shoulders back. "You need me. I might be able to help."

Bastian and Robyn looked at each other. She shrugged. When Bastian looked to Finlay, he knew the boy wouldn't be dissuaded. He also knew they were wasting precious time.

"Okay," Bastian said. "But if I tell you to run, you run. Both of you. Got it?"

They nodded.

And even though they were heading toward their inevitable doom, Bastian felt a strange warmth in his chest knowing that they were both behind him.

They stopped on the other side of the lake, managing to find a small hillock covered in tombstones and fog that was just out of sight of the manor. Finlay cast a protection circle around them, and Bastian cast another, smaller circle within it, this one glowing purple with dancing glyphs and runes shimmering in the sky.

Finlay gave him an appraising look.

"It's for descending," Bastian quickly explained. "It protects even in the underworld."

But will it protect me from the shadowman? No, that isn't important—the only important thing is getting Harold out of there.

"If I die—" Bastian began.

"You're not going to die," Robyn interjected. She stood just outside the circle, twin flames now dancing above her head as she scanned the horizon for trouble.

"But if I do," Bastian pushed. "Tell my aunt I love her."

Finlay stared at him for a long moment. Then he laughed, trying to turn it into a cough.

"What?" Bastian demanded.

"I'm sorry," Finlay said. "It's just . . ."

"It's just *so* cliché, dude," Robyn said. "But yes, if you die we'll tell her you loved her. But again—you aren't dying. Not on my watch."

"Or on mine," Finlay said. "You'll be fine. Doubt is the seed of death."

He stood within the circle, with Bastian. And maybe it was the circle's magic, or Bastian's imagination, but he swore it was thirty degrees warmer in there because of it.

Bastian nodded and lay back on the grass. The ground was soft and wet beneath him, instantly soaking through his clothes. But where he was going, the cold and the damp wouldn't bother him. There, the cold and the damp of the mortal world would feel like a California beach.

He looked once more at his friends. Robyn, watching the hills. Finlay, watching him.

Finlay took Bastian's hand, just briefly. His touch was warm, and the look in his eyes made Bastian's breath catch. "Good luck," Finlay whispered.

Bastian nodded and closed his eyes.

Steadied his breathing.

Forced away the fear and the doubt.

Focused on Harold.

Just Harold.

I'll save you, Bastian thought.

And he descended.

Fog billowed around him as the mortal world bled into the *terra sine forma*. His friends faded from view, as did the comforting blue ring of Finlay's protection circle. All that remained in this rolling, gray-washed landscape was the glimmering purple of Bastian's own circle.

He looked around him. There, on the horizon, was Gallowgate. It was impossible to miss, even in the underworld. The hulking Gothic manor pierced through the gloom like a black beast, and threads of blue Ætheric energy crisscrossed and spiraled in a dome around it. The wards burned bright blue, like a sapphire sun. All that power . . . even to him, it felt like a beacon.

"I'm here!" Bastian called out. His voice echoed in the otherwise-empty landscape. Where was the shadowman? Where was Harold?

For a moment, Bastian's heart dropped. What if it was already too late? What if Harold was already lost?

Doubt is the seed of death, Finlay had said.

"Where are you?" Bastian yelled. "Don't tell me you're scared!"

"Oh, I'm not scared, young Sebastian," came a voice through the mists. It wasn't the shadowman. "Not in the slightest."

Bastian turned.

There, translucent and fading, floated Harold.

And behind him, a serene smile on his face, was Virgil.

61

Bastian nearly jerked back to his body from shock.

"No," he gasped. "No—what are you doing here? I thought . . ."

"That I was confined to the academy?" Virgil asked. "You thought what I told you to think."

"But what . . . why?"

Harold's eyes fluttered open. When he saw Bastian standing there, he cried out, "Run!"

Virgil snapped his fingers. A pulse of purple light washed over Harold, and his eyes fluttered back shut.

Bastian's thoughts raced.

"The shadowman . . ."

"The *maleficarum*," Virgil corrected. "It will come. When it is called. But for now, Sebastian, I wanted us to talk. Just the two of us."

He floated forward, leaving Harold suspended and comatose behind him

Bastian flinched back. But Virgil didn't pass through his circle. No, he reached out a transparent hand and caressed the glimmer of purple approvingly. Maybe it was Bastian's imagination, but Virgil appeared more opaque, more solid, down here. Sparks rained down under his fingertips.

"Your father would be proud of you," Virgil stated. "You were a quick student, Sebastian. Not as quick as him, of course. But none were. Your father, he was one of a kind."

"What's going on?" Bastian asked. "Why are you here?"

Virgil smirked. "As I said, you aren't *quite* as quick as him. I'm admittedly shocked that you've outlasted the maleficarum so long. Very few can. Perhaps it is mere luck. Or perhaps there is more to you than meets the eye."

"It was you," Bastian gasped, realization dawning. "You were the one who summoned the sha—the maleficarum?"

"Not quite," Virgil said. "But I must say, learning of its existence turned out to be quite fortuitous."

"But you said you could call it."

"No, Sebastian. I said it would come if it was called. *You* are the beacon it is drawn to. You are the one it was created to kill. No other—not even the one who created it—can control it now. That circle you stand in, well—it shields you from its view. For now. I suppose you could continue hiding from it, should you wish. Go back to your body, come up with a better plan. You have all the time in the world, but your friend here . . . You know what happens to those who are in the underworld too long, Sebastian. Unless you do as you're told, and quickly, you won't have much of your friend to bring back."

Bastian could have sworn that Harold had grown even fainter during Virgil's speech.

"Just let him go," Bastian said. "He has nothing to do with this."

He balled his fists, and tiny purple lights flared around his knuckles. Virgil just smiled.

"I'm afraid not. It took a great deal of coercing to get the maleficarum to give him to me. No, your friend will not return to the living until you have done what I need you to do."

"You want me dead?" Bastian asked. "Why? All those nights I was alone with you . . . if you wanted to kill me, why didn't you do it then?"

"Kill you?" Virgil asked. "Is that what you really think this is all about?"

Bastian stared. "It came after me at my aunt's . . . it's been hunting me ever since."

Virgil shook his head. Bastian kept looking at Harold. He had to get his friend out of here. There had to be a way. If only . . .

An idea sparked. He didn't know if it would work, but he had to try.

"I do not want you dead," Virgil said. "When you told me it was hunting you, I knew I had an opportunity. An opportunity not only to train you quickly without raising your suspicion, but to get you to fulfill your destiny."

"I don't understand . . ."

"Think about what you *are*. What only *you* can do."

"I can descend . . ." Bastian whispered.

"Precisely. The maleficarum wants you to pass through the Final Veil. As do I. But where the beast wants you to fade away, I, my dear boy, want you to *return*."

Bastian could only stare. None of this made any sense. The maleficarum wanted him dead, and so did Virgil, but Virgil wanted him to come back? What for?

Once more, Virgil seemed to read his mind.

"I knew you would never pass the Final Veil unless coerced or dragged," Virgil said. "You are far from my ideal subject. But when you appeared in my study, I knew your father had died, and our plan had failed. So I had to prime you to be his replacement."

"My father," Bastian gasped. "What does he have to do with this?"

Virgil smiled wide and spread his arms. "Everything, young Sebastian. He and I had grand ideas. Ideas that would have changed the world. Sadly,

306

your father was too weak to bring them to fruition. But *you* can continue his work, can follow in his grand footsteps. I just need you to go past the Final Veil. I have a . . . friend . . . waiting for me. I would go myself, but I'm afraid that without a body, I am of no use to him." Bastian could have sworn that Virgil's eyes turned to shadows at the mention of his *friend*. Even in the underworld, Bastian shivered.

"Why would I help you?" Bastian said. He looked to Harold, knowing full well his words were weak.

"Because I know how to retrieve what you want the most," Virgil replied. "If they are truly dead, I can help you bring back your family."

62

The circle wavered, just barely, just for a moment, as shock rippled through Bastian.

After his studies, after Harold's grave warning, he'd given up on the hope that he could see his parents ever again.

"Yes, young Sebastian," Virgil continued, his voice cajoling despite the darkness in his eyes. "There is more to your power than treading the lands of the dead. Under my guidance, your father came to understand this. You can do so much, Sebastian. With me guiding you, we can perform *miracles*."

Bastian's head swum.

Did Virgil truly mean that he could bring back his parents? Was that what Virgil and Bastian's dad had been working on?

Under my guidance . . .

Virgil's words sparked a note of fear in Bastian. He knew that there were spirits in the underworld that could possess you, but he had a feeling Virgil was speaking about more than a wraith, dangerous though they might be.

He had a feeling that whatever *miracles* Virgil was talking about, they weren't the kind he'd want to enact. He also knew that his dad would never have done something like that. Not unless he'd been coerced or possessed.

"Who is this friend of yours?" Bastian asked.

For the first time in their meeting, Virgil's confidence faltered. Just for a moment, he actually looked afraid.

"His name is forbidden," Virgil said. "To know his name is to know madness."

All this time, Bastian had thought that the maleficarum and all those ghosts were wanting to take him to some*one*. They kept mentioning their master. But what if it was a some*thing*?

Realization dawned.

If Bastian passed through the Final Veil and came back, he had no doubt that he would be bringing this *friend* with him. Is that what Virgil had wanted his dad to do?

Harold flickered.

Bastian pushed the hundred questions aside. He had to save his friend. And he would have only one chance to do so.

"I know you have questions," Virgil said softly. "Of course you do. All you need to do is lower the circle, and you will find all the answers you've ever dreamed of."

Bastian swallowed.

He knew what he had to do.

"Okay," he said. "I'll do it."

Virgil's smile widened.

Bastian reached out to the Æther and dropped the circle.

The purple shield fell in a curtain of sparks, a soft hiss. A second later, he heard the unmistakable, victorious wail of the shadowman. The familiar black-ink smudge appeared in the darkness, a few feet away. Tendrils coalesced and congealed into the spindly shape of the shadowman . . . the maleficarum.

"You can take me," Bastian said. He looked over to Harold. "But you aren't hurting anyone else."

309

With a snap of the Æther, he summoned a protection circle around Harold's floating form, ensconcing him in purple light.

"No!" Virgil yelled. But it was too late. Virgil himself said the circle was the only thing keeping Bastian safe from the maleficarum—it would hide Harold just as well.

"Stupid boy," Virgil said as the shadowman stalked forward. "You only delay the inevitable."

"Maybe," Bastian said. "But I'm done delaying this."

He reached out and called forth the River.

Black water surged up from the lake, seething around his legs as he forced the River toward the maleficarum. But now that he was no longer warded by his protection circle, the maleficarum wasn't waiting around.

While Virgil growled about Bastian ruining everything, the maleficarum attacked. It scuttled forward on six legs, no longer pretending to be human. Its masked face was split wide, its tongue lashing, hissing like an angry serpent.

Bastian conjured his own fireball, a purple billow of Ætheric flame that, he knew, only existed in the underworld. He thrust it at the maleficarum. The creature darted to the side, and the flame hissed into the surging waters, but Bastian had another conjured before the first dissipated. This time, when he threw it, it hit one of the maleficarum's arms. And unlike the flames Robyn had wielded in the mortal world, when this fireball hit the maleficarum, it left a mark.

The maleficarum screamed in pain as the flames burned through its arm, searing it off entirely.

"*You will pay!*" the maleficarum screamed as it lunged toward Bastian. "*I will rip you apart!*"

"No!" Virgil yelled out. He floated above the River. "We need him in one piece! If you destroy him, you ruin everything!"

But the maleficarum wasn't listening. The monster was out for blood. Its tongue lashed forward, smacking Bastian in the chest and sending him into the River.

Water thrashed around him, tumbling him in hissing static darkness. He tried to swim to the surface, but he couldn't find which way was up, and distantly, he was aware of the maleficarum stalking toward him. He gave a great kick, and managed to surface just for a moment, just long enough to see Virgil screaming at the maleficarum, while the monster thrashed its tongue this way and that through the water, trying to find Bastian.

Downstream, only a few yards away, was the gray-black wall of mist that signaled the Second Veil. The maleficarum lunged toward him, and Bastian reached out with the Æther. But he didn't send his bindings around the maleficarum.

Right before Bastian sank back under the roiling waves, he snared on to Virgil.

If he was going under, he was taking the construct with him.

Virgil yelled out, and the maleficarum followed like a mindless dog, screaming as it chased Bastian through the waves, toward the Veil.

Then Bastian felt the cold chill of the Second Veil wash over him, and everything went silent as the grave.

63

Black trees of gnarled flesh pierced from the churning waves, tumbling past him in the blur. The water was quicker here, hungrier. He felt the Third Veil nearing, and knew that if he didn't act fast, he would fall past it and begin to forget who he was, and why he was here.

With a great wrench of willpower he forced the River to subside, just a little, just enough for him to stand. The waters still tugged at his feet, still dragged him onward, but he tried to hold strong. Virgil silently struggled against Bastian's bindings a few feet away, but the magic snared him tight. He would go where Bastian led.

Farther upstream, the maleficarum rose, its legs elongating so it cleared the water by a good yard. It watched him with that split porcelain doll face, its tongue lashing silently through the waves.

Bastian flung a ball of purple fire at the maleficarum. The beast dodged to the side, and the fireball hit one of the nearby trees. Rather than burning or disintegrating, the tree began to writhe silently in pain. Bastian realized these weren't trees at all, but monsters of charred skin and rolling eyes and reaching arms, all horribly contorted in the shape of trees. All in agony, and in complete silence. His stomach churned.

You cannot run from me, echoed a voice in Bastian's mind. The malefi-carum. *I know your thoughts. Your passions. Your fears. I know how to make you beg for death.*

The maleficarum stood on its two hind legs, folding back in on itself into the semblance of a man, its pale white porcelain eyes staring at him as its tongue curled around it like a serpent tasting the air.

This land will devour your screams, it said. *It will rip them from your soul, until you are nothing but a husk. Until you cannot even cry out for mercy.*

Bastian took a step back as the maleficarum approached. Something wet and cold snaked around his arms and legs. The tree. It had grabbed him with its slimy bark, holding him in place.

The maleficarum reached into the heavy shadows of its own chest as it neared.

It pulled out a small rectangular object.

A photo frame.

It was the photo Bastian had dropped into the marsh when he first arrived at Gallowgate: him and his parents by the fountain, laughing. Except now, as the maleficarum neared, the picture changed. His parents' faces contorted in pain and fear. They screamed silently, as the child version of himself cried out.

You have caused so much pain, the maleficarum said. *Give in, and I will take you to the ones you've lost. Give in, and the pain will end. But should you continue to defy me . . .*

The maleficarum cracked the photo in two and tossed it into the waves. He knew it was impossible, but Bastian swore he could hear the photo screaming. The message was clear: Even in death, I can cause suffering.

It is time to stop running, the maleficarum said. *You are alone. You have lost. It is time to face your destiny.*

Stop running. The words echoed in his head. But he didn't hear the maleficarum's voice anymore. He heard his parents.

He had been running ever since his parents had been killed.

Until Gallowgate, he'd felt hunted and alone and scared.

It wasn't just the maleficarum, but all the horrors of life that had scared him—the fears of losing his aunt, of being beaten up. Of being different. Of always being alone.

But as he stood in the bowels of the underworld, facing a monster that haunted his dreams, he knew he wasn't alone. He never had been, and he surely wasn't now. He'd carried his parents' memory and the magic of their legacy in his veins without even knowing it. And now, he had the strongest friends he could have asked for, friends who had become his family. Friends who were counting on him to come back.

He wasn't going to run.

And he wasn't going to go down without a fight. He just had to convince the maleficarum and Virgil otherwise. Or else this would never work.

He forced his gaze down, tried to make his face look defeated. It wasn't as hard to act as it might have been before. Virgil had taught him to quell his emotions, and despite his resolve, doubt still gnawed at his heart. He bowed his head and nodded in defeat.

The maleficarum closed the space between them as the tree relinquished its grip. The tree squirmed behind Bastian—for a moment, Bastian wondered if it was readying to ensnare him again. Then he realized it was trying to get away from the maleficarum.

The maleficarum grabbed Bastian's arms and lifted him high above the water. Lifted him so Bastian could stare down its endless gullet.

Very good, Sebastian, the maleficarum said. *Your destiny awaits.*

It wrapped its tongue around Bastian's body like a rope, and carried him down the River. Bastian didn't struggle. Didn't fight. He held on to the threads that bound Virgil, and together, the three of them descended deeper into the underworld than Bastian had ever dared to go.

64

When the *Memorius Velamentum* passed over him, Bastian was blinded by its brilliance.

Where the first and second levels of the underworld were gloomy and dark, the third level, the *terra sine memoria*, was the purest, brightest white.

Because the third level was blanketed in snow.

Pure, crystal white snow glittered as far as he could see, disappearing into a pale blue sky that looked like the hottest part of a flame. Large crystals the size of humans and houses glimmered in the glow, each of them clear and pure as ice, as diamonds. The River snaked silently between the crystal towers, the only darkness in the otherwise radiant landscape. The malefi-carum sloshed downstream. Here, Bastian saw other shapes in the water. Shards of crystal, floating with the current, like small ice floes.

One passed by, and he saw that it wasn't just clear ice. Images moved within it. Images of a smiling family at supper, shifting to a graduation ceremony, to a table laden with presents.

Memories. These were memories.

As the water lapped at his ankles, which just brushed the top of the waves, he saw small fragments like glitter washing off of him, coalescing in the stream, becoming small diamonds.

He knew, distantly, that the River was already taking his memories. And now that he was outside of his circle, there was nothing he could do to prevent it. He had to act, and he had to act fast.

With a wrench of power, he forced Virgil down into the River.

The construct might not have had a soul, but it was a being of memory and thought and magic. Here, memories were what the River craved most.

There wasn't a splash, wasn't a scream. Virgil submerged under the water without a sound. Purple light flashed and bubbled beneath the surface as the construct struggled to break free. But he had taught Bastian well, and Bastian didn't let go of the power.

It wasn't foam that frothed up to the water's surface, however. But crystals. Thousands of tiny shards of ice that floated up and swirled together, forming small floes that floated downstream. Bastian glanced at Virgil's memories, just for a moment.

In one of those shards, he saw his father's face reflected back. His father as a boy, about Bastian's age, smiling and laughing in the psychopomp's study. Bastian's heart burned. *What happened to you?* he wondered, just as he felt the question slip away.

The maleficarum looked at the space where Virgil had once been, the collection of ice floes that drifted downstream and gathered against the banks, mingling with other crystalline towers or forming new ones. Within seconds, all that was left of Virgil were shards of ice.

But . . .

Who was Virgil in the first place? The question wafted idly through Bastian's brain. He vaguely remembered Virgil being a teacher. Or was he the bus driver back home? He couldn't remember, and he also couldn't force himself to believe it was that important.

The maleficarum continued downstream.

This will all be over soon, Sebastian, it said. *All your struggles, all your fighting, all that pain. All of it could have been avoided. But soon, soon you will struggle no more.*

316

Struggles? Bastian wondered as another crystalline shard floated away from him. *What struggles?*

There were so many beautiful ice crystals around him, and the otherworldly sky shone so bright he couldn't imagine feeling anything but peaceful. It was best to just let this strange creature guide him downstream. That was where he was meant to be, after all.

The boy looked down at one of the larger crystals floating beside him.

In it, he saw a great, Gothic manor, surrounded by trees and glimmering lights. And then he saw people reflected within it. A boy with a big goofy smile and a strange mask like a bird's head in his hand. A girl with fierce eyes and pink streaked through her hair. Another boy, with wavy brown hair and glasses and a cautious, open smile.

And as the crystal began to float away, the boy in the River felt something grip his heart.

Meaning.

A meaning not to succumb to the descent. A meaning to fight back.

The crystal began to dissolve—not into the rushing River, but back into Bastian's body.

Harold.

Robyn.

Finlay.

They were all waiting for him. They were why he was down here in the first place. Fighting. For them.

The meaning filled him with warmth, a warmth that the icy floes of the *terra sine memoria* couldn't bleed. And with it, he felt his power, his plan. He held on to it with all his might. It wasn't time to act. Not yet. Not yet.

Ahead of them rose the Final Veil. A curtain of glimmering crystalline

317

mist that fell not down, but *up*. Disappearing into the blinding heavens above.

And maybe it was Bastian's imagination, but he swore he heard it, even though it should have been impossible. He swore, deep within him, as if it came from his own heart, he heard the musical billow of wind chimes. Calling him. Telling him that beyond that Veil, everything would be okay.

When the maleficarum was only a few feet away from that final curtain, the Veil from which no one—no matter what Virgil had said—could return, Bastian acted.

He reached for the Æther. It pulsed through him, stronger here than he'd ever felt it, as if he were closer to the source than ever before. It hummed through his veins, burned like beautiful lightning, as purple flames billowed up around his body.

The maleficarum recoiled. Its tongue snapped back as Bastian burned, brighter than a star, brighter than the dazzling ice floes, floating above the River and facing down his foe. With another lash of power, Bastian wrapped the maleficarum in cords of burning purple.

The maleficarum screamed inside Bastian's mind, but Bastian paid it no heed. He tightened the bindings, forced the beast down into the River. The shadowman struggled. This close to the Final Veil, it was stronger, too. It pushed against the bindings, strained against Bastian's might.

An arm snapped through, and it whipped out toward Bastian like a lasso. But Bastian raised his hand, and purple flames billowed before him. Where the maleficarum's arm hit, the fire disintegrated flesh.

Bastian wrapped more threads around the maleficarum, binding it in a cocoon of purple.

If you destroy me, you will never see your mother! the maleficarum screamed. *You will lose her forever!*

The words passed through Bastian. He could never lose his family. He carried them with him. Always.

With a force of power, he shoved the creature down into the waves.

He felt it struggle. Saw it writhe in the darkness below, illuminated by the strands of Bastian's magic. He saw it drift downstream.

He felt it pass through the Veil.

For the longest time he floated there, surrounded by silence, by forgotten memories, holding on to the threads of power that faded as the maleficarum . . . dissolved. As whatever happened beyond that Final Veil happened to it.

And then, when the final threads faded, Bastian let the power go.

He reached down into the River and picked up a shard of ice, a crystalline memory of his friends, of his family. He held it close to his chest, and with their faces guiding him, he trudged back toward life.

65

"Can you believe all this?" Robyn asked, leaning over Bastian to grab an éclair.

Weeks had passed, and the end of the term had finally dawned. The dining hall was transformed for the Naming of the Guard. Silver and metallic black streamers arched over the windows and spun across the ceiling, while jeweled bats flocked and swirled with their wind chime wings. Everything was decorated in the colors and sigils of the four disciplines: emerald green serpents for Alchemists, arched scorpions on goldenrod for Conjurers, dusty blue spiders for Summoners, and pale red moths for Necromancers. The flames in the hearths pulsed between the four colors, and on the tables, the silver dishes were laden with foods fit for royalty. The amount of delicacies and decorations put all their other meals to shame.

Everyone within the hall was wearing their best. No burn marks on the Conjurers' jackets, no rips in the shawls of the Necromancers, no ectoplasmic stains on the robes of the Summoners. Heck, even the Alchemists had managed to find aprons that weren't covered in dirt or soot.

"Always was my favorite part of the year," Harold said. He helped himself to another round of dessert—chocolate mousse and a decadent three-tiered cheesecake.

Bastian grinned and politely declined the ghost that came past with a tray laden with freshly baked cookies. He'd already had half a dozen. Any more, and he was going to explode.

He and Robyn just watched Harold mow down his food with fervent abandon. Bastian could have sworn that Harold's appetite had tripled since coming back from the dead. Then again, if he'd been trapped in the underworld, he probably would have been relishing every mortal delight he could, too.

They had tried their best to keep what happened out in the moors secret. Which, of course, meant that everyone knew about it the next day. Both what happened to Harold, and how—precisely—Bastian had gotten him back. So much for keeping Descending a secret.

Once the maleficarum and Virgil were gone, Bastian had returned to the *terra sine forma* to find Harold still floating in his protection circle, though he was nearly transparent. Just as with Finlay, bringing him back was more an instinct than a knowledge. Bastian had grabbed Harold's arm and reached for the thread connecting him to his own body and pulled them both through.

He'd woken up in the marshes, to the embraces of Finlay and Robyn. Harold had woken up in the nurse's ward, an event that had—according to Nurse Joanne—scared her to death (though she of course was already dead). By the time Bastian and the others had run to the ward, Harold was awake and gulping tea and, although a little pallid, excitedly telling Madame Ardea about being in the underworld, and Bastian's daring rescue.

He didn't seem to mind his near-death experience nearly as much as Finlay had.

Madame Ardea's expression had been grim but somehow mildly amused by Harold's tale. When she saw Bastian, she pulled him aside and asked him a thousand questions. He'd answered those that he could, and promised he wouldn't descend again. Somehow, she never answered a single one of *his* questions, and had left before he could force one out of her.

That had been weeks ago, and in the run-up to the end of term exams and the Naming, he hadn't been able to ask her a single thing. He hadn't had the chance, or the brain space.

He would have thought that the events in the underworld would have changed the course of the year, but only a few days after, things returned to normal. And by normal, that meant preparing for exams, which thrust all questions about the maleficarum and his family out of his mind.

All he could focus on were his studies, and studying in public was harder than ever, since everyone kept asking him to retell the story. Harold had been more than happy to pick up the slack. In fact, he'd become a bit of a celebrity himself. He was the only other one who saw the events firsthand, after all.

He just tended to leave out the bit where he was unconscious for most of it.

Amazingly, Bastian had passed his exams—much to the surprise of everyone, including a very grumpy Professor Fennick—but he definitely hadn't excelled. In anything.

Which made him wonder if he'd be invited back next year at all.

For as beautiful as the dining hall was, he was still dreading the Naming.

Madame Ardea stood and rapped a knife on her glass. She was in the robes of a Summoner, long layers of black belted with leather, her dagger and bell hanging at her waist and her hair in an intricate braid. All the teachers were assembled. Even Willow was there, floating beside the table with a pensive look on her transparent face.

Madame Ardea smiled warmly when she looked around the room.

"We have braved another year," she said. "Another year of victories in our unending fight against the restless dead. Tomorrow, you will return home to your families; some for a summer, and some for good, though the

322

halls of Gallowgate shall remain forever open to you. But first, our most sacred of ceremonies. You have fought long and hard this year, harder than most, and have faced nightmares none of us could have imagined. Your skills are an honor to us all, and tonight, we honor *you*.

"First-years, I speak to you directly; this has not been an easy path, and I dare say it will not get any easier. When your discipline has been chosen, although you will still study the four pillars, your work and focus will intensify beyond what you believe you are capable of. But we have watched you all year, and we know the power that lies deep within each of you. Tonight, when you are Named, you will have yet another family, and another purpose and path through life. From here on out, your studies will be specially tailored for your individual craft, and we expect you to carry out that expertise with enthusiasm and pride. It is now in your hands to defend the world of the living from the ever-present dark. Tonight, you take on the mantle of Æthercist. Tonight, your life changes forever.

"Now, let the Guard be Named!"

She took a roll of parchment from a nearby ghost and began calling out names, beginning with a small white boy named Martin Adair. When he reached the front podium she Named him as a Necromancer and handed him a small pin. The older Necromancers clapped as he walked back to his table, blushing furiously. Next came Sayuri Amaki, who was Named a Summoner.

When Robyn Corsair was called to the front, Bastian felt his heart hammering in his throat.

"Conjurer!" Madame Ardea declared.

The Conjurers went wild, whooping and clapping like they'd won a football game. Robyn came back with a huge grin on her face, clutching the scorpion pin to her chest.

The rest of their class made their way to the front. It was funny, but after banishing the maleficarum, Bastian felt more connected to them than ever before. It felt like they were all a part of something, and it was more than just a fight against the dead. It felt like they were in a fight for the living, and that difference meant all the world.

For the first time in his life, surrounded by kids his age, Bastian actually felt like he belonged.

"Finlay Glass," Madame Ardea called.

Bastian looked over to see Finlay stand. Andromeda patted him on the back as he nervously made his way to the front. After their time in the marshes, he and Bastian had been spending more and more time together. Finlay had even helped him study for Summoning the last few nights before exams.

Andromeda never said anything, but it was clear she didn't approve of it.

Finlay got to the front, and Madame Ardea proclaimed him Summoner. Bastian found himself clapping even louder than the upperclassmen. Robyn caught his enthusiasm and winked at him.

Andromeda was soon called up, and Named Conjurer.

"*Great*," Robyn muttered beneath the applause. "I get to spend even more time with her."

And eventually, Harold was called to the front.

Harold practically leaped from his chair, beaming over at the Alchemists who were all smiling at him with knowing, excited grins. Harold had well surpassed even his advanced-level Alchemy exams. For what seemed like the first time ever, he walked with his shoulders back and head high. He was finally coming into his own.

"Harold Watts," Madame Ardea read with a small smile on her face. "We Name thee . . . Necromancer!"

The hall was silent.

"What?" Harold gasped. Bastian could hear him all the way in the back. He felt the same word catch in his own throat.

"As I said, Harold," she said. She held out his pin. "You are to be a Necromancer."

Fervent whispers echoed through the hall. Everyone knew Harold was meant to be an Alchemist. Everyone knew that was his calling. So why . . .

"There has to be some sort of mistake," Harold said. "I'm an Alchemist. Check it again."

"There *is* no mistake," Madame Ardea said. Her words were firm. "You are Named a Necromancer. Now please, take your pin and return to your table."

Harold took the pin in a shaking hand. He seemed to deflate into himself as he walked back. A few Necromancers awkwardly clapped. But everyone else—including Robyn and Bastian—remained in shocked silence.

"Are you okay?" Bastian asked when Harold sat back down. He felt oddly guilty. Was this because Harold had been trapped in the underworld? Was this somehow his fault?

Harold didn't say anything. He just stared at the red moth pin in his hand in shock.

"Sebastian Wight," Madame Ardea called.

The hall went deathly silent.

Bastian patted Harold on the shoulder and awkwardly made his way to the front. Suddenly, all his confidence and good feelings had vanished. If Harold was Named a Necromancer, what would his own fate be?

When he reached Madame Ardea, he was shaking from head to toe.

"Sebastian Wight," Madame Ardea repeated. She looked him straight in the eye. "Psychopomp."

The school erupted into applause as another banner unfurled along the wall: a heron holding a lantern in its beak, on a field of purple. Just like the symbol on the door to the study.

Madame Ardea leaned forward and handed him a purple pin with the same heron emblazed on it.

"The path of gallows beckons you," she whispered, clasping his fingers over it. "And no matter how much I may wish otherwise, you cannot deny its call. Just remember: You fight for the living. Always for the living."

It sounded like a warning.

66

Harold was in a state of shock for the rest of the night.

While Bastian was packing up the few things he would take back to his aunt's, Harold just sat on Bastian's bed, surrounded by Bastian's clothes, staring at his pin. It should have been an exciting moment. Their last night at school, a break from their studies. And, more importantly, Aunt Dahlia had offered to host Harold over summer break, so they got to spend the entire summer together. But Harold looked like he'd just been handed a death sentence.

"There has to be some sort of mistake," Harold said for the millionth time.

Bastian didn't know what to say. He'd already tried comforting Harold, but it hadn't helped. The only thing that would make Harold feel better was being Named an Alchemist.

Harold looked over to his desk and shelves of herbs and vials and Alchemical machinery.

"I almost want to blow it all up," Harold grumbled.

"Don't you even dare," Bastian said. "Those things smell horrible when they're *supposed* to be burning."

Harold just muttered something under his breath and went back to rolling the pin over and over in his palm.

A knock sounded at the door. And since Harold clearly wasn't going to human anymore tonight, Bastian dropped his socks into the steamer trunk (supplied by the resident ghosts) and opened the door.

It was Madame Ardea.

Harold jolted upright when he saw her.

"Did you change your mind?" he asked.

She sighed.

"Harold, my darling. It is not my mind that needs to change. Professor Luscinia confirmed this herself. You are destined to be a great Necromancer."

"Maybe she got it wrong."

"She is never wrong," Madame Ardea said. "But you are welcome to pester her yourself. I'd like a word with Sebastian, if you don't mind."

Harold nodded and hurried out the door. Madame Ardea watched him go.

"I do hope he learns to accept his path soon," she said. "Life is so much more difficult when we refuse to see or believe what we are."

She looked at Bastian knowingly.

"Which is why I am here, Sebastian. I must apologize to you. I've done nothing but keep secrets from you all year, and all because I thought—I'd *hoped*—that keeping your destiny from you would help keep you safe. I was wrong. And I ask for your forgiveness."

Bastian was shocked to silence. Madame Ardea didn't seem to be the type to ever apologize. He was only able to nod.

She swept into his room, ignoring the piles of dirty clothes and stacks of books and paper, and sat down on Harold's bed. She gestured for Bastian to sit across from her.

"Descending is the most terrible of the skills ever taught at Gallowgate," Madame Ardea said. "Just as it is the most powerful. It is not a fate I would wish on anyone. By now, I assume you know that Descending cannot be taught to just anyone. You must have the inherent knack for it, and for that, you must have experienced death firsthand."

"But . . . I thought that everyone here had?"

She shook her head sadly.

"No, Sebastian. To be a Psychopomp is to walk between the worlds of the living and the dead. And so, to become a Psychopomp, you must have died in your younger years . . . and returned back to the land of the living."

Bastian's throat clenched.

"But how . . ."

Madame Ardea sighed.

"To understand that, you must first know the truth of what happened to your parents. Your mother and father were never shot, as you yourself had begun to doubt. No. Your mother was killed defending you from the maleficarum."

Bastian leaned back in shock.

"But I remember—"

"You remember what you were meant to remember." Madame Ardea's eyes truly did look full of sorrow. "Your aunt was a skilled Æthercist and a strong Necromancer. In your more advanced studies, you will learn that Necromancy can be used for more than communing with the dead. It can control souls, even those within a body. And it can make them . . . remember things differently. It is how we Æthercists have gone so long outside the knowledge of mankind.

"We knew it would be too much for you to remember what horrors truly befell you. So your aunt decided to give you a different memory. One that would raise fewer questions. And nightmares." She looked at him, as if waiting for him to ask a question. He was too shocked to say anything.

"A maleficarum is created with only one purpose: to kill its target. It will stop at nothing until that has been accomplished. It wasn't after your mother, however. It was after you. And it succeeded. When your aunt found you, you weren't breathing. You had died, Sebastian. And somehow . . . you came back. That was when your hair turned white, when your fate at Gallowgate was sealed. The maleficarum, of course, had thought you had been killed, and its work complete. So your aunt shielded you from its gaze the moment she could, and—with my help—kept up those wards until it found you once more."

"Until I descended," Bastian whispered, remembering how quickly the shadowman had found him once he'd slipped into the underworld back at his normal school.

She nodded.

"You descending rang like a beacon to the maleficarum. After that . . . well, after that, there was no hiding you any longer. But I still had hoped I could keep you from your father's path. I had hoped you would show an affinity to another discipline. I was wrong."

"Why?" he asked. "Why didn't you want me to be like him? What did he do?"

Madame Ardea's expression grew even more shadowed.

"Edgar was a gifted student," she said. "The first Psychopomp our school had seen in many years. When he graduated, we knew he would do wonderful things. And he did. He married your mother, and they had a beautiful baby boy. He shared so much of his discoveries in the underworld, advances that helped us gain the upper hand on many dangerous spirits.

But after a time, something in him changed. Your mother came to me, once, a few months before she was killed. She was scared. Said that he had begun dabbling in things that should be left for dead. That he had been spending more and more time in the underworld.

"And then he did what is unforgivable. He killed. He killed many people. All in the name of his underworld pursuits. And with those deaths, a great scourge of the dead rose throughout the world, a haunting the likes of which we had never seen before. Your mother fled with you here, and we protected you both while the battle raged. We were ultimately victorious, but the price we paid was steep.

"We had hoped you would both be safe after that, but somehow . . . you were not. No one knows who summoned the maleficarum, or why it targeted you. To summon one is a most vile and difficult act of magic, an act of utter desperation. It appeared mere weeks after the battle was won. Your mother was the final casualty. After that we decided that Descending was too dangerous. We struck it from the records, and from the halls of this school."

Bastian looked to his feet. He didn't want Madame Ardea to see the emotions and questions warring within him.

"Did my father . . . Was he a bad person?"

It was the question that had eaten at him since his confrontation with Virgil, and it was made worse by Madame Ardea's words. But he couldn't let himself believe his father would have killed or unleashed so much evil. He must have been possessed.

"I cannot pretend to know your father's heart, Sebastian. But there are things in the underworld, creatures and spirits of which we have no name. Horrors our minds cannot comprehend. It is my belief that your father encountered one such spirit, and that it began to take control of him. Your father was a good man. He loved you dearly. Which is why I believe it was not truly him in those final months. He had lost himself to something else."

Virgil's friend, Bastian thought.

It had infected his father's heart, had made him do things he wouldn't have done otherwise. And it must have been what summoned the maleficarum.

That was the only logical explanation.

He just had no idea *what* or *who* it was.

Madame Ardea shook herself.

"That is why, in the coming years, my one prerequisite for your continued studies is total transparency. I cannot risk losing you to the denizens of the deep like we lost your father. It is a dangerous world down there, Sebastian. And the farther you go, the more dangerous it gets."

Bastian nodded.

But how could he promise that, when he had so many questions, when he felt filled with so many secrets?

"Tomorrow you will return to your aunt," Madame Ardea said. "And although the threat of the maleficarum has passed, you must promise me not to descend outside of school grounds. I believe that might be why so many vengeful spirits were able to get past our wards this year. Every time you descended, you created a rip in our barriers. I know you did not mean it, but I think it best for everyone if you just . . . abstained for a few months. Can you do that?"

"Yes," Bastian managed.

"Good." She stood and walked over, placed a hand on Bastian's shoulder. "And take care of Harold this summer, will you? I would never forgive myself if one of his experiments blew up your aunt's house."

With a sweep of her robes, she turned from the room and was gone.

It was only after the door had shut behind her that another realization dawned.

Neither she nor the maleficarum had mentioned that his father had died.

67

"You ready?" Bastian asked.

It was dawn, and their room was halfway packed. Harold had come back late in the night, unsuccessful but somehow not as morose as he had been. Bastian had barely slept; he kept wondering what had happened to his father. He must have died in the big battle. There was no way he would have just vanished and not tried to find him. Right?

Thankfully, the excitement for summer—and having a friend like Harold staying with him for it—helped ease his anxious questions. A little.

Harold sat down on the lid of his trunk and Bastian helped latch it shut. Seriously, Harold was bringing, like, all of his Alchemical equipment to Aunt Dahlia's. Bastian would have a hard time holding true to his promise of preventing Harold from blowing anything up.

"Ready," Harold said when the trunk was latched. "You're *sure* she's okay with me staying over?"

"Positive," Bastian said. "She loves company, and *I'll* love her having someone else to discuss tea with."

Harold managed a grin.

"But," Bastian continued. "I don't think she's going to love it if you bring all your herbs home. You do realize they smell, right? Like really, really bad."

"I use them to mask your BO," Harold said with a shrug.

Bastian tossed an old sock at him.

"Gross," Robyn said from the doorway. She looked between the two of them. "Also, how are you two not packed yet? I've been done for the last hour."

"We keep getting interrupted," Bastian said.

She just smiled mysteriously. "Well, prepare yourself for another in three, two . . ."

She opened the door wider, and Finlay stepped into view.

"H-hey," he said. "Am I interrupting?"

"Nope," Robyn said. "Was just grabbing Harold so he could help me gather some mushrooms for my dad. I'm still really bad at remembering which ones are edible and which ones make you die a painful death."

Harold looked at her.

"But you aced that part of your exams . . ."

"Come *on*, Harold!" Robyn said. She strode in and grabbed Harold by the arm. She blew Bastian a little kiss. "If I don't see you before you leave, promise you'll write this summer. Or, like, astral project over to say hi. We can be ghost pen pals."

Bastian grinned and gave her a quick hug before she led Harold, still protesting, from the room.

"So," Finlay said.

"So," Bastian replied.

"Are you ready to go back?"

"I think so," Bastian replied. And for the life of him, he couldn't figure out why this was so awkward, why Finlay kept avoiding his eye. They'd spent the last few weeks working together.

Then again, this was the first time they were actually alone, doing something other than study.

"I just, um . . ." Finlay looked around. Then he looked at Bastian—really looked—and Bastian felt his heart flip. "I wanted to apologize. For being so distant with you earlier. I was . . . I was scared."

"You already apologized," Bastian said. "I totally get why you'd avoid me after that underworld thing. It's in the past."

"That's . . ." Finlay hesitated. "That's not entirely why I was scared of you."

"Oh," Bastian said. "Then why—"

He looked at Bastian, and that look said everything.

Oh.

Finlay swallowed. "Okay. Well . . . um . . . cool. I guess I'll see you in a few months, then."

"Yeah," Bastian replied.

Finlay hesitated. Then he stepped forward and wrapped Bastian in a quick, awkward hug.

Bastian froze for a moment. Then he felt himself melt, and returned the embrace.

"I'll miss you," Finlay said.

"I'll miss you, too," Bastian replied, surprised to find just how much he meant it.

Then Finlay stepped away, blushing furiously, and with an awkward little wave, left.

Bastian stood there, still tingling from the hug, his heart swelling and breaking all at the same time.

When he finally turned around to continue packing, he found that he wasn't really all that excited about leaving.

He was mostly just excited for the summer's end, when he could finally come back home.

ACKNOWLEDGMENTS

This book was born during the coldest, darkest month of the year, in a tiny town on the coast of Iceland. From there, it was written and rewritten multiple times, in multiple countries, during multiple periods of lockdown and quarantine and freedom. Which is all to say, there are a great many people to thank for being there along the way.

First, to my companions and coordinators at the NES residency in Skagaströnd. With a special thanks Janette, Sue, Sarah, and Kerryn—we braved blizzards and swam under the northern lights and kept each other grounded during the darkest nights . . . and then dispersed to the winds when Covid disrupted everything, forever. Save for those final few days, I couldn't have hoped for a better place for such a strange tale to be born.

To Will, fellow author and ride-or-die, for reading so many horrible first drafts and still managing to keep me optimistic. I owe you more coffee and scones than is probably healthy for a human.

To my family, for always supporting me, no matter how far my travels took me or how strange my interests seemed to be at the time.

To my goofy partner, Carleton, not only for all the amazing art you've made for this book, but for being my number one fan. And for being able to make me smile no matter how grumpy I may be. (And readers: I am grumpy a *lot*, so this is no small feat.)

To my Seattle writing community, new and old, for all their support and insight over the years: Levi, Lish, Martha, Kristin, Danielle. You've helped make this rainy city home.

To Kirsty, who convinced me to lean in to the macabre and quirky imagery. To the Adams and Julie, for keeping me company even when we were quarantined in our flats. And to Glasgow in general, for gifting me the name for the academy.

To my agent, Brent, for believing in this story from the moment I pitched the idea, and through every draft in between. I couldn't have done it without you.

To my brilliant editor David, not only for his insight and enthusiasm on this and all my other stories, but for taking a chance on a tale as strange as this one. Here's to many more books and adventures!

To the entire Scholastic team, with a special shout-out to Jana, for wholeheartedly supporting my books from the very beginning. I've said it before, and I'll keep on saying it: working with you all has been absolutely life changing.

And finally, to you, dear reader. I know authors say this all the time, but truly—if you are reading this, thank you. Whether an old fan or new, your support and kind letters have meant the world, and has constantly reminded me of the connective power of words. I hope I can keep sharing these tales with you for many years to come.

ABOUT THE AUTHOR

K.R. Alexander is the pseudonym for Alex R. Kahler.

As K.R., he writes creepy tales for young readers, including the smash hits *The Collector* and *Darkroom*. As Alex, he writes fantasy for adults and teens, including *The Runebinder Chronicles* and *The Immortal Circus*. In all his tales, his focus is on ensuring that every reader gets to see themselves as a hero.

The embodiment of a Sagittarius, Alex is most at home either pursuing a distant horizon or cuddled up by the fire reading a book. He constantly travels the world seeking new tales; from Hawaii to Iceland, Scotland to Seattle, Iowa to Amsterdam, he is always looking for the next adventure. To quote Mary Oliver, "I know several lives worth living." Which is probably why he truly thought he would be a contortionist when he grew up. Or a musician. Or a silversmith. Or a . . .

Right now, however, he spends most of his time with his partner in Seattle, surrounded by rain and trees and good coffee. You can learn more about him and his adventures at www.cursedlibrary.com.